THE WRECK OF THE *SIDONIE STONE*

Perle Butcher-Lyons

Published by

Inknbeans Press

Cover art: Evonne the art elf
The Wreck of the Sidonie Stone
Copyright © 2011 & 2014 Perle Butcher-Lyon
And Inknbeans Press

ISBN-13: 978-0692285039 (Inknbeans Press)
ISBN-10: 0692285032

To Bobbie
From the year the Sidonie Stone sank
To the year it sailed again

In 1936 the world was in turmoil; depression swept over the land stealing jobs and hope, and from Europe came rumblings of another war. Women had few choices: they could teach, nurse or marry, and none of these options brought a guarantee of a better life. Chances for success and for happiness were still in the iron grip of men...

Chapter One
The Wreckage

It's a funny thing how shock can twist up a reasonable mind. I've always thought I was a rational, practical person, and that my thoughts and actions were reasoned and appropriate to the circumstances, but that rainy morning just before dawn, I wasn't sensible of the fact that I had survived when the sea sucked the *Sidonie Stone* from under my feet. I wasn't thanking God for my rescue any more than I was thanking the men who had pulled me out of the water. I didn't even have the sense to be frightened or angry. No, I was thinking that winter was early, reaching her icy fingers over autumn before summer had fully surrendered the year. I was thinking that the woollen blanket someone had dropped over me was rough and smelled like a wet horse. I was thinking that the little spot of light there in the outer reaches of the harbour was moving back toward land too soon. I was thinking that the wind kept whipping my wet hair against my face like the tentacles of some undersea monster. I certainly wasn't thinking that I could have died, and that my husband was dead.

"Come away from there, now, Miss Stone. Come back to the fire and get warm. There's nothing to be gained by catching your death of pneumonia." Hands reached for me.

I shrugged them away. "It's Keel," I hissed, still watching the progress of the men out there around the rocks where the mast of my fishing vessel had listed hard right and gone under just a moment ago. "Mrs. Cainan Keel." There, if I say it out loud, I reasoned, it had to be so. It was true, in the most liberal sense, that Cainan and I were married; having raced around the Bay De Verde Peninsula to St. John's against a headwind just to stand before a magistrate last night – was it only last night?

The rain stung my face as I turned to take in the huddle of men in yellow macs near the pit fire. *None of them will believe we were married*, I realised, *because it didn't take place in the Church.* Despite the strong Anglican influence throughout Newfoundland, Random Island is a stronghold of the Catholic Church, so Cainan's plan to marry officially in St. John's before going to a priest had made sense last night...or was it just that I wanted it to make sense? He had insisted that no one inside Trinity Bay would dare defy his parents and perform the service, and that was probably true. And he had me convinced that he could manage the helm against the worst weather. That, obviously, was not true.

The dinghy was coming closer now, filled with five hopeless looking men. Seeing them made me feel a new level of hopelessness of my own. Cainan was gone, and it was unfair. More unfair than his death was that we had never had a life together. I hadn't minded the rushed words in a grimy office because Cainan had been there and promised everything would be all right. I hadn't minded not having all the trappings of a bride. The only dress I had – my mother's and too short for fashion or modesty, and that sad little pancake of a hat that had long ago lost its jaunty feather – was no bridal finery, but that didn't matter, because Cainan was holding my hand, and looking into my eyes. The ring he pushed onto my finger was probably brass, but it shone in the lantern light as brightly as his eyes. The bouquet of buttercups was squashed and battered, but in his pocket was a paper averring that we'd made the requisite statements and promised to remain wed.

The headwinds came around as we were coming back. One minute Cainan had been standing at the wheel, smiling, looking so proud and the next a squall was raging at us like an angry mother, and the *Sidonie Stone* was turned against the rocks just as we came in sight of Hickman's Harbour, ripping the hull with a roar that surely could be heard all the way back to St. John's.

When I looked around, trying to stay above the black water, the deck was empty, the wheel spinning wildly.

I don't know who sounded the alarm, or how anyone found me, but if those men in the little boat didn't find Cainan, I might as well be dead, too. "Oh, Cainan."

"Come on, now." Someone new pulled at me. It was Mr. Idle, a former competitor of mine, now forced by poor economy and government interference to live up to his name. "There's coffee by the fire. It's hot, just what you need. Your hands are cold as ice." He pushed again. "Come on, now, Miss – Mrs. Keel. There's no profit in letting yourself die, is there?"

Reality was starting to dull the edges of shock as I looked at him. "What profit is there if I live, Mr. Idle?" I waved a hand toward the sea that had taken everything. "I've got nothing left to live for. Nothing." Those tentacles of hair were in my eyes again and I pushed at them, impatiently. "My father is gone. My boat is gone. And Cainan...oh, Cainan."

Like most men, the threat of womanly wailing unnerved Mr. Idle, and he grew brusque in defence. "What were you thinking to be out on a night like this? You've spent enough time on that water; you knew the wind were having its due."

I didn't need his censure at that moment, so I returned to my vigil. He wouldn't have understood if I'd told him why I was out there; it would have made no sense to him that it was my only chance for happiness. A man like Mr. Idle understood fish and boats and the struggle to make a living in hard times. He wouldn't understand that Cainan Keel, heir to the wealthiest family on this side of Newfoundland, had been forbidden to see me anymore. He wouldn't understand a lovers' pact to do whatever was necessary to circumvent his parents' interference. To him, their objections might have seemed reasonable. It didn't matter to them that I came from good, French stock, that I'd inherited the second largest fishing vessel working Trinity

Bay. They had only cared that I was neither Catholic nor rich, and therefore I was beneath their notice, and most certainly not to be noticed by their son.

It had been Cainan's idea to take the boat around to St. John's, arguing that once we were legally married the local priest would convince his parents to give us our wedding in the Church. I knew better, I saw the red skies the night before, I saw the white caps when we passed the far side of Random Island. I knew that it was a mistake to go out, even if his parents' trip to Ontario was only an annual event and we'd have to wait another year to make our love legal. But, Cainan Keel, with his eyes full of laughter and his heart full of music, was my weakness, and even though I knew it was a mistake, it was still my only hope of happiness.

Men were dragging the dinghy up onto the beach, shaking their heads. So much for hope.

Cainan Keel was a popular boy around the harbour, and no one wanted to tell his mother that he was gone – especially if he was leaving a widow. Not, of course, that his family would believe that.

Matilda Harper Keel was undoubtedly the driving force of Hickman's Harbour, in all good causes and arbiter of all good behaviour. Her husband, known as Mr. Keel or Yer Honor, had been mayor of the town for years. Their daughter, Mavis, had married a Very Important Man from Canada, although his name and the nature of his importance had never been revealed. There was another son, their eldest child, enticed away to join the Blue Puttees even though he was barely fifteen. He died at Gallipoli like thousands of other sons of the Empire. His death made Mrs. Keel extraordinarily protective of her surviving children – especially Cainan.

Now me, on the other hand, I was far from popular. I had only lived here a few years, and this was a society so insular a family might not be considered 'local' until they could count or two or three generations born there. I suppose I shocked the sensibilities of everyone from Matilda Harper Keel right down to Mrs. Keel's washer woman by taking the helm of the *Sidonie Stone* after my father died and making my own living instead of accepting marriage from one of the boys in town who thought the *Sidonie Stone* would make a fine dowry. I wore trousers, never did anything to display my femininity and was inclined to be a little sharp tongued if someone tried to take advantage of me. In short, I was the scandal of Hickman's Harbour, and everyone seemed pretty grateful to me for giving them something to whisper about behind closed doors.

As I said, shock can twist the thoughts of even the most reasonable minded.

The men abandoned the dinghy on the beach and walked up to the fire pit, another clot of yellow rain gear, none of them risking even a glance my way. It didn't matter. I probably wouldn't have looked back. I was still staring out to the furious, grey-white water, wanting to believe there was still a chance for Cainan. The sun hadn't breached the horizon, but there was enough light to see across the cove, and the broken mast on the rocks; that was my future, my hope creaking and groaning out there. That was my father's legacy, my inheritance, my living, my life.

The wind had shifted enough to drive the rain into my eyes, but I wouldn't look away – not as long as there was a chance that Cainan might rise up from the water. If he did not, I didn't know what to do. I couldn't survive in Hickman's Harbour, probably not anywhere in Newfoundland without that boat; jobs for men were scarce enough, who would hire a woman? I had no one left in France, and didn't know how to reach anyone from my father's family. It was devastating to be twenty two years old and utterly alone

One after another, the men began to gather near me, then around me; Milford and Shadwell had both worked for me for a while before I caught them helping themselves to the best of the catch and selling it on the side. There were Madden, and Al Rowley, two men from the market who always complained about my prices. There was Mr. Frisk, from the Fishing Commission and Diggs and Mr. Idle, two men for whom the economy had been especially harsh. They circled me, none of them particularly sympathetic to my situation. Standing on the outcropping of rock beyond them all, his back to us, was my biggest competitor, Jaggar Cingesleah.

He had not joined the men in their desperate search for Cainan. He climbed up on the rock, stationed himself in a position of surveillance, his hands behind his massive back, his sharp nosed profile directed at the horizon, and there he stood throughout the turmoil and drama of the ill-fated rescue. With a shudder, I realised that he had turned, at last, and was looking at me. Huddling deeper into the sodden blanket, I looked away.

If there was a soul less liked along the island than me, it would have to be him, with his aloof manner and craggy appearance. He was wealthy, that was well known, and he was the pariah of his family – that was merely well rumoured. There was a woman in St. John's, or was she in the United States, or were there two of them? No one knew for sure, but mothers would drag their offspring aside when he walked down the cobbled village streets, and the men would find other places to be when he was around. The little children, probably the most daring of the citizenry, made up rhymes about Jaggar, the Dagger.

I looked at Mr. Shadwell, who was standing nearest. "Is there no hope?"

He shrugged, spraying salty water into my eyes. "Don't appear so. Poor Mrs. Keel."

I knew better than to believe the sympathy was for me. Surely he meant Cainan's mother, who had despised me on sight. "Yes," I repeated, "poor Mrs. Keel."

"What were you doing out on a night like this?" Mr. Madden demanded raggedly, elbowing his way through the gathering to face me. He was the first to let his emotions show, for he was an emotional man. "That Cainan's too smart to be out in gale warnings. Was." The accusation was clearly that I had somehow lured Cainan Keel to his doom.

Behind them, Jaggar Cingesleah dropped from his lookout on the rocks, cutting through the group to snatch up my hand before I could react and pull away. He held it up to show off the wedding ring. "If you'd bothered to take a good look, you'd see they eloped." He dropped my hand just as roughly, and removed himself from the group as purposefully as he had entered it.

I suppose they reacted to his announcement with disbelief and surprise, maybe even denial, but I didn't hear them.

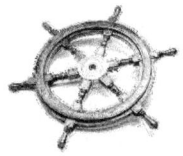

I woke up in a place as dark as my dreams had been, with air so still I almost daren't breathe. My clothes had been removed and in their place was an old fashioned chemise several sizes too big. I was on a feather ticking, under a pile of quilts, and I'd been there long enough to warm even my icy fingers and toes again. Somewhere nearby, someone with heavy steps paced restlessly. I had no idea where I was. My head hurt too much to try and muddle it out. My arms and legs ached too much to tolerate the effort of pushing the quilts away. My throat was too raw to call out, all that came out was a pathetic little groan.

The pacing stopped. A deep voice said something too low for me understand, and the door pushed open until a massive silhouette hovered over me, outlined by a light from beyond the door. "Well, are you awake?" the voice asked.

"Yes," I whispered. That is, I suppose I was awake, but the situation did have all the eerie, inexplicable properties of a very bad dream. "Yes, I'm awake."

The figure took a step back. "And do you know who you are, now?"

"Of course. I'm Sydney Stone." What do you mean, do I know *now*? "What I don't know is where I am. This isn't my house."

"It is not," the voice agreed, and it was then I recognised the sharp edges to the words. It was Jaggar Cingesleah who stood over me, so I must be in his house. "You have been here some days," he continued dispassionately. "You could not be left alone."

As he finished speaking, another figure entered the room. This was a shorter, rounder shadow, which moved with a swishing of fabrics. "Well?" the shadow asked. "Does she know herself?"

Jaggar Cingesleah withdrew from the bedside, making room for the woman. "She knew her name but not that she had been ill. How long before she is fit to go home?"

"Yer too impatient, boy; you always was." A chair was dragged up to the bedside. "And what for? It's not as if she put you out of your bed."

The chair protested the weight placed upon it with a loud creak, and the face bent over me. In the poor light, I saw a face as sharp and sober as Jaggar Cingesleah's. "Are you a doctor?" I croaked.

The sharpness and sombreness softened with amusement. "Not a bit. I'm a housekeeper-" she gave a nod over her shoulder "-and nanny before that. I'm Merdyce Widecomb, but you can call me Dycie. Everyone does." She brushed callused fingers over my brow. "Hmm, still a touch of fever." She stood. "I'll get that medicament the doctor left."

"But, why am I here?" I called out as the face moved away from the light. Things were very out of place. "I should be at home. I've got a business to –"

Mr. Cingesleah's face replaced Merdyce's above me, a frown giving his sharp features a sinister appearance. "You have no business left, Mrs. Keel. The *Sidonie Stone* sank a week ago."

The shattered pieces of my life came hurtling back at me: Cainan, the storm, the rush to St. John's and back. The wreck. Cainan. Cainan!

I must have made some sound, for I was screaming in my head, and Merdyce rushed back to the bed, pushing Mr. Cingesleah away, roughly. "You see how you are?" she complained. "It was too much effort to put things a little more kindly, was it?" She cradled my head in her broad hands. It was a comforting gesture, but wasted. I was not to be comforted at the moment. "D'ye delight in making a poor girl cry, Jag? Go downstairs now where you won't be in the way."

He stalled. "But, I've-"

"Go, boy."

Even in the midst of incredible grief, I couldn't help admire the way this woman called Jaggar, the Dagger 'boy', and dared to give him orders. "Oh, Merdyce, what do I do? I have nothing."

"Nonsense." The old woman brushed my tears away as if they annoyed her. "You have your life, mercifully. We wasn't any too sure we could say that the most of this week. But, you're fine now. And there are always friends to look after you."

"No." I pulled away from her. "I have no friends. No one in this town has ever liked me. I'm just like Jaggar, the Dag-" I broke off, embarrassed.

"Ye make a fine pair, neither the most popular folks in these parts," Merdyce agreed, evenly. She actually smiled, amused. "So, mebbe you're best suited to being friends."

"Friends? I don't like him and he doesn't like me," I argued, wishing I could just hide from the agony of reality in sleep a little while longer, but I had no business, no husband and no friends, and sleep wasn't going to change that.

"Hush, now, hush. A girl can't afford to hate everyone," Merdyce told me, pouring a greenish liquid into a big pewter spoon.

"I didn't. I loved Cainan." I felt more tears spill. "Oh, Cainan."

"Is she going to spend her waking hours bawling like that?" Mr. Cingesleah demanded from the doorway.

"Didn't I say to go downstairs?" Merdyce said with an authoritative edge to her voice. "Here, now, child, the doctor left this for you. Take it, that's a good girl. Now, for some restful sleep." Merdyce bent over me, arranging quilts as lovingly as any mother. "Just sleep."

"Oh, Cainan."

From the landing beyond, I could hear Jaggar Cingesleah and Merdyce Widecomb argue loudly, but their words seemed to gradually fade away, to be replaced by soft and urgent promises, treasured memories of a laughing eyed boy with hair like ripe wheat. Cainan, with his ready humour and tender kisses, had filled my days with stolen moments of happiness I never thought I'd ever share with anyone. Cainan didn't care that I went about Hickman's Harbour in a man's trousers and coat, or that my father had died under somewhat suspicious circumstances (some had suggested piracy), he didn't care that I wasn't Catholic nor eager to swear my loyalty to the British Crown. He loved me. We had risked everything to be together and we'd lost it all. Oh, Cainan. Cainan.

"Easy, now, shhh." Strong hands held me. "It's over now. Shh."

I reached out helplessly, struggling up from the icy black waters of a nightmare. "*Je ne comprends pas,*" I whispered. "*Je ne fais pas.*"

10

"*Je sais*," the husky voice soothed. "*Silence, maintenant. Il va aller bien. Arretez-vois de pleurer.*"

No one had spoken so softly to me, or said such comforting words to me since my mother had died. I opened my eyes to find I was in Mr. Cingesleah's arms, my cheek pressed to the warmth of his bare chest. "Oh," I sighed, straightening painfully, drawing quilts up to cover myself. The chemise had slipped off my shoulders, leaving very little of me concealed. "Oh."

"Are you through with the nightmares, now?" The gentleness that had smoothed the harshness in his voice was gone. "A man can't get any sleep with you yelling the house down." He stood, and in the half light of the moon through the shutters, I could see he wore only long winter underwear, which revealed almost as much of him as the chemise had revealed of me, and far more than I ever cared to see of any man but Cainan. "Are you?" he repeated roughly.

"Yes." I eased backward gingerly. "It won't happen again, I assure you." I was mortified to have awakened him with my grief, mortified that I had responded to his unwillingly offered comfort, mortified that both of us were in such a state of undress and mortified that he didn't seem to care. "In fact, I will be out of your house tomorrow."

"You'll go when you're able," he answered sharply, turning on his heel. He left without looking back.

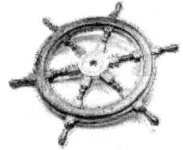

I was still awake when the silvery moonlight gave way to a gunmetal grey dawn. Outside the round window over the bed, I could hear the sounds of buoy bells and creaking hulls and men calling to one another as they pushed out to sea. It was such a familiar, normal symphony of sounds; I'd known it from the day my father had brought us here, and he set out to make a living from the *Sidonie Stone*. Over the years he'd tired of the working man's life, and as likely as not the *Sidonie Stone* remained in harbour while all the other boats went out. When he died, I did what I had to do to survive: make the *Sidonie Stone* a going concern. I didn't know much about fishing, but I learnt. I had to. I was successful until that day when Cainan and I slipped away. Oh, Cainan-

Stop it! I told myself fiercely, throwing back a mountain of quilts. *You don't have the luxury of self-pity anymore. You have to find a way to rebuild your life.* Gritting my teeth against aching muscles, I stumbled around. My clothes were nowhere to be found in the sparsely appointed room, so I wrapped one of the quilts around me and poured water from a pitcher into a waiting basin. There were homemade heather soap and fresh, coarse towels, so I scrubbed vigorously, grateful for the sting of cold water. A hairbrush had also been laid out so I applied it thoroughly to undo the damage of wind, rain, a week in bed and a natural inclination to curl.

It felt good to be up and moving with purpose again. I felt quickness in my limbs and could think again without being muddled by grief. Circumstances were undoubtedly bad, it was hard enough to make a living anywhere these days, and to make a living from the sea took a big boat with long, strong nets and a big hold. Jobs in other industries were just as scarce, and I really didn't have many other skills. I had to find a way to get another boat and get it back out to sea.

It wasn't entirely hopeless. I had managed to save a little money despite the Provinces' ever tightening fishing regulations and the poor economy, and there was the insurance on the *Sidonie Stone* – I had always made sure that was paid first. I would get another boat and go away;

begin somewhere new, somewhere that had no tragic memories; somewhere people wouldn't blame me for Cainan's death. Somehow I would manage. Even in a depression – as they were calling the loss of jobs and failing of banks – there were possibilities for someone with a little intelligence and a willingness to work.

The effort caught up with me abruptly, and I felt faint, staggering against the table where the pitcher and bowl rested. *No weakness*, I scolded, catching the bedpost for support, *you must get out of here today, and as much as Jaggar Cingesleah resents your presence here, he won't let you leave unless you are fit.*

"I am fit," I said aloud, just to hear myself say it, but the words began a spasm of lung burning coughs, and I reeled against the table again.

The door crashed open and Mr. Cingesleah's eyes went first to the empty bed, and then across the room to where I was trying to right the pitcher before it splashed over the floor. "What are you doing out of bed?" he demanded, dragging a woollen work shirt closed, as if in the morning he felt a need to preserve his modesty.

My hands flew to the tuck in the quilt, making certain that I was properly concealed from his angry eyes. "I'm used to getting up at this time," I told him, trying to choke back another fit of coughing. "Where are my things so I can dress?"

"Get back in bed," he ordered, working buttons into place. "You've been stricken with pneumonia. You've been out of your head with fever for a week. You have no business being up."

My eyes smarted from a desire to cough, cry and throw things. "But, business is why I must be up. I have to find some. I would like my clothes."

He looked at me, hands on hips. "What are you trying to do, kill yourself, too? I told you; you've been very sick. You are still sick. You could die." There was no compassion in the words or the disgusted glare. He pointed. "Get in that bed or I'll put you in."

I worked myself upright, stiff, awkward, but upright and matched his glare, spark for spark. "You'll not lay a hand on me. Now, please, get me my things."

His eyes widened in surprise. Then they narrowed into even tighter slits. "By God, woman, you can barely stand. Swallow that damned pride and get back into bed." He took a step toward me.

"Keep your hands off," I warned, barely above a raspy whisper, "or you won't have any hands at all."

"Here, what's going on?" Merdyce appeared at the door, tugging on a red flannel wrapper, her hair in a frilly cap, her breath coming in heavy wheezes, much like mine. "Jag! What are you doing in here, bothering the poor girl?" She gave him a push with both hands. "Get on with yer."

He turned, shoving his hands deep into the pockets of his denims. "Ah, I haven't time for all this. *I've* still got a business to run."

Merdyce had her arms around me, urging me back toward the bed. "And what are you doing up, poor thing? Here, lie down, now, that's right." Quilts were pulled up to my chin. "Now, what about some breakfast?"

I shook my throbbing head.

"Oh, surely a little tea? Mebbe with some honey?"

Tea had never been my favourite drink, though I'd gotten fairly proficient at preparing it for my father, but, laced with honey, it might be very soothing for my throat. Besides, it might put Merdyce in a more obliging mood if I cooperated a little, so I nodded, meekly. "Merdyce, where are my things?"

"Your things?" Merdyce echoed.

"Yes. Yes, my clothes. The clothes I was wearing," I said, impatiently. "What happened to them? I'm sure I didn't come into this house naked."

Merdyce managed to look both scandalised and regretful at the same time. "I never saw a silk dress that could stand up to sea water," she answered, vaguely.

"Oh," I said, sadly. I had so few things of my mother's that even losing a dress that was woefully out of fashion was painful, and it was, after all, my wedding dress. I closed my eyes, feeling defeat sweep away my new-born resolutions. "I must get something to wear. I can't very well go home naked, either."

"Well, you're not going anywhere, right now," Merdyce said firmly. "You've been so sick. You need to regain your strength."

"I'd regain my strength a lot faster in my own home," I argued. "I don't belong here and we both know it."

"I don't know anything of the sort," Merdyce sniffed, bringing more medicine from the side table.

"Oh, I know you don't agree," I returned, trying to be patient, a mighty struggle for me at the best of times. "I was talking about Jag – I mean, Mr. Cingesleah." I looked toward the half open door, wondering if he were lingering outside, eavesdropping. "I know he resents me being here. And it's not right, me being here in a bachelor's house like this," my voice dropped to a raw throated whisper. "People will talk."

"Oh, they're already talking, Miss," Merdyce assured me, holding out the spoon. "The way the two of yas eloped is the nine day wonder around here. Then to wreck that big, fine boat..." Merdyce wiped a drop of the green syrup from my chin with a corner of her apron, "well, you can imagine."

I eased back in the bed wearily. The truth was no kinder when Merdyce said it.

She wasn't through saying things, either. "There you was, fainting away in the middle of the beach, and might well have died." Her voice took on a note of contempt. "Ten grown men standing around, staring a girl in a heap on the wet sand. The only thing to do was pick you up and carry you home. And that's just what he did," she concluded with satisfaction.

"Who did?"

"Jaggar did when he saw no one else was going to help. Not even that blockhead could walk away from someone in such a state." She pressed the stopper into the bottle firmly, shaking her head. "It's not like him being a hero," she admitted. "Jaggar generally keeps himself to himself, but he said he couldn't turn his back when he saw that everyone else did, too."

That surprised me. I hadn't quite thought through any other circumstances that would have landed me on the Cingesleah patch, but the idea that he had rescued me from the indifference of the entire village just didn't add up. "Well," I concluded, shifting around under the quilts, "I think he'd be very pleased if I'd get up and get out of his house. I think I will – today." I tried to sit up, but was instantly overruled by protesting muscles.

"There, now." Merdyce pulled the quilts back into place. "See what comes of such big talk? I reckon Jaggar can stand you a few more days. But, now you have come round again, is there someone we can fetch for you?"

I like to think I have a methodical mind, and I used it: what did I need to start rebuilding my life? "I suppose I need to see my father's old solicitor. He wrote the will, and made all the arrangements for the insurance."

Merdyce shook her head. "You're such a smart girl – everyone says so. Even Jaggar's allowed on many occasions that you're no fool, and can manage yourself better than most men. Of course that was before you run off with that silly boy."

"Cainan is a fine – was a fine young man," I snapped. "And he loved me."

"Well, love is a powerful thing," Merdyce agreed, doubtfully. "What's the name of this solicitor? I'll send Jaggar off for him after tea."

I might have argued against involving Mr. Cingesleah any further in my affairs, but even he would agree the sooner I saw to these details, the sooner he'd be free of me. "Grayson. Angus Grayson."

"I know him. He's not five miles from here," Merdyce said, with more confidence. She shook the spoon at me. "Now, no more talking. Save your voice for seeing Angus. Your throat must be on fire now."

I'd never had someone coddle me in time of need, and I couldn't help being grateful that in my greatest need, Jaggar, the Dagger, brought me into a house where someone like Merdyce was willing to look after me.

I must have slept for it seemed no sooner did Merdyce reach for the door, but she was coming back through it with a tray bearing tea, milk and honey. "Jaggar'll go for Angus this noon," she announced.

I rubbed weakly at my eyes and struggled to sit up without losing the chemise in the process. "I can't very well be receiving him this way," I muttered.

"Always looking for things to worry over," Merdyce tsked. "We'll work it out."

Impulsively, I reached for her hand. "You're such a comfort to me, Merdyce and I've been so grumpy and unforgiving. Tell me, what should I do now?"

Merdyce looked down at the ring on my hand. "Get well, first off," she advised. "Things will work themselves out in the end."

"Oh, I've already begun to plan," I told her, as she held out the cup and saucer. "I'm going to take the insurance money and my savings and go away. I'm sure I won't have enough to go back home, and all my mother's people are gone now, but I'll find some place...someplace where no one knows me and nothing can remind me of Cainan."

"Is that what you really want to do?" Merdyce asked, horrified. "Child, there's another war coming to Europe, there's no doubting it. Germany's back in the Rhineland and the Eyetalians are in Africa. No, better to stay here, we won't be going to war. Newfoundland gave up too many of her sons to the Great War. It will be safer to stay here."

"No, it wouldn't be safer for me to stay here, not at all," I insisted. "I need to go if I have any hope of rebuilding from my...my misfortunes." I wasn't quite ready to call them mistakes.

"And there's nothing here, no one that you'd miss?"

I emptied the cup – such a delicate thing to belong to such a rough and raw man – and handed it to her. "No. No one here has ever liked me."

"Oh, that's just-"

"No, it's true, and I understand it. No, I do," I added, seeing the doubt in her eyes. "You see, my father was there when the people marched on Colonial Hill that day. He made speeches that a lot of people resented. He called them weak toads, willing to be stepped on by the Crown just for a crust of bread. People don't forget a thing like that. Why do you suppose we settled so far from St. John's? And when he died, I didn't behave like a lady and sell the *Sidonie Stone* and retire to a cottage to wear black and knit." I sighed again. "No one here has ever been kind to me – oh, except you, Merdyce. You've been wonderful to me, kinder than any other soul I can remember since my mother died, but I can't stay here just for that, can I?"

Merdyce's old blue eyes had welled with tears. "I hate to think of you going off to an unknown place all alone. You're still so young, and you just lost your husband – such as he was. You need to marry again and let someone look after you for a while."

"That's old fashioned thinking, Merdyce. I'm twenty two years old; I've run a business for years. I had to grow up and learn to look after myself when *Papa* died. I don't need anything – or anyone."

Chapter Two
The Recovery

"Do you really mean I cannot get any of the insurance money for three years?" Disgust and indignation blended into the incredulity I felt. "That's the most ridiculous thing I've ever heard. My father left me that boat and I've been using it for business ever since. No one said a word about *that*."

Angus Grayson pushed his wire rimmed glasses higher up the bridge of his narrow nose. Clearly, it gratified him to make this speech – it was evident in every syllable. "I'm afraid that is so, Miss Stone – that is, Mrs. Keel. You see, your father's...er, body was never found, so there can be no presumption of death for seven years. Since he is not yet legally considered dead, you aren't entitled to any clear inheritance for another...ahh..."

"Two years and eleven months," I supplied tightly.

"Just so. And since the insurance claim is on inherited property, it falls under the same restriction." He squirmed in his chair. "Naturally, the funds will be placed in trust for you until then."

"That's certainly good to know, but how am I supposed to live until then?" I demanded, twisting knots into Merdyce's grey dress shawl. "I haven't got enough cash in the bank to live a year - no matter what economies I make – much less three years. I'm not trained for any other kind of work." I might have sounded calm, but inside I was raging...and frightened. "I know fishing, Mr. Grayson. Nothing else."

Mr. Grayson's nose wrinkled, causing the glasses to slip down again. He shook his head and began tapping paperwork into precise sheaves. "You can't be entirely without resources, a pretty young woman..." one look at me and he let that idea go. "Well, what about your new in-laws?" Something flickered in his eyes – amusement? "They must have the means to look after anyone lawfully related to them."

I saw the amusement, I even understood it. I resented it, but I understood it. "That was rather mean, wasn't it? You know they'd like to give me nothing more than the taste of their door. You know as well as anyone else for fifty miles around that Cainan and I eloped without his parent's permission. They didn't like me before, they didn't approve of me, and they certainly won't recognise the marriage unless and until they're dragged into court." I could tell by the unguarded expression in his face that he knew the details of our elopement as well as anyone, perhaps better than I did. I gave him my most disdainful stare. "I have no expectations regarding his parents."

He shifted again, clearly uncomfortable. "Do you expect to take this matter to court?"

"And have my private sadness dragged into court right behind? I couldn't!" I blurted. The idea of our tender love being turned into fodder for gossip and public titillation for an even wider audience was unbearable. "I won't do that."

Mr. Grayson looked at the papers in his hands, avoiding my eyes. "Not even for the sake of...er...future heirs?" The tips of his ears were turning pink.

"Future...you mean children?" I'm sure more than my ears were turning pink. "We weren't married that *long*, Mr. Grayson."

"Oh?" He looked up, puzzled. "Well, if that is true, it will be very easy for his parents to have the marriage annulled and then you would have no claim at all."

"You mean because we didn't..." my whole body felt hot with shame, "the marriage isn't valid?"

"I'm not saying that," he hedged, "but I am saying the law can be very queer about elopements. I could look into it for you." He stood, adjusting his glasses again, clearly eager to get out and traffic some juicy gossip. "I'll keep you informed. I wish you luck." He put out a hand.

It was all I could do to accept it. "Luck won't put dinner on my table, Mr. Grayson, nor give me a table to put it on."

Sydney Stone Keel got only what she deserved – the belief was painted in brilliant hues across his face. "Good day, Mrs. Keel. I'll be in touch." He turned away, and hurried down the stairs with quick, loud steps which announced his great desire to quit the house.

I wasn't left alone long enough to determine what I thought, or how I felt. The door pushed open again without a heralding knock, and Jaggar Cingesleah filled the frame. He looked tired and windblown, his thick sandy hair falling into his eyes, his mouth a tight, haggard line, his eyes clouded and unraveling, but fixed on my face as if he expected to find tears or joy or anything other than the bewilderment he found. "What did he tell you?" he demanded.

Another time I might have been annoyed, or even amused by his assumption that he should know my private business, but at that moment I couldn't rouse any sort of feeling, other than the sense of disquiet his presence always brought me. "Nothing good. He said the insurance money will be put in a trust for me, but my father can't be legally considered dead for seven years. Something about..." my fingers fluttered impatiently, "common law."

"That makes no sense," he pointed out, darkly. "You've made a living off that boat since you were seventeen."

I confess it surprised me that he knew that particular statistic. "Oh, that was all right, apparently. But, the people who make these decisions seem to feel that the insurance money constitutes profits from the sale of the *Sidonie Stone*, and that I'm not entitled to have it until I have my father declared dead *in absentia*."

Mr. Cingesleah rubbed his eyes with the back of his hand. "Then how are you expected to survive?"

I shrugged, resolutely. "That is not part of common law; therefore it is of no concern to those who administer it."

"What will you do?"

I kept my expression as calm as I could. I could never reveal my fear or uncertainty to him as I had to Merdyce. "I'll manage."

He shook his head, not bothering to disguise his disgust. "Stubborn."

"Stubborn? Why? Because I won't go weeping and begging to his parents? Is everyone stubborn who doesn't turn himself over to charity?" I pressed a finger to my chest. "I have made my own way since I was seventeen. I'll make my own way, now."

He seemed distracted momentarily; I wasn't sure if it was some unpleasant memory or that he wasn't certain what I had said, since the accent of my childhood tended to become more prevalent when I was agitated. He must have sorted it out because his huge shoulders rose and fell in a sigh of resignation. "I have been well aware of your struggles to survive, Mrs. Keel." He said the name so formally it was actually bitter to my ears. "You and your business have been a thorn in my side for over four years. It was a relief to see the *Sidonie Stone* sink."

Fire raced through me from head to toe. "You son of a – a - beast!" I swore, looking for some object within reach that I could hurl at his arrogant face. "What could I expect from Jaggar, the Dagger, than to gloat in someone else's misfortunes? Cold, cruel, uncaring-"

He was laughing at me! "So you *do* possess feelings. I was beginning to think your heart was as stony as mine." He cocked a finger at me. "And I might point out that those very epithets you just flung at me are the same things that are said of you. Right now, down in those streets," he pointed that finger toward the window, "people are talking about you – and not very kindly. They talk about the way you didn't even weep when they told you there was no hope of seeing your beloved again. They talk about how you installed yourself in another man's home. They are even, today, talking and wondering why you would send for an attorney, speculating that you might be suing his parents for a large sum of money.

I didn't hear the townsfolk's complaints. My heart had been ripped into pieces by his first accusation. "How dare you imply that I don't mourn Cainan? I love him, I l-loved him...more than...than..." again the tears threatened and I had to stop.

He twisted his hand from the window toward the bed. "Spare me. I've been subjected to enough of your histrionics the last week. I do not imply that you felt nothing for your ill-fated love. I am only saying that I am probably the only one who has ever seen any evidence of your grief." He flipped his hand back toward the window. "It appears to the rest of the world that you are as hard hearted and mercenary as me."

I dragged the corner of Merdyce's shawl across my eyes. His assessment hurt. "Oh, I don't care what anyone thinks," I sniffed.

He frowned in disapproval. "A little sympathy would do you good right about now; people are far more likely to extend themselves for a sympathetic character." He shifted in the doorway. "And you may as well put away your pride, as you are going to need *some* help. I'm surprised you haven't flung yourself deep into a plot to relieve some other poor fool of the burden of his vessel so you could get back into the business of plaguing me, rather than this silly idea of running away to a place where no one yet knows of you."

"Merdyce shouldn't have told you that," I said, my face burning.

"Of course she should have done," he snorted derisively. "Dycie, the silly creature that she is, worries about you. She thinks your plan is foolhardy and dangerous. I pointed out that you were no stranger to either, but she's still worried."

"Beast," I repeated, with faltering viciousness.

He continued to look at me, unmoved.

24

"I can assure you," I said, compelled to end the conversation with the upper hand, "that if I were so inclined to overthrow a man, steal his business and reduce him to subjugation, you are the one I'd most enjoy seeing vanquished."

He smiled at me as if I had shared the final line of a lengthy joke and confirmed that he had cleverly foreseen the correct punch line. "Why do you suppose I've got you under my eye right now? I wouldn't like to wake up a week from now and find that the *Gabriella* was flying under your flag." He eased away from the doorframe, as if to depart, allowing me to absorb his remarks.

With that change in the wind, I tacked in another direction, lowering my eyes, pulling my mouth into what I hoped was a coy smile, looking up through a veil of lashes as I had seen other women do. "Do you really think me capable of doing that to you?" The sugary soft voice sounded alien in my throat.

His expression was now far from unmoved. "More capable of that than this vain trick," he answered angrily. "You're a brand new widow, Mrs. Keel. Show some decorum and don't try your feminine games on me." He turned and stomped down the stairs as quickly and as loudly as Mr. Grayson had done.

I fell back into the pillows, exhausted, face still hot, tears still threatening, and wondering what had convinced me to attempt such a transparent and silly stunt. I would never have done such a thing with Cainan. I would never play tricks on any man – even a man like Jaggar Cingesleah. I don't know why I derived such pleasure in his confidence of my abilities, no matter how unwarranted; it certainly couldn't be that I would ever entertain the idea of doing someone – anyone – out of a hard earned business. I may have lost my own, but that was down to fate and my own follies. I really wasn't as cold and despicable as Jaggar, the Dagger thought.

Merdyce brought up another cup of tea and honey later on, a brown paper wrapped bundle tucked under her arm. "Jag said he'd not tolerate you entertaining anyone else wearing my shawl," she announced, putting the bundle in my lap.

"Did you extend my most humble regrets?" I asked, dourly, tugging at the strings which tied up the package. "I don't suppose he cares that I didn't have any other options at the time."

"Don't be snippy, Miss," Merdyce answered, setting the tea cup at my side. "Just open it. Jaggar sent me out for it 'specially. Go ahead, take a look," she insisted when, at the mention of Mr. Cingesleah's name, my hands stilled over the paper.

I opened it, reluctantly. It was not, by anyone's standards, a frivolous or feminine frippery, suggesting an evening of sexual delights. Nor was it a somber and sensible flannel nightgown. It was a floor length gown of Indian cotton. The rich pattern was made up of rust and indigo, neither gaudy nor muted. With a high collar fastened by a gold clasp, and long, flowing sleeves, the garment would be suitable for entertaining almost anyone, yet comfortable enough to sleep in. It was ideal for a girl laid up in bed.

I had never been a follower of fashion, but I knew the merchants of our little fishing village better than most, so I had a good idea where Merdyce had found it. At the far end of the high street was a shop that featured goods from Asia and Africa. The scent of sandalwood always wafted down the street on a mild day, and bells hanging from silken cords in the window frame rang out at the slightest breeze, becoming a cacophony of brass and silver on a stormy afternoon. There were always strangely carved figures of jade and ebony, bolts of embroidered fabric, packets of strong smelling tea and tall, thick candles on display. It was not a shop for the budget conscious and I had always wondered how such an exotic trade could end up in Hickman's Harbour and remain there despite the rising poverty.

"Ain't it nice?" Merdyce demanded, spreading the cloth out with a satisfied smile. "When Jag described it to me – he saw it in a shop window on his way home – I didn't think it was right for you nor any other woman in these parts, but when I sees it, I knew it was exactly right for you."

I knew her claim didn't hold true. Jaggar Cingesleah couldn't see in that shop window on his way from the docks any more than I could see the Eiffel Tower from the window over the bed. He went in search of something for me and that's what he found. I pushed it away. "I can't accept this," I said firmly. "It's expensive."

Merdyce shrugged the fact away as she pushed the package back into my hands. "Hardly a thing," she lied. "Take it. He'd never understand if you refused.

"Oh, no," I muttered, "*he* would."

"Oh, well, if it's just your pride-"

"It's not my pride," I protested, pushing it away again. "It's…all right, it is my pride, but it's also not decent. A woman mustn't accept expensive gifts from a strange man – not a nice woman, anyway."

Merdyce looked at me as if I was speaking another language, but she smiled. "Oh, so it bothers you to take it as a gift. Well, pay him back when you get your settlement. He'd be willing to wait, I'm sure."

I caught myself fingering the fabric longingly. It recalled the pleasant memories of gifts my father used to bring me from his travels. It even had the spicy fragrance of something carried halfway around the world to make a lonely little girl smile. I hated to give those memories away. "Very well," I decided, "give me the bill. I'll see he's repaid as soon as I'm able to leave this house."

"I'll have to fetch it up from downstairs," Merdyce answered, gathering up the paper and string. "Try it on. D'ye need some help?"

"No, no, I can manage, thank you." It would be nice to put on something close to my own size. I pushed the quilts back and swung my legs to the edge of the bed.

Merdyce moved out of the way, taking the wrapping paper, the untouched tea and her satisfied smile away with her.

It was no great effort to get out of that blousy chemise. All I had to do was let my arms fall to my sides and allow the cotton shift to drop to the floor. I pulled the new gown over my head and let it flutter into place like a brilliantly coloured and aromatic cloud. One glance in the mirror above the washbasin told me it suited my dark hair and pale skin, and definitely improved on the image of a helpless female in borrowed clothes.

I had long ago accepted I would never be considered beautiful. I had my mother's high cheekbones and my father's wide set eyes, and my skin was as white as bone china, despite all the hours I had spent exposed to harsh elements. A century ago, my complexion would have been highly prized, but in the present day I was often likened to a ghost. Having hair so black it was nearly blue and wind reddened lips only emphasised the paleness of my skin. Despite all of that, the gown seemed to give me an exotic look that might even be considered lovely to some tastes.

I had ignored the heavy footsteps beyond my door as I admired the fit and colour of the dress, and only turned toward the door at the sound of it being pushed open. For a moment, we stared at each other, his eyes as black as coal, mine as grey as carbon steel. Then he broke the gaze, letting his eyes travel from the indigo hem to the out of control curls and back to my face. "I see you got it," he observed, curtly.

"You might have knocked. You couldn't have known if I had finished dressing, or if I had even accepted it."

His chin lifted sharply. "I do not need to knock on any door in my own home," he answered with equal sharpness. "And it doesn't matter anyway. You are dressed."

"Yes." I ran my open palms over the rippling fabric, no longer interested in an argument I had no hope of winning. "It is very lovely."

He lowered his chin for a moment; for him it was a grand bow. "Happy to oblige."

"Oh, it won't be an obligation," I informed him, bending stiffly to scoop up Merdyce's chemise, left on the floor. "I will pay you back." I wadded up the grey cotton and stuffed it under a pillow. "The full value, just as soon as I can."

He gave me that half motion shrug that could almost be called a trademark, his eyes once again taking in the full picture. "I doubt you could afford the value I put on that thing."

"Affording is not the matter under consideration, Mr. Cingesleah," I told him, trying to keep my voice as cool as a morning at sea. "No matter what it cost, I will repay it."

He lifted his eyes Heavenward as if he felt very put upon by a higher power. "As you choose, Mrs. Keel." His eyes dropped to mine again. "Do you suppose, as you have managed to dress, that you could come down to tea this evening? I'm sure Dycie would appreciate not having to climb the stairs with a tray."

I felt thoroughly rebuked for my infirmity. I lifted my head, proudly, as if I thought I could look down my nose at him. "I will be down at once."

"That's very kind of you," he drawled.

I felt my temper rising and struggled not to reveal it in my voice. "I should like to point out that I never chose to be waited upon, Mr. Cingesleah. I always serve myself in my own home."

"But, of course you would, Mrs. Keel." Without a twitch of a smile or a snicker in his voice, he still made a mockery of my name.

I clenched my teeth, wishing I could think of a way to knock that smug look from his sharp edged face. "Very well, I'll be down shortly. You may be excused now, Mr. Cingesleah."

For a moment, something bright flashed in his eyes, and he bit down on his lip as if to keep from laughing. He bent forward, sweeping one arm outward actually achieving an elaborate bow. "Oh, thank you, m'lady." He pulled the door closed as he backed out. I could hear him chuckling as he crossed the landing.

"Ooh, that man! At least my mother would have been proud that I didn't lose my temper." I splashed water on my face and then, rolling up the sleeves of my new gown, scrubbed my face, neck and arms vigorously. I brushed my hair and twisted it up in pins I found in a drawer of the wash table. I'm not sure why I went to such efforts for *him*. It might have been invoking my mother's teachings, which included, among other things, endeavouring to look one's best in company. That made the attempt doubly ridiculous since I spent most of my days in a man's overall, with grimy cheeks and flyaway curls.

Outside the door for the first time since my arrival, I found myself on a wooden landing with a low ceiling, as if under the eaves of the house, and smooth white, slightly rounded walls. I knew this house well enough from the outside, for it was strikingly different from every other house on the shore, and stood out even a mile from land, but I had never been curious about its interior. The stairs wound down in a circle, ending in a big, bright and warm kitchen.

Merdyce was at the black wood-burning stove, but she looked up as I reached the bottom stair, and pointed, wordlessly, toward a swinging door. A glance at the stove confirmed my suspicion that she had held back serving until I appeared.

Through the swinging door, and down a dark, short corridor, double doors stood slightly ajar, far more in reproach than welcome. Mr. Cinglesleah was sitting at the head of a long table; it reminded me of a monastery where my father and I had sheltered during our trip across war tattered Europe. It was not ornate, but it was impressive: smooth and polished black as his eyes.

His face was a vivid description of irritation and impatience. "Well," he sneered, as I pushed inside and considered the room, "I'm so glad you could make it." With a fork in his left hand, he indicated a place set for me on the bench at his side. "I was about one moment away from coming up there to drag you down."

I took my seat at the place he indicated. There was a cream coloured mat of some woven material I'd never seen, and dark crockery bowls and plates of an indeterminable colour laid out. In the centre of the table between us, was a broad green bowl filled with buttercups which gave the whitewashed walls and dark furniture a stark simplicity and a splash of joy. Despite the host's dark visage at the moment, the room seemed to suit him. "This is a good room."

"It does well enough," he grunted, reaching for a basket made of that same woven material, and offered me bread that was dark brown and crusty. "But," he added with that mocking note that seemed ever present in his conversations with me, "I'm gratified you approve."

I sighed. "I was trying to make pleasant conversation."

He gave me a modified version of his shrug as he spread butter sparingly across a piece of bread. "Please don't feel you must for my benefit." He took a big bite. "I prefer to eat in silence."

"Very well." I took up my napkin and dropped it into my lap. When I looked up, he had turned to look over his shoulder toward another door.

As if responding to some telepathic command, Merdyce appeared, a steaming platter in her hands. What she set before us was a magnificent display of food: beef and vegetables seasoned and roasted, almost too beautiful to eat.

This wasn't exactly what I would have ever described as 'tea.' The most I'd expected was bread and jam, and perhaps some hot soup, the staples of my own evening meals. This was more like a fine Sunday dinner. "Oh, Merdyce. It looks wonderful."

Mr. Cingesleah shot me a glance that seemed half amused, half pitying.

I knew what he was thinking; that I could never afford such indulgence and pride demanded that I dispel that idea directly. "After all, when one is cooking for oneself, it's too much trouble to put together such a lavish meal. This is a real treat."

"I expect bread and water would be a treat after the week you've had," Merdyce observed as she spooned carrots and celery and potatoes onto my plate. "But, Jag's a meat and potatoes man, so you can always count on a meal like this here."

"Meat and potatoes man, am I?" he said, lifting the carving knife. "This she says of a fisherman."

Merdyce responded with a playful ruffle of his shaggy blonde hair.

I admit I was surprised by the genuine affection the two held for one another. When Merdyce gave her previous vocation as nanny, did it mean she had cared for him as a young child? I'd heard of men who retained or rehired the matron of their youth to manage a new generation or simply as a charitable act, but Mr. Cingesleah had no children and he certainly didn't seem the sentimental type.

He smoothed his hair down roughly, and wiped his hands on his shirt before reaching for the knife again. With the cutlery in his hands, he gestured toward the platter. "What would you like?"

Realising, belatedly, that he was talking to me, I pointed vaguely. "Thank you." This man was more bewildering by the moment.

He put a generous slice of beef, dripping with juices, on my plate. "You seem preoccupied, Mrs. Keel," he observed, preparing a portion for himself. "Anything you would care to discuss?"

"No." I picked up my fork resolutely, and took a bite. "Mmm, this is delicious."

He gave himself an equally generous serving. "Well, if you have anything you feel you must say, by all means, blurt it out."

I arched a brow. "I was under the impression that you deplored table talk."

"I like even less the worried frowns and pensive sighs," he countered, dipping bread into gravy. "If you must make sounds at my table, then at least let them be intelligent conversation."

I wasn't aware that I had been making any sort of sigh, pensive or otherwise. I looked up at the connecting door while I searched for a reply. "Isn't Merdyce going to eat with us?"

He shook his head. "She prefers the kitchen."

That comment reduced my opinion of his generous nature significantly, and I scowled. I couldn't help it.

He scowled back. "She suffers from rheumatism, if you must know. She likes to sit near the stove, because the warmth allows her a modicum of relief."

I lowered my eyes, contritely.

He was quiet for a moment, allowing me to simmer in my embarrassment, before he asked, "have you decided where you plan to end up on the dole?"

I gave my plate a guilty glance, knowing there were hundreds of people right there in Hickman's Harbour barely surviving on the sustenance provided by the government, but my guilt was overridden by my pride and irritation. "Nowhere," I assured him icily. "I am not dimwitted, Mr. Cingesleah. I know how to run a business. And if there is no business to run, I can learn another trade. After all, I managed to pick up the pieces of my father's business and make it thrive."

"There's no doubting you have a keen head for business," he admitted with the beginning of a smile that should have made me expect the next line. "It was only when you let your fool heart out of the box that you ran that thriving business onto the rocks."

I put my fork down with a bang. "Shall I continue to suffer your nasty remarks? What is it to you, anyway, what I did or what I do? I don't need you to point out that I made a horrible mistake. I knew when Cainan proposed that scheme it was too dangerous, but I went anyway, and I will have to live with that for the rest of my life."

He wasn't impressed with my passionate protest. "It was his idea, was it?" He chewed thoughtfully. "It figures. He was an impetuous and selfish brat from childhood – he got that from his mother. I don't know where you got it, but you've got that same nature, if you think you can simply stroll off into the sunset and find yourself on your feet at sunrise."

"I only have to manage for a few years," I reminded him, dangerously close to tears at the thought of Cainan. "I'll do just fine, thank you."

"You'll be in the workhouse in a month," he predicted darkly, jabbing another forkful into his mouth. "Or worse."

I gasped at the implication. "Mr. Cingesleah!" I stood up, eyes blazing. "I've been on my own for more than four years and I've never taken a thing I couldn't pay for, and I don't intend starting now."

His black eyes slid over my face and down my body, almost insolently, before resting on the plate before me. "Is that a fact?"

My cheeks began to blaze, too, as I realised he meant every gesture he made to be a charity. It would have given me so much satisfaction to strip off that gown and walk out of his house, naked, but not enough satisfaction to overcome modesty. I fixed my eyes on his, coldly, as I put the napkin down deliberately. "I do not intend starting now," I repeated, and turning on my heel, I left *him*.

Chapter Three
The Recommendation

I threw things into boxes and barrels carelessly, blind with hurt and anger. I had been through entirely too much in the last ten days; an ill-advised elopement, the wreck, the loss of Cainan, being so ill, the abuse of Jaggar Cingesleah and then, having survived all that, I returned to my little house at the back of the high street to find a Notice To Quit nailed to my front door.

I had gone to the bank in the hope of getting a loan against my upcoming settlement, but I was abruptly and uncharacteristically denied. Although I had done my business there for four years, I barely had a chance to put the request together before I was turned away with the haste of a housewife having discovered a rodent in the pantry. I had no other course but to close my account, and take my cash back to the Cingesleah house. There I left enough money to cover the cost of the gown and ten days' worth of accommodation based on the fees at the local inn. This, done over Merdyce's loud protestations, nearly depleted my cash, and I wasn't too certain what I would do once I was pushed out of my home, but the gesture had given me a great deal of satisfaction all the same. Let him accuse me of accepting charity now!

My miserable reverie was interrupted by an insistent pounding on the door. "I've got three days to get out of here," I grumbled, dropping a stack of my father's books into a crate. I didn't even bother to look up. "You'd better not bother me until then."

The pounding continued, growing louder and more determined until, with a sigh that warbled with a threat of tears, I surrendered and pulled back the bolt.

Before I could even lift the latch, the door swung open as if a hurricane was coming through and Jaggar Cingesleah filled the doorway, his face purple with rage. "What the hell is this?" he demanded, flinging money to the floor.

I watched the paper flutter downward. "You know perfectly well what it is. I said I would pay for my accommodations, Mr. Cingesleah, and I did. I would have thought that was obvious."

"I'll tell you what is obvious: You are the most stubborn, most ill-mannered female in the world to insult my hospitality this way," he snarled.

"That was hospitality? I thought you meant it as charity." I bent and scooped the bills together, holding them out to him as I stood. "Thank you just the same, but I don't need charity."

He didn't take the money. He was no longer looking at me, his black eyes sweeping the clutter and confusion of my packing. "So, you're really going."

I sighed and picked up the writ I had torn down from the door. "In this case, it is not my decision."

"Oh, I see." His voice softened as he took the notice from me. "You could have spent this," he paused to nod at the money in my hand, "on your rent."

"Believe me, I thought of that," I assured him. "But it seems it was not about the money. I was paid through the end of the month anyway. The landlord promised me I'll get that back in due course, but he's afraid that, without the *Sidonie Stone*, I won't be able to continue to make a living." I blinked back tears for about the thousandth time. I absolutely would not give into tears in front of him. "It seems to be a common theme today. No one wants my money – not even the bank."

He made a sound under his breath and I knew that, whatever he said, it was vulgar. "So," he puffed out breath, "now what will you do?"

"Just as I had planned," I told him, struggling to keep my voice calm and unemotional, even though I really wanted to scream and rage. "I'm going to go away – someplace where no one knows me. I'll just have to do it a little sooner than I had thought. Now, please," I reached for his hand and pressed the cash into his palm, "take this and go." I waved toward the stack of books at my side. "I have a lot of work here, as you can see."

He closed his fingers around mine, holding tightly. "I don't want this. Take it back."

I struggled to free myself from his grip. "I don't accept charity, Mr. Cingesleah. I thought I had made that clear."

"Oh, yes, you made it very clear," he rasped, angrily. "It was not charity, Mrs. Keel. It was an act of kindness." He pulled the wad of bills from my fingers and shook them in my face. "You ought to learn the difference." His fingers tightened as I tried to slip away.

"In your case, they look mighty similar. And anyway, on what grounds would you be kind to me?" I continued to fight his hold. "We're not related, and we certainly wouldn't rank as friends."

"Damn you." He grabbed my free hand and pulled me closer, effectively holding me in place. "Must you categorise everything? Must everything be in black and white for you? Can you never accept anything at face value?" He waited a moment, but I didn't reply, so he went on, on a sigh. "Very well, the grounds are that it offended me to see someone – anyone – in need, and no one around willing to lend a hand. I've been down, my dear – oh, yes, I have," he insisted when my eyes widened incredulously. "I was down lower than I hope you will never even be able to imagine, and I wished so desperately that there had been just one person who cared enough for mankind in general to lend me a hand, just to get me on my feet again. I had to crawl for a long time before I could walk again, and I swore I'd never step over another soul as they crept around. Is that reason enough for you?" He released me, abruptly.

"Y-yes." I backed away from him, straightening my father's old work shirt, which hung on me like an empty sail, and ran nervous fingers through my hair. "I'm sorry if I seem ungrateful, Mr. Cingesleah, but I've been on my own too long not to question everyone's motives, especially the motives of someone not generally known for his generosity or kind heart. And...you were very cruel to me," I added in a small voice.

His brows rose, as if my accusation surprised him, but just as quickly he lowered them and frowned. "I suppose it might have seemed that way – although I didn't think would be at the time. I thought, being the sort of pragmatic woman you've always appeared to be, that you'd prefer honesty – even cold edged honesty – over the lachrymose bleats of pity and false sympathy."

I swallowed, ashamed. It was hard to believe, but he had just made his hard hearted behavior seem almost kind. "You're right," I said quietly. "I would have done." Through gritted teeth, I added, "I'm sorry."

He shrugged that painful apology away. "Very well, then, how much money have you got left?"

Reluctantly, I told him.

He took the money from his fist and wrapped it into the writ from the landlord. "Now you have this much more." As my hands were pulled behind my back to avoid being caught again, the money, in his hand, just hung between us, and he shifted his frown to it. "Although, this won't even get you off the island. If I were to offer you-"

"No!" I cut him off, horrified. "Regardless of your motives, Mr. Cingesleah, I could never accept a loan."

"Silly fool," he snapped. "Why don't you listen to everything a man is trying to say before you speak? I was going to offer you a job."

I staggered back into a crate. "A...a job?"

He nodded. "You've already proven you have a head for business – maybe a better head for this business than I do. I know traps and lines well enough, much better than I know ledgers and books. Come keep the books and help with trading the haul for the *Gabriella*."

I blinked at him, stupidly, wondering if this was just part of some sort of bizarre, grief induced dream. "You would trust me to keep your books after what you said about stealing another man's business?" I whispered.

He put the folded writ, and the bills, on the top of the stack of books. "You wouldn't be stealing from me, Mrs. Keel," he said evenly. "If you did, you'd really be stealing from both of us. And in case you thought you might try, I'm going to put a proviso on this offer."

I stiffened, warily. "What proviso?"

"That it will become a twenty four hour a day job, Mrs. Keel." The black eyes swept up over me, meeting and boring into mine. "I propose a legal merger."

The way my father died had taught me one thing: if something appears to be too good to be true, it is. "There's nothing to merge. I have nothing to offer. I won't get the *Sidonie Stone's* insurance money for several months."

"So, you won't have anything to offer for several months." He shrugged again. "You'll give me something to hold as collateral."

"Impossible. I haven't got of value to hold." I gestured at the boxes, crates and piles around the room. "You could have this whole room for about five dollars. What could I possibly offer?"

He smiled. It was a smile different than I'd ever seen on his craggy features, but then, I hadn't seen all that many. "You."

"Me?" I gasped when I realised his implication. "I don't know what you think of me, Mr. Cingesleah, but I do know you're wrong on one big point. I would never-"

"Shut up!" he barked, and my argument was effectively silenced, mid-word. "I was not going to suggest anything so crude as the surrender of your virtue, if it still exists. I was going-"

"Damn you!" I flew at him with the only weapon I had, fingers bent, nails ready to score. "I've had more than enough of you and your nasty, evil thoughts. Take them and your vile offer and get out. Get out of my house!"

He fended me off with ease. "All right, I'll assume this display of passion is your version of maidenly outrage. I apologise for my assumptions, but you *are* married, Mrs. Keel." He glanced away, only for a second. "Or rather, you were, and it's a long trip back from St. John's, even under power..." He let the explanation go when he realised I had collapsed against him in exhausted tears. "Easy now," he advised, letting his arms hover over my heaving shoulders helplessly. "Don't cry, Mrs. Keel, don't cry. I only mean that people can't expect a couple as in love as you were to wait any longer than necessary."

I pushed away from him, wiping tears with the back of my hand. "I'm sorry. I'm just so..." I turned away, "tired. Very tired." I sighed. "We wanted to wait until we'd seen a priest. It mattered so much to Cainan, and he felt we weren't truly married until then. He knew once we had a legal marriage, the priest would have to bless us, too. It was worth waiting for that."

He tugged a surprisingly clean handkerchief from his hip pocket. "Yes, the Keels have always been so prominent in the Church," he conceded. "Does that mean you were planning to accept his faith?"

I shook my head against the handkerchief. "We never discussed it." I gave my nose one last, thorough rub. "I don't know. I suppose." I looked up at him. "Does it matter now?"

He wiped his frown away and shook his head. "I suppose it doesn't. Now, about my offer..."

"Why?" I asked, idly folding up the soft white cotton square. "Why are you offering me so much help? You've already done more than anyone else." I looked up at him, knowing my expression must be an unattractive blend of

curiosity and contempt. "You don't owe me or your con-
science any more. Why get further involved?"

Mr. Cingesleah judged his words carefully before
speaking. "I won't insult your intelligence by pointing out that
you are very young and, at present, a very helpless woman.
Even though I'm sure you don't agree," he rushed on as if
he expected an argument, "I can't help seeing you that way.
After all, you just lost your livelihood and your husband and-"

"If one more person reiterates my misfortunes, I can
promise I will scream until the rafters come down," I vowed,
tears once again starting to fall.

"Very well." He backed away slightly. "At any rate, I feel
compelled to smooth your path some, if I can." He watched
me for a moment, and could see that he had yet to move
me, so he decided on a different approach. "Now, the truth
of the matter is this: You're good at what you do, but you
have no way to do it for nearly a year. In that year, trying to
survive in this economy, there's no telling what could
happen to you. Let's be realistic, Mrs. Keel. No matter how
clever you are, no matter how hard you're willing to work,
there are no jobs. Men are losing work up and down the
coast, in factories, shops and on their own boats. What
chance do you have of finding work when even young, able
men cannot get jobs?" I started to splutter and he held up
his hand again, but only showing two fingers. "The *Gabriella*
might be the single largest vessel still operating in Trinity
Bay, but there are men down in St. John's and other ports
with more square feet of board because they have fleets. I
want the biggest fishing concern in the whole of
Newfoundland, and with your help, I can have it. So, I propose a trade. I give you the support and shelter you need,
and you help me turn the *Gabriella* into the flagship of the
largest fishing fleet in the North Atlantic."

I wasn't crying anymore. I was listening in rapt
fascination. He had just expressed, in very eloquent terms,
my own burning desire, the one I had cherished from the

day my father was buried. He had always talked about having the biggest business out there, and even though he'd never been willing to work for it, I was. Together Jaggar Cingesleah and I could have it. "That's quite a job."

He nodded. "It is. Are you up to it?"

"I'm not sure," I hedged. "It depends on what you expect from me and what I can expect from you."

He shrugged again, that half shrug. "It's hardly sinister. I need a full partner. I need someone who is as committed to this goal as I am. I need someone who rises before the sun to check weather charts, the way I know you do. I need someone who will stay after the haul is brought in to look for damage in the lines, as I've seen you do. I need someone who will burn the midnight oil, keeping records straight, as I'm sure you do. I need someone who won't shrink into insignificance whenever a buyer starts to haggle, who will fight for the best prices, every day. In return, you'll be a full partner in what will soon be the largest business in Newfoundland. You'll have a place to live, and food and clothing, protection from the scorn, gossip and recrimination that run rife in this town and, someday, another *Sidonie Stone*. That's what you can expect from me. What do you say?"

It still sounded too good to be true. I sighed. "I'd say I'm crazy not to leap at this chance, but..."

"But?" he prompted.

"But, what if something happens to change your mind? What if you decide you want to move on to something else? Or with someone else? What if we want to dissolve this partnership?"

He shook his head with conviction. "Not this partnership, Mrs. Keel. I don't happen to believe in divorce."

I jerked upright. "Divorce?" I repeated with a squeak. "What are you talking about?"

He met my stare with a frank, even expression. "I'm talking about marriage, Mrs. Keel. I won't take you into my

43

house or my business any other way. Between us, we have caused enough tongues to wag already. I know that we will never have the marriage you and Keel might have had – I don't hope for it, and you don't believe it could happen. But, I am confident that we can have a solid relationship nonetheless, based on respect and our mutual goals."

"But, suppose," I pressed both fists against the packing crate, feeling almost faint with confusion. "Never mind."

"What?" I could feel his dark eyes scouring me, as if he could fill in the 'never mind'. "Suppose what?"

I lowered my eyes to avoid his piercing gaze. "Suppose we are unhappy."

The suggestion seemed incredible to him. "How can we be?" he argued. "I derive my happiness from my boat and from being out on the sea. I derive my happiness from being a success." He crossed his arms over his broad chest. "I've always supposed you felt the same. If we are working to increase the business that makes both of us happy, how can we ever be unhappy?"

"How can you ask a question like that?" I demanded. "Haven't you ever been in love?"

The black eyes veiled instantly. "I'll make a bargain with you, Mrs. Keel," he said, coolly, "I will not pry into your marriage again, if you never ask me that question again."

A heavy silence came over the room. I stood, twisting the handkerchief in my fingers forlornly, exhorting myself to be the reasonable, rational person I'd always striven to be. I had to concede that the offer was beyond generous – it bordered on miraculous. I knew I did not have the capital to survive a complete relocation while I waited for the insurance claim to be processed, and I had feared what might happen to me as a result of such a retreat – though I'd never admit that to *him*. Yet, he had asked for so much in return, without seeming to want any of it. Marriage to Jaggar, the Dagger? Unthinkable!

"Well?" His voice rumbled through the silence like thunder. "What is your decision?"

I kept my eyes on the floor. "I can't give you an answer this minute." I risked looking up. He was looking annoyed. "It requires some consideration. After all, it's not something to be entered into lightly."

His mouth twitched. "The marriage or the business?"

"Either," I returned, uncomfortably, "both."

"Stop looking at it that way," he suggested. "Think of it as an investment in a very profitable enterprise." He unfolded his arms and spread his hands. "That's all it is, really; an investment."

"I wouldn't even enter into an investment based on a five minute conversation. I'm not like my-" I cut myself off.

He tilted his head, thoughtfully, as if absorbing information I had not given. "Well? How much time do you need to...reflect?"

I looked around the cluttered room, as if I'd left the answer somewhere, I just didn't know where to look. "Could you give me an hour?"

He looked around the room as if trying to assess if I could pack up and run away in an hour. "Very well. An hour. Shall I call back then?"

"Thank you." He had picked up the money and held it out again, but I resisted. "I haven't said yes, yet, and if and until I do, that's still a payment of debt."

He made a face, but tucked the money, still wrapped in the Notice to Quit, into his pocket, and turned away, pulling the door open and striding out without so much as a nod in my direction.

With him out of the room, there was enough oxygen to breathe again. I filled my lungs and settled back against the crate of books with a loud puff of air. "What do I do?" I asked the room. With no answer forthcoming, I scrubbed at my burning face with both hands and began to stack books again.

It wasn't until I'd put all the books away and pulled the wooden lid over the crate that I saw them: three pieces of paper covered with intricate blue and black ink, with a picture of the King in the middle. Thirty dollars! I glared at them and then at the door. He'd left them behind deliberately, I was certain.

I suppose there are some who would think I used that money as a ruse to track him down in the street and make him give me a better reason for saying yes, but such ideas never entered my mind as I yanked the door open and stormed out into the misty, muddy street. In fact, his actions had turned my thoughts to quite the opposite conclusion. I meant to throw it back in his face and refuse the offer.

I was coming around the corner at full steam when I saw a figure backing out of a shop, an intimidating sight despite the ludicrous oversized hat and veil, and the unexpectedly out of fashioned skirts billowing and swishing over the wooden walk. I would have backed up the way I'd come, but the woman saw me, raised one pointing finger and effectively pinned me in place. "You!" she said in a voice colder and deeper than the Atlantic Ocean.

"M-Mrs. Keel."

"Yes, that's right," the woman agreed, pulling her veil back as she crossed the street. "I am Mrs. Keel, not you. How dare you?"

I shook my head, bewildered. "I…I…"

"You've been all over town with your ridiculous lies."

"I…what lies?"

"Calling yourself Mrs. Keel. Putting on airs. Presuming to lay claim to our family." Mrs. Keel had crossed the street and stood face to face with me. "How dare you?"

"I haven't been…I haven't…Cainan and I *were* married," I insisted. "I am Mrs. Keel, too. But, I don't want anything from you. I haven't been spreading lies." I didn't mean to shrink back from her, but her face looked like a grotesque mask of grief with blood red eyes and pulled back lips.

"Liar," she pronounced. "You were no more married to my son than I am to this post." She put her gloved fist against the lamp post. "You won't get a thing from us – do you understand? Not one thing. You take your stories and your lies and get out." She pointed dramatically toward the harbour. "I never want to see your face again."

I pulled myself upright. "You cannot force me to leave. I have as much right to live in this town as you."

"Rights? You have no rights. You have no income. You have no home. Oh, yes," she nodded, almost smiling, "I know about that, too. You'll end up on the street begging – or worse. And then you'll be run out of this town, just as you deserve."

I made myself smile even when every muscle in my face protested against it. "I'm very sorry to disappoint you, Mrs. Keel, but I will not oblige you. I *will* stay. I *will* have a home and an income." I paused, finding my resolve. "In one thing I will accommodate you. I won't be calling myself Mrs. Keel for long." I pushed past her. "Good day."

I managed to get all the way to the pub at the end of the high street before I paused to wipe away tears. My head was buzzing with anger, fear and indignation. To think I had ever hoped for that woman's love and approval!

"I said I would call back."

I turned sharply at the reproving voice. "I know." I slid the cuff of my work shirt over my cheeks just to make sure there were no more tears. "You left this behind." I held out the money.

"So you ran all the way after me, in that state, to return it? It could not wait until I came back?" He seemed amused and willfully misunderstanding my 'state.'

"Well…" oh, what happened to my ability to speak? "I didn't want you to think you could…that I would…here." I pushed it into his hands. "It's an obligation." Before he could respond, before he could even take hold of the money I'd pressed on him, I was running away, flying down the street, not caring what people might think. I knew I looked unkempt and wild. I felt as if my soul was unkempt and wild – why shouldn't I look that way, as well?

It was starting to rain by the time I reached my front door and shoved my way inside, ignoring the mud I tracked across the floor as I paced. I was hurt and humiliated by Mrs. Keel's words, and a little frightened by my own. I had to accept his proposal now, but what if he had changed his mind? How would I live? Mrs. Keel clearly had the power to find out everything about me, and she certainly implied that she had been responsible for my eviction. What else could she do?

Mr. Cingesleah appeared at my door, pushing it open easily and stepping in from the downpour. "Excuse me," he murmured, "but I was getting wet."

I willed myself to stand still and keep my expression disinterested. "Of course, I would offer you some tea, but…" I didn't need to finish the sentence as my kettle peeked out of the top of a packing box.

He declined with a short jerk of his head. "Have you come to a decision? Have you been able to look at this as an investment in your future?"

I inhaled deeply and held it for a count of ten while I tried to look at it from that point of view. It was difficult when all I wanted at that moment was refuge. Still, an investment did not seem to entail any personal intimacy, the thing I'd dreaded most from an association with any man other than Cainan. "Very well."

"Good." At once his voice became terse and professional. "Since you've indicated you're not Catholic, I see no point in planning a wedding in the Church. We can marry at the courthouse." There was a hint of satisfaction in his voice. "I daresay he won't argue when *I* want his services."

My eyes narrowed in irritation. "How did you know that the Justice refused to marry us?" Dear Lord, did everyone in this town know all my misfortunes and failings?

He shrugged. "Why else would you make the trip all the way around to St. John's? With our Local Lord Mayor Keel tucking half the politicians of Newfoundland in his pocket there really wouldn't have been an official from here to there who would dare go against his word."

"It sounds as if you've had dealings with Mr. Keel," I observed dryly.

"Almost as often as you have, Mrs. Keel. Mrs. Keel," he repeated and the half smile that began on his face faded. "I do not intend to call you Mrs. Keel the rest of my life."

I laughed in disbelief. "You mean, you just proposed marriage to me and you don't even know my name?"

He was not laughing, however. "I didn't have the advantage of choosing someone the local children have immortalized in rhyme. For years, I had only heard you referred to as 'that Stone girl.' If I had not seen the name of your boat, the way people spoke of you I'd have taken it as a description and not a proper noun. Once, when you were ill, I asked your name, but your voice was so raspy, I couldn't make it out." He waited a moment. "Look, I really don't know your name."

I stopped laughing. "It's Sydney."

"Just like the boat?"

"No." I spelled it. "My father named the boat for my mother. Sidonie was her name."

"I never cared for that trend of women taking on masculine names," he complained.

I tried to match his shrug. "I'm sorry you don't approve, but in France Sydney is not a masculine name."

"France?" He seemed startled by my response. "What has France to do with it?"

Oh, *now* we're going to get to know one another? I settled against a packing crate, rubbing my eyes. "I was born there. I didn't come to Newfoundland until I was fourteen." I paused, trying to remember. "I think you came here the next year."

"Yes, I know you and your father were here when I came. I always assumed you came from Quebec, given your father's accent." His eyes seemed to glaze over once again, pulling him away to a different time. "I believe your father died shortly after I arrived." He focused on me. "I was struggling to establish myself, despite the economy and the Fishing Council, and I remember thinking – rather cruelly – that I might have a better chance when your father died. But, there you were, picking up the pieces and making the *Sidonie Stone* an even bigger threat to my success." He shook away the memories. "Let me see," he rubbed his chin with long fingers, "you must be out of this house by Thursday, so we will marry on Wednesday. I'll arrange for someone to come and move your things. You shouldn't be doing it," he argued over my protest, "you're not strong, yet. You come along with me now and we'll make up a room for you at the house."

"I don't need to go today." Somehow that came out churlish, and I struggled to rephrase it in a way to reassure him that he did not need to put himself out over my situation. "That room I had before was fine." *And, now that I think about it, it was far away from you.*

"Oh, no." He looked mildly affronted. "The only reason you were put up there before was that it was above the kitchen and so it was extra warm. The doctor said you must be kept warm or you would die." He frowned. "You don't need that now, and there are two decent bedrooms for guests. Come along now and look at them." He glanced around the cottage, and spotted the door to the bedroom. Manoeuvring through the cartons and crates strewn about the space, he pushed the door open and gave it a cursory study. "You have a small bed. No matter." He returned his attention to me. "What do you need to be comfortable tonight?"

I had been ignoring him, considering the money he had put down on the table. I hadn't seen him do it, yet it had been done with care, for the currency was smooth and stacked with precision. I looked up at him. "Could I ever buy my way out, the way other business partners do?"

His frown deepened. "You would want to compete against your husband?"

"That's not what I meant."

He waited a moment, as if he expected me to spell out what I meant. "No, Sydney, we will always be married." He crossed the room, bent slightly to take my shoulders and pulled me upright. "Come on, it must suit you as it does me. Tell me, can you ever imagine yourself loving anyone else as you loved your Cainan Keel?"

I shook my head.

"Then why languish away dreaming of a love that is dead and you can never duplicate? Why not take advantage of a marriage which has everything else to offer – especially for a strong, independent, clever girl like you?" He finished with what he must have meant to be an encouraging smile.

I could see the logic. The difficulty was that I never thought of logic as a key ingredient in marriage. How could this man enter into the union so callously? Had he, somewhere in his murky history, also known an irreplaceable love?

"Sydney?" he prompted.

"I…oh, yes," I said, capitulating. "You're right, of course. Now is not the time to cherish silly, girlish dreams. This is a very practical solution to a bad situation. It's not as if we have to be terribly in love in our private lives, isn't that so?" I darted a glance at him, only to catch him with a scowl where the smile had, only a moment before, struggled. "Is something wrong?"

The scowl vanished almost guiltily. "No." He straightened, twisting his broad shoulders as if they ached. "I just find it unpleasant to be accused of trampling on cherished, girlish dreams.

I reached out, impulsively and almost touched him. "I didn't accuse you of that," I said swiftly. "I only meant that – oh, what's the use?" His expression did not invite my comfort. "Don't worry over it. You're absolved." I waved my outstretched hand.

"Very well, come on." He put out his own hand. "Merdyce is keeping tea until I return. There's bound to be a place waiting for you."

I hung back from his hand, startled. "You discussed this mad scheme with her?"

"Of course." He gestured impatiently for my hand. "She thought it was a fine idea. She'll help you arrange for your room and get ready for the marriage. In all honesty," he lowered his voice conspiratorially, "I think she's looking forward to having another woman in the house."

I glared at him, resisting his hand. "You two had it all figured out between you, didn't you?"

"You needn't make it sound like a conspiracy, Sydney," he answered irritably. "We were just being logical."

"And you just assumed – logically – that I would accept this cold blooded proposal."

He set his mouth hard in strained patience. "I assumed you were going to react like a reasonable, sensible young woman." He glared back at me. "I should have known I would be more likely to find a mermaid in Hickman's Harbour than such a creature. As for being cold blooded... well, you could hardly expect me to blow in here and sweep you off your feet with declarations of love, could you? As charming as some men find batted lashes and pert remarks, we hardly spent enough time together to be friends, much less kindle a romance."

"Batted lashes! Pert remarks!"

"All right, I take that back, if you're going to be a petulant child about it. But, at least be honest enough to agree we're not the best of friends."

52

"No, we're not." I pressed my hands to my anger hot cheeks. "And that is why I don't understand how you can be so certain that this will work."

"I can be so certain because we both want one thing in life more than any other: success. Success in the fishing business, success that will make people recognise us and treat us with grudging respect rather than fear and contempt." He nodded confidently. "We both want that, Sydney, and that is why we're both agreeing to this marriage."

I found my gaze dropping to avoid his, and it fell upon the Notice To Quit lying next to the stack of notes, taunting me. The landlord had made it clear he *knew* I would do something disreputable in his house, and Mrs. Keel had made it clear she wouldn't let me have any peace or chance to succeed in this town. Well, I wasn't going to do anything disreputable, now. "People will talk, you know," I said at last. "Especially since I just..." I bit my lip as I thought of poor, dead Cainan. "People will talk."

As if reading my thoughts, Mr. Cingesleah gave me an unexpectedly winning smile. "Not if we don't give them anything to talk about. Is there any harm in giving this town a little show to appreciate?"

"A show? What kind of show?"

"Oh, I don't know." He waved a hand toward a window. "A wedding party, the sight of a happy couple now and then? Why not have a model marriage beyond my door – excuse me, our door?" he amended.

"I'm not sure about a wedding party." I chewed on my lip. "But the rest of it would be all right, I suppose." I looked up, resigned and ready to answer any challenge, especially one issued by the whole bloody world. "No, there is no reason, and if they do talk...so what? In a year's time, we'll be serving their words back to them with a silver spoon."

Mr. Cingesleah took my hand and squeezed it. "That's the spirit, my girl. And we're going to do it, too, you wait and see." With my hand firmly in his, he led me to the door, throwing it open on a sleepy, murky mid-afternoon. The rain had stopped, mud filled the cobbled street and shadows filled the alley, but as he opened the door, a little ray of sunlight broke through the grey clouds and sent a shimmer of gold dust through the misty air. "There's the future, Sydney," he said, waving at the sight. "Are you ready to march right into it?"

I pulled free and ran back to snatch up the money and shoved it into the pocket of my trousers, took a deep breath, thought a prayer for Cainan's soul and marched past him into the golden light. "Follow me, Jaggar Cingesleah," I called over my shoulder, "we've got work to do."

Chapter Four
The Wedding

Among the inlets and harbours of the Newfoundland coastline, Hickman's Harbour looked as if it could have been torn out of a book of maritime history. Nestled between grassy hills and the grey ocean, the houses were rough boxes, staggered along the edges of the harbour; coming in from the open sea, it always appeared that they were bobbing along the shore. The facades were flat and usually painted white or bright colours to be visible from the deck of a boat, wooden shutters sheltered small windows and bright doors opened out onto cobbled streets, all meant to weather storms and high seas just steps away.

The only house that stood out on this vista was long and low, with burnt sand stucco porticos and a red tiled roof which looked as if it belonged on the coast of the sunny Mediterranean instead of the Northern Atlantic. It sat on a small bluff above the high street, as if looking down its stubby, rounded nose on the town. I remember how my father reacted when he first saw it, pointing excitedly as he turned to me, shielding his eyes with his other hand, and letting the wheel spin against his hip. "That's a fair house for us, don't you think, Syd?" He pressed both hands on the wheel, firmly. "That's the house for us, by God. We'll live there someday, I promise you that."

I was old enough then to know his promises were as likely to linger as a paper sail, so I never put much faith in that one. A few days after we'd settled, we climbed up the bluff and looked at it, and my father was crushed to find it was barely more than a shell. Later we heard rumours that it had been started just before the Great War by a famous author who thought the solitude of a tiny fishing village would inspire him. When the Empire called for her gallant men, he picked up a gun, like thousands of other Newfoundlanders, and he died on a foreign shore before he could finish the house. It had been in a state of ruin for almost twenty years because no one had the inclination or money to repair and complete it.

Oh, Papa, I thought, as we trudged up the road, *this is one promise that actually came true.*

"When I first arrived here," Mr. Cingesleah said as we reached level ground, "I lived on my boat. I didn't have the funds to live anywhere else. When I decided to move to solid ground, this place was the only thing I could afford. It was an eyesore then, let me tell you."

"Yes," I agreed, considering bright tiles around the entry. This had all been mud and stone when I saw it last. "My father and I came up to look at the place when we first arrived. I don't think that part of the house was even there then."

"It was just a field," he agreed. "I had to go to St. John's to get the original plans, but over the years I devoted every spare moment and penny to turn it into the villa it had been intended to be."

I turned to look down at the town, and realised I could see all the way out to the Bay. It was beautiful.

As remarkable as it was on the outside, it was even more impressive inside. The rooms were long and low, with more of those bright tiles on the floors, and exposed beam ceilings. The heavy, Spartan theme of the dining room was carried throughout all the common rooms. There were tall, narrow windows fit into unexpected curves of the house, looking out across a bluff of buttercups and violets to the harbour. The huge, domed ceiling kitchen was dominated by a black iron stove and a dough table that rivalled the dining table in size. A small bed and bath suite behind the kitchen gave Merdyce privacy.

The bedrooms were on the main floor, as well as two unexpectedly modern bathrooms, with copper tubs and oil water heaters, along with what Merdyce referred to as 'the necessaries.' The foyer was grand, tall and round, defined by colourful tiles half way up the walls, and around the windows. The mudroom had plenty of pegs and shelves for rain soaked coats and muddy boots, and a pitcher and basin waited to wash away the stink of fish at the end of the day's work.

Despite its unusual floor plan and materials, as well as its prospect on a high piece of ground, it was not a cold house. The walls were thick, the windows narrow and the wood burning stove in the centre of the main room cast its warmth in all directions. The attic room, which I would always think of as my own, was small and cosy and had the warmth of the kitchen below.

I would have been happy to return to that room, but Mr. Cingesleah had suggested it would be unseemly for a bride to sleep in the attic. He could not be argued from that position no matter how hard I tried.

Merdyce had given me the tour of the house primarily to let me choose a – to use his words – more seemly bedroom for my use. She didn't seem a bit surprised when we appeared together for tea, and Mr. Cingesleah announced that we would be married in two days' time. She merely smiled smugly, as if she had arranged the whole thing, and once tea was finished, took me on the tour.

There were indeed two suitable guest rooms downstairs. The first room, just to the right of Mr. Cingesleah's bedroom, was large and open, with more of those tall, narrow windows. There was a large cupboard on one side, and a connecting door to a bath. It would have been ideal, in my opinion, except that on the other side of the bath was another door, connecting it to his bedroom.

The second bedroom, while adequate, was much smaller, wedge shaped to fit into the curve of the house created by the circular foyer and parlour. It had only one window, which faced the craggy, tall-grass covered hills above the village. It had a small closet and bare wooden floors, no bath of its own and none of the charm of even that attic cubby, but there was a lock on the door – a feature I couldn't help favouring over charm, cupboards and a bath.

"You can't want this room," Merdyce protested. "There's not enough room for a mouse in there. I'd never have even shown it to you if I thought you'd consider it." She plucked at my sleeve. "It's so dark in there and there's nothing to see from that window. Best take the other room. You'll be happier there."

I held my ground. There were all sorts of happiness, and being well removed from the master of the house was, to me, the best kind of happiness. I couldn't put my finger on just why I wanted many doors, walls and locks between us, after all, he'd given me his word that this was just a business arrangement, and he had a reputation for being as good as his word. I suppose it was because I'd lived alone for so many years, and was accustomed to my privacy.

Merdyce didn't understand that at all. "Privacy?" she repeated as if the word were foreign to her. "Married people don't need privacy. You weren't counting on privacy from young Mr. Keel now, were you?"

Mr. Cingesleah had come out of the room at the back of the stairs (I'd later learn this was his office), and he looked down the hallway at us. "Merdyce," he said tersely, "we've agreed not to discuss Mrs. Keel's first marriage." His eyes flicked toward the partially opened door. "And if she has a preference for that room, then by all means, get it ready for her. Her things should start arriving tomorrow, and she'll need a place for them." He cast me a funny look. "I always thought the other room was more pleasant, but it *is* her prerogative." He said this somewhat reproachfully, and I wasn't too sure which of us he was scolding.

I nodded a bow toward him. "Thank you, Mr. Cingesleah."

He gave me that now familiar shrug. "We make the best of things, Sydney. It is how we become successful." He paused, and there was a feeling in that hallway that something else needed to be said by someone, so we both filled the pause with stammers and mumbles. "By the way, I did speak to the magistrate this afternoon," he said, at last. "He's agreed to the arrangements."

"Arrangements?" I echoed, bewildered. What arrangements would require the magistrate's approval? And when did he have time to make them, much less get approval for them? I'd only just agreed to his offer, and we came to his house, directly. "What arrangements?"

"Oh, just more than a civil ceremony," he said, blandly. "I thought we could use the courtroom instead of his office. It's a little grander. And perhaps bring along some flowers, have some music, that sort of thing. Surely you missed all that the first time."

I glanced toward the empty room I had chosen. It was true that those previous proceedings had been rushed and sterile, but I had no remorse at the time. I thought I had all the time in the world to celebrate my marriage, and now, just two weeks later, it was hard to believe I had ever been married. To hear Cainan's mother talk, I suppose I hadn't been. "I suppose," I murmured.

"I thought we were not discussing her first marriage," Merdyce puffed, indignantly.

He did not answer her, but sent a rueful smile to me. "Is it any wonder I've never had need of a wife?"

Merdyce made a sound of protest, but he ignored her and returned to his study. "I wouldn't mind a pot of tea, Dycie," he called as he walked away.

I looked at Merdyce. Earlier, he had mentioned having another woman in his house. What had he meant? It was clear that Merdyce would understand the significance of such a remark, but I knew Mr. Cingesleah would resent any prying questions. I decided not to pursue it, but all the same, I went upstairs that night, wondering.

Perle Butcher Lyon

I was folding the ancient Aran jumper my mother had lovingly knitted for my father and putting it into my valise, when I heard Merdyce's heavy steps and equally heavy breathing on the stairs. "Are you awake, Miss?"

As I had stripped down to the essentials, I dived for the quilt at the foot of the bed and wrapped myself in it, suddenly feeling very shy. "Yes, come in."

Merdyce pushed the door open, glancing over her shoulder toward the stairs. Reaching for the clothes in my arms, she said, "Let me take those things downstairs and put them away for you. It will be one less thing to do when your furniture arrives." She was speaking a little louder than necessary, and not even looking in my direction as she pushed the door shut. Turning back to me, she pretended not to notice that I was gaping at her. "May I be frank?"

I recovered enough to manage a jerky nod.

Merdyce settled herself into the rocking chair and wasted no time launching into what she had to say. "When Jag first discussed this proposal with me, I didn't want to think about details; I just wanted you to have a safe place, and I thought the two of you could throw in together to beat this sorry state of things. But now..." she drew breath, noisily. "You aren't the first Mrs. Cingesleah," she announced, her hands twisted into my jumper as she struggled with the truth.

I had the answer to some of my questions now and found that I didn't particularly like them. "Well, he won't be my first husband, either. Not...officially."

Merdyce shook her grey head. "Not the same thing at all." She looked down at her gnarled fingers, clutching and fussing with the cables of the knit, and she looked up at me again. "I believe the first Mrs. Cingesleah is still alive." Having made that statement, she sat back, freed from the guilty knowledge, and waited for my reaction.

I dropped heavily to the bedside, gripping the quilt as tightly as Merdyce gripped the jumper. "You mean…he's divorced," I whispered, shocked.

Merdyce screwed up her mouth in a grim frown. "I hope so," she said, fervently.

I clutched at the edges of the quilt until my knuckles were white – probably as white as my face. "What does that mean?"

Again Merdyce glanced toward the door, as if she suspected Mr. Cingesleah was hovering just outside. "She left him. She just…" one rough old hand floated toward the window, "walked away in the night." Her voice dropped even lower, so that I had to lean toward her to get the last details. "He came back from a trip and she was gone."

I settled back on the bed, overcome with horror, confusion, sympathy and, perhaps the tiniest bit of satisfaction. Divorced? A runaway wife? "How dreadful."

Merdyce's hand straightened as if to say 'wait!' "That's not the worst of it."

I winced at the words as if a doctor had brandished a long, sharp needle, with every intention of sticking me. "You mean, there's something worse than that?"

Merdyce nodded. "She spread rumours about his business and hinted at some unsavoury activities he might be involved in. His business was destroyed and he was left with practically nothing. No wife, no home, no money and no reputation."

I sat up again. "But how can you spread rumours about a fisherman? No one cares what he does on land, so long as his fish is fresh and his prices are fair. My father proved that. What business could be destroyed by her rumours?"

"He wasn't a fisherman then, was he?" Merdyce countered with a hint of pride. "He was a banker in Canada then – in Montreal – but when she got through spreading her poison, there was none that would trust him with their money. The only thing he had was the *Gabriella*, sitting in dry dock. His uncle died the year before and left it to him. He put her to sea and ended up here, studying tides and migrations and weather and a lot of things I never did understand. But, he's never given up his dream to go back there more successful than he ever was before."

I was amazed. Rough edged, rough mannered Jaggar, the Dagger, was once a banker, once a respected member of financial society? He was once a man who wore fine suits and spent his days among the moneyed and important? Impossible. Yet, it would explain a lot of things about that brooding, surly man and his dreams for success. "Oh, that is so sad. But, Mrs. Cingesleah...what happened to her?"

Merdyce's shrug was reminiscent of her employer's habit. "I'm not certain. I know that just after he managed to scrape together the money to finish this place, he went back to Quebec. I thought he meant to bring her back here, seeing how he worked so hard to make such a fine house, but who knows? Perhaps he gave up his fine ideals about divorce and went back to petition for one. I never dared ask. I know the night he returned, he took off his wedding ring and threw it in the fire, but he never said another thing about it – or her, or what happened in Quebec. I wouldn't bring it up to him now for love nor money." She levered herself out of the chair, hugging my jumper to her bosom. "But, I thought you ought to know the whole history."

"Thank you," I whispered. He must have gotten the divorce; he wouldn't dare commit bigamy...would he?

Despite Merdyce's confidences, I married him on Wednesday morning, as planned, though it was far from the hurried and furtive ceremony Cainan and I had celebrated. The judge agreed to let us use the courtroom, though it allowed for an audience from the gallery, which made me very uncomfortable. Mr. Cingesleah wore a black suit that made the notion that he had once been a banker almost believable; he looked very tall and distinguished.

I hadn't given any consideration to my own costume, but Merdyce insisted we do something. The idea of going into shops and trying on things was abhorrent to me, so Merdyce offered to go through my wardrobe to find something suitable. Needless to say, she found nothing, except a dress of my mother's, one kept wrapped in paper, and memories. It was not white, but it was made of pale pink satin and lace, from the days of my father's courtship. I never saw my mother wear it, but I had seen her take it out of its box occasionally, and hold it against herself, and sway before a mirror, smiling, but with tears in her eyes. It was too long for current fashion, with those ridiculous puffed sleeves of the Gibson Girl era, but with a little sewing wizardry, it became acceptable for occasion such as this wedding.

Somehow, Mr. Cingesleah had gotten some advanced knowledge about the dress, for the morning of the wedding, a crown of pink roses was delivered for me to wear, along with a single, long stemmed rose with matching ribbons. I think I was more surprised that he was able to find roses – let alone pink ones – than I was in the gesture itself.

Mr. Cingesleah left early that morning, and later on a hired car came to deliver us to the courthouse.

A crowd of curiosity seekers had gathered in the lobby, drawn by the smell of gossip. They all ooh'd and ahh'd at our arrival, probably surprised to see me in a dress, much less in lace and flowers, clutching my mother's Bible. I heard someone jeer 'It's the widow Keel.' Merdyce got in

63

front of me, my wrist clenched in her hand, and pulled me through the crowd as if she expected them to start pelting me with rocks and rotten fruit.

At the door of the courtroom, Merdyce gave a breathless account of the assault, and the judge promised to have the lobby cleared after the offices were completed, but he didn't sound very convincing.

The judge arranged us before the bench in the front of the courtroom, under the eyes of those crowded into the balcony, and somberly exhorted us on the duties and obligations of marriage, warning us of the gravity of our vows and putting a slight emphasis on the fact that it was a lifelong commitment to one another. Behind us, witnesses mumbled and Merdyce sniffled softly.

Mr. Cingesleah was suitably somber about the proceedings, too. His vows were repeated in a grave murmur, his dark eyes never leaving my face. I don't know why that gave me an odd little flutter in my middle. To my great surprise, at the appropriate moment, he produced a ring from his breast pocket, a narrow circlet of diamonds fit into gold. He said nothing as he took my hand and found that I had not yet removed the band Cainan had given me, nor did he waste time waiting for me to remove it then. He simply slid his ring on beside it, his mouth a thin line of determination.

There was a round of shocked buzzing when the magistrate declared us man and wife, and when Mr. Cingesleah took me in his arms and kissed me. It was a kiss meant only for show, I understood that, but the touch of his lips on mine seared my mouth and I pulled back in alarm. Cainan's kiss had not burned that way.

He released me, without the cutting comment I expected, without even a frown of displeasure. Instead, he lifted his eyes to the balcony, twin blades of defiance, as if daring the world to try and knock us down now that we were both on our feet. It made me proud to walk out of that room on his arm.

Mr. Cingesleah left me in the lobby to take Merdyce to the hired car, parked down the road from the courthouse. I wanted to go with them, feeling conspicuous and exposed on the courthouse steps, but they both insisted my dress would be ruined walking through the mud. Those who had dispersed on the judge's command, milled around the bottom steps, casting looks at me and shaking their heads. Before long, the gathering parted and a woman climbed the stairs, her red eyes and rage visible even beneath the black veil.

"You animal! You quean! You whore!" she swore, and with a sweeping arc of one black gloved hand, slapped me hard enough to send me reeling backward.

I put up my hands, not to strike back, but to ward off another blow.

There was not another one coming. Having struck once, the distraught woman seemed content to continue her volley of words. "You must have your men no matter what the cost," she accused. "First you take away my precious..." her voice caught for a moment, "baby. You steal off in the night with him and before we can even understand what you've done, you snatch up another man. You won't be happy until you've destroyed them all." Catching my shoulder, Mrs. Keel shoved me around to face those gathered below. "Look at her and lock up your sons, your brothers, your husbands. She'll ruin every one of them."

Dozens of people stared up at me, and I had no answer. From Mrs. Keel's point of view, and undoubtedly from the view of those looking at us, I must have been on a mission to have a man, any man, and as many as I could get. Why else would I rush from one marriage to another? "M-Mrs. Keel," I began, wondering what I could say to justify my behavior. "You must know that I loved Cainan."

"Love?" the woman hissed. "Love him?" She was teetering toward hysteria now, and people were edging up the steps to watch how things would play out. "You didn't

65

love him. You loved his money, his name, his position. You loved what you thought he would give you in this town: respectability. You've got a heart of stone, and you could never truly love anyone." She flicked a hand toward a black Willys-Knight roadster rolling up to the courthouse steps. "I didn't believe such a heartless woman could exist until I watched with my own eyes while my son's widow married another man, only days after my son was taken."

There was a general round of reaction, surprise and disapproval, rippling through the crowd. Surprise, perhaps because Mrs. Keel actually admitted that Cainan and I had married, and disapproval that I had married someone else so soon.

The only thing that kept me from breaking free from her grasp and running as fast and as far as I could, was the sweet bit of irony in Mr. Cingesleah's arrival, easing over the side of the car and taking the steps on a march. The car at the curb was a 1932 touring car, much nicer than the 1928 Ford Model A which the Keels drove with such pride.

"If that was truly the case, Mrs. Keel, then you would have every right to sit in judgement," he said, as he reached the top of the steps, holding his arm out to me. His fingertips brushed almost tenderly across my cheek where she had struck me, before he drew me to his side. "As it is," he continued, shifting his gaze to her, "it is you who deserves judgement." His voice remained even and clear enough to be heard, yet his words made it cold and threatening. "You were the one who refused to acknowledge that your son chose this woman as his wife – until now, that is when it suits you to make a spectacle of yourself calling her names. You were the one who abandoned your own son's widow, after she'd lost everything. It was you who spread your poisonous ideas around, forcing her out of her home and any hope of survival. And yet, you present yourself now, on our wedding day, to accuse and cast aspersions on her character, in front of witnesses, just to make a scene."

He paused for effect and there were murmurs among the crowd that seemed to discomfit Mrs. Keel. She began to mouth some rebuttal for which she never quite found her voice. "You have no right to say anything to her," he continued. "Sydney did nothing wrong in marrying me, and since she has done, I'll thank you to leave my wife alone from this moment on. She is no longer any concern of yours." His voice hardened into a sword. "And if I ever see you strike her again, I will not hesitate to have you arrested for assault." Letting his final words settle on Mrs. Keel so roughly that she nearly tumbled, he slid his arm around me and guided me toward the car.

The crowd parted before us, wordlessly.

As Mr. Cingesleah handed me into the car, I risked a peek up the steps. Mrs. Keel was standing still, hands clenched into fists at her breast, staring at the place where we'd been standing, as if stunned. I knew I shouldn't feel smug about my circumstances in the presence of a woman who had lost her child, but I just couldn't help being a bit pleased to be getting into that car at that moment. I'd seen such a car in newspaper adverts and associated them with wealthy Americans. It seemed unthinkable and therefore especially delicious to discover a 'mere' fisherman could acquire one in a place where automobiles were rare; almost none were kept for anything but labour.

As he adjusted a blanket over my lap, Mrs. Keel seemed to recover and shoved her way through the crowd to catch his arm. "And you're no better, Jaggar Cingesleah. What did you possibly hope to gain by marrying her? She has nothing now. That filthy boat is gone and she'll get nothing from us. Nothing!"

For a moment, he looked down at her, his face a strange mix of confusion and contempt. I tensed, waiting for him to repudiate the marriage based on this information. But his face relaxed into something like a smile. "On the contrary, Mrs. Keel," he said, showing far more tolerance than could be

67

expected from almost any man, and most especially not from the irascible Jaggar Cingesleah. "She still has all the things a real man would want in marrying her; she has warmth, charm, intelligence and compassion. She's also..." he turned his head to include me in the remarks, "magnificently beautiful, inside and out." He shrugged away Mrs. Keel's hand. "And that, Mrs. Keel, is something your child would never have been able to appreciate."

I watched him move around the front of the car, surprised by how genuine his speech sounded. I confess there was a small but growing part of me that wished he really felt that way, that the kiss and the speech weren't just for show.

"You'll never be happy with her!"

I turned to look back as the car began to move forward. Mrs. Keel, a woman renowned for her grace and poise, was suddenly reduced to a ridiculous figure, running after the car, her dramatic veil flying, shouting at us. "She'll never love you. She'll never love you. She was in love with Cainan. You'll be sorry! She has nothing. Nothing!" She might have said more, but the rumble of the powerful engine drowned out all sound, except the rubber tires on the uneven street.

I turned back in the seat, my head bowed, embarrassed for the woman.

Mr. Cingesleah rolled to a stop at the end of the street and lifted up out of his seat. "You're wrong, Mrs. Keel," he said, loudly. "She has me." And with that he put all eight cylinders to work to send the car screaming away from the scene.

Merdyce had wanted us to have a wedding party, but neither of us could think of people to invite. Merdyce argued that we could have used the old assembly room above the pub, and just having a party would be an open invitation to the town. It didn't need to be fancy, she insisted, but it would be a good chance to set the world straight about our marriage. When we both rejected the idea adamantly, she persisted that we needed *some* celebration, so Mr. Cingesleah suggested an inn across the bar in Clarenville, and I agreed for the sake of domestic harmony.

We drove in silence most of the way, the conversation being limited to his solicitations regarding my comfort, and apologising when the big roadster bounced into and out of a pit in the road.

Clarenville was hardly St. John's or even Gander, but it was a nice, bustling town on the main road to St. John's, as well as a stop on the new railway. The inn, at the top of the high street, was unremarkable on the outside, but had a fine reputation all the way to St. John's. There was a man in old fashioned livery at the door to announce us, and then take the car away. There was another man, in a modern suit, to direct us to our table: next to a window with a breathtaking view of the lighthouse and the bay. A third man hurried forward with menus and to recommend wines.

From the moment we had encountered the coachman, Mr. Cingesleah had turned on a charm that I had only suspected he possessed, smiling, patting and looking pleased. He ordered champagne and toasted our happiness just loud enough for patrons at other tables to hear. "May we never know regret," he said over his raised glass.

"Hear, hear," I murmured, raising my glass to my lips. I felt conspicuous and I didn't like the feeling.

"Tell me about yourself," he said with forced brightness. "I know you're French and not quite twenty two and you have a strong spirit. Tell me the rest."

I sipped slowly, wondering where to start. There were so many pieces of my life and they did not add up to a whole. "There isn't a great deal left to tell," I hedged.

"On the contrary," he scolded gently, "I suspect there is a great deal. How did a French girl – and not a Quebecois – end up on this half empty island in the North Atlantic? Where did you learn your business skills? Where did you develop such a will to survive?"

I took another sip, hoping to lubricate a tongue mysteriously tangled under his black gaze. "Well…I suppose I should start with my father, then. He was born in Nova Scotia, but my grandfather arranged for him to go to school in Scotland. When the war came, his grandfather sent him home. My mother was on the same ship, going to family in Quebec. They met, fell in love and eloped as soon as the boat landed in New York City. They lived a while in America and then returned to Nova Scotia, where I was born.

"My mother longed to go back to her family in France so, when the war ended, Father put us on a boat back to Europe." I slid a finger along the rim of the glass, making it sing for a moment – one piercing yet mournful note. "My father followed a few months later, but he was restless there. He would often disappear for a few days or a few weeks. In those days there were lots of ways to make money helping connect people with family, black-market supplies, government payout schemes." I lowered my eyes, embarrassed. It was no secret my father had been somewhat unscrupulous in his behavior, but I'd never really thought just how much he danced on the wrong side of the law until I began to account for my life. "Most of the time, growing up, it was just my mother and me. Her family had been broken up and scattered around during the war, and the family home was mostly in ruins, but we made up a nice apartment there and waited for my father to return."

I sighed and pushed the glass away. "Oh, I know it sounds like a novel, doesn't it? But it wasn't a bad life. We never did without and sometimes we had more than enough. My mother wanted to teach me through her own mistakes and urged me to think for myself and not depend on a man for my happiness and well-being as she had done. She got me some books and I studied..." I gestured faintly, "all kinds of things, art and language and business and accounting. She wanted me to be prepared as she had not."

"She did a good job," he allowed. "And then?"

I shrugged. "There isn't much more. My mother died when I was thirteen. Somehow my father got word and came back to Annecy, where we lived, and for a time tried to stay there with me. He was a shopkeeper, a grocer and then a postman. But he wasn't good at anything like that so he collected some money owed him and sold some things..." I stumbled a bit over that painful memory. Some of the things he sold had been in my mother's family for generations, things that I had cherished as much as my mother's memory.

"Anyway, he brought me back to Nova Scotia and bought the *Sidonie Stone* – well, it was called something else then, but he renamed it in my mother's memory. He decided he didn't want to live under provincial law so we came up here. You know the rest." I waved off his offer for more wine. "What about you, Mr. Cingesleah?"

He laughed. The sound surprised me and I arched a brow. "That question amuses you?"

"No." He pressed his napkin to his lips as if to stifle any further mirth. "It was the way you asked it, or more correctly, the way you addressed it. You called me Mr. Cingesleah."

"It is your name," I protested, feeling my cheeks pink up at his tone.

"Surely you're too modern a woman to address her husband in such a formal manner."

"I...I hadn't been given leave to call you anything else."

"Indeed?" Both of his brows went up. "I didn't think you needed my leave. Very well." He raised his glass, as if toasting our future again. "I hereby give you leave to call me Jaggar...that is, if you will."

I nodded. I didn't like it. Calling him by his given name just stripped one more layer of formality away from our relationship. Calling him by his given name was just a step away from emotional intimacy and there was no need for such intimacy in a business partnership. "Very well, Jaggar, what about you?"

He put the glass down and settled into his chair. "Well, the family's originally from Wales, but my grandfather fell in love with a distant cousin by correspondence and eventually came to Cape Breton to marry her. They had two sons; the younger died in the war, but the elder son married an American woman and they settled in upper New York. That was my father. They had four daughters and one son."

"You?"

His face darkened. "Oh, no, my elder brother." He reached for his glass, and pulled his hand back, changing his mind. "His wife died and he sent my brother to school in England and took his four daughters to Cape Breton to stay with his parents. He then went all over Canada and the northern part of the United States looking for work.

"Eventually he got word that my grandmother had died and my grandfather couldn't care for the girls, so he returned home. On the way he stopped in Quebec. There he met the woman who would become my mother, and they married and had me. Eventually all of the family was reunited in Sherbourg, except for my brother, who chose to stay in England. My four sisters, all of whom spent the greater portion of my youth telling me how to live my life, married and made the men as miserable as they had made me, thus convincing me that I would be very happy doing something that did not require a woman's hand or opinion." He reached again for his glass, this time smiling. "And now look at me."

I did look, wondering where his first wife came into the picture. "It won't be so bad," I said weakly.

"Oh, no." His eyes slid over me. "Not bad at all. You look very pretty today, you know? I meant to tell you earlier. Despite Merdyce's mysterious workings with lace last night and the fact that I arranged for you to have flowers, I was almost convinced you would still arrive at the magistrate's office in one of those jumpers and trousers. I don't think I've seen you properly done up in a dress before." I appreciated that he did not allude to the mess I was in the night of my marriage to Cainan.

"I only had a few of my mother's old dresses," I explained, shifting self-consciously in my chair. "This one is from when she was just a girl. I have another that was the last dress my father bought for her...well," I corrected myself, "I had it. Silk doesn't stand up to sea water." I sighed, regretfully. "Living with my father, it was just easier to wear the kind of thing he wore. After all, working on boats and in fish stalls for more than five years and having no social life, there hasn't been much need for dresses."

"Well, that should change now, don't you think?" He let his eyes go over me again and when he spoke, there was a note of surprise that offended me, a bit. "You've actually got something of a figure, Sydney. I would never have guessed in those shapeless clothes you've been wearing."

I lowered my eyes, too bewildered and bewitched by the unexpected compliment to remain wounded. "Thank you."

He was amused by something. "You're welcome," he chuckled. He picked up his fork as our plates were set before us. But before he put a bite in his mouth, he darted me a challenging look. "Is there anything more you would like to know about me?

Yes, are you divorced? But I shook my head. "I suppose I'll learn things as we go along."

He nodded. "You certainly will."

Chapter Five
The Rumours

The meal was probably the best I'd ever had: a full five courses with a mint sorbet between the meat and salad courses and a dense *pain chocolat* at the end. It was the sort of meal my father loved to boast about, and more than once he'd end a lengthy description of such a meal with a promise to take me to a fine restaurant someday.

I should have been embarrassed that I cleared each dish, but I doubted I would ever have such delicacies again and Jaggar seemed glad to see me taking pleasure in the food. He kept ordering things I'd never had before and urging me to eat it all, right down to the sugared almonds the maitre d'hotel gave me as a token of good luck in my marriage.

Finally, I could not take another bite. I settled back in my chair, almost faint with a pleasurable and unfamiliar sense of fullness. "What a sight I must be," I sighed.

"Yes," he agreed, lifting his coffee cup. "You are the very image of a properly spoilt bride."

"Yes," I echoed. Calling me a bride stripped away another layer. I sat up, looking around the dining room, subconsciously seeking escape.

Thankfully, he misunderstood. "Well, why don't you freshen up while I take care of the bill and call for the car?"

I nodded and he rose with me, discreetly indicating where I might find facilities to meet my needs.

While I wasn't particularly interested in the ladies' lounge, at least it was a place to sit for a few moments and have my thoughts to myself. Unfortunately, the chairs were occupied by a group of women of assorted ages, from a girl still in pigtails to a woman in a hat large enough to conceal a cat, and though they fell silent as I pushed the door open,

75

their chatter continued as soon as I locked myself into one of the stalls.

The wooden door felt smooth and cool and I pressed my cheek to it, trying to gather my wits and gauge my senses. I had no idea how long I stood there, and I might easily have gone on standing there for an hour but for the sound of a familiar name.

"Well, you know how she gives herself airs, doing all of her shopping on the mainland because no shop in all of Newfoundland could possibly have merchandise to meet her standards," one woman was saying without a hint of shame. "My husband heard from a grocer in Clarenville that they owe every shop from here to Boniface Bay. The Keels, for all their fine talk and superior airs, are as poor as the rest of us."

"They say he lost all his money in bank speculations," someone else contributed.

"The only hope they had was that boy of theirs," the first one returned. "He was supposed to marry money and save them all."

"Who has money like that these days?" snorted another woman – possibly the woman in that hat.

I couldn't stifle my gasp of surprise. Could any of that be true? My poor Cainan was expected to marry for money like a prize winning bull?

There was a swishing of fabrics and a flurry of hushed words, and the sigh of old springs as the door to the lounge swung open and shut.

I waited a moment for my heart to stop pounding and went out to splash water on my face before returning to the dining room. The party of gossipy women was nowhere to be seen, but Jaggar was at the table, settling our bill. He looked up and started a smile, but must have thought better of it, for it faded quickly.

"Ready to go?" he asked, gathering my things from the table top.

"Yes, thank you." I took my bag and shawl and let him lead the way to the lobby to wait for the car.

"Did you have a nice time?" he asked.

"Yes, thank you." I looked around the lobby uneasily, wondering if any of those women knew who I was and what part I had played in this rumoured downfall of the Keels.

He frowned down at me. "Are you all right?"

"Yes, tha-" I cut myself off and forced a smile. "I'm sorry. It was such a big meal, and so lovely, I think I'm just a trifle overwhelmed."

He accepted the excuse and indicated that the car had been brought to the door.

When we had arrived at the inn and Jaggar had turned on the charm and the chatter, I had predicted that, as soon as we left the inn, he would fall into silence. I was right. He took me back to the car and drove the whole way home without uttering anything more than the most necessary words to me. I didn't try to encourage further conversation, either. Even if I had been in any frame of mind to talk about anything other than the disturbing gossip I'd heard that afternoon, the roar of the engine in the open cab made every word an effort. If I had even attempted to be heard, the first words out of my mouth very well could be: Did you ever get that divorce when you went back to Quebec?

It was after dark when we arrived at the faux villa on the bluff above the harbour. Merdyce waited on us with a tray of tea, sandwiches, a bottle of sherry, and her discreet absence. As Jaggar assisted me with my wrap, he noted the housekeeper's contributions with a nod. The tea was still steaming so Merdyce must have waited by the window until she saw the lights coming up the hill before she took the kettle off the fire.

Jaggar filled cups for both of us, and sat down in a chair by the fire. It was a big, ungainly piece of furniture, half leather, half wood, looking as if it once belonged in some medieval castle. Yet, it fit well in that oddity of a home, so out of place in a small fishing village. He settled back, resting his heels on the stone hearth, watching me as I remained at the entrance, considering the house, the furniture and the host.

That is, I suppose he must be considered the host. It was his house and nothing had been mentioned by him about sharing assets above the business itself. I wished I'd gotten a better idea what would be expected of me after business hours.

He gestured with his cup, indicating another chair. "Come in and sit. Drink this while it's hot. It will be a clear night, and you know what that means."

I shivered, as if to agree. A clear night was a cold night, and a cup of tea by the fire was the very thing for such a night. I picked up the cup and saucer left for me and perched on the matching chair. Neither tall enough nor wide enough to sit in the chair as intended, I sat uneasily on the edge, my feet not quite reaching the floor. I didn't look at him and he did not look at me. If this was the future of our lives, this was going to be some marriage.

"You know, you were really splendid this afternoon," he said lazily, his eyes still fixed on the steam rising from his cup. "I should have told you so earlier, but with that confrontation with…with your former mother-in-law, I forgot."

I looked up, sharply, at the mention of Mrs. Keel. Did he know of their financial situation? Would he be able to tell me if it were true? It wasn't wise to ask, I decided, especially after he'd just called me splendid. I wasn't exactly certain what I'd done to be perceived as splendid, so I did what I'd been doing since we left the inn: I nodded.

Jaggar acknowledged my nod with an amused twist of his mouth. He might have thought he was smiling. "You may rest assured you will have no other mother-in-law to contend with. My mother is gone five years at least, and even if she were still alive, I think she'd like you." He sipped tea – an oddly dainty gesture from such a large, rough edged man.

"She would have found you...appealing," he said, deciding on the word with pleasure. "You're very much alike in all the important ways."

I nodded again, not knowing what to say.

"You are allowed to speak in my presence," he concluded with a wry chuckle.

I took him in with an angry stare. There was no need to say such a thing to me, and especially not in such a mocking manner. Couldn't he understand how out of place and uncertain I felt? "That's very good of you," I snapped.

When I saw the surprise in his expression, I softened my voice, contritely. After all, he had a right to be tired and edgy, too. "There's something I should have said earlier, too. I appreciate that you came to my rescue during that confrontation."

He made a dismissive gesture with his cup. "You didn't need rescuing. You hit a squall, but you would have found your course soon enough." He emptied the cup. "I only acted as would have been expected of me."

"I had no expectations of you."

"Perhaps not, but did we not agree that beyond those doors," he paused to nod toward the massive, ornate doors of the foyer, "this was to appear a model marriage? A model husband would not allow anyone to speak to his model wife that way, regardless of the woman's ability to deal with the situation on her own."

"Oh, I see." I had to acknowledge his point, but still, I was disappointed. "You did it for your sake, not mine."

"Oh? Is that how you see it?" He put the cup into its saucer with care. "Well, you didn't do too badly by it, either. The whole place will be agog over our love story."

"Love story?" I stared into my tea cup, and decided to put it down before I dropped it – or threw it at him. Cainan and I had a love story. This wasn't a love story. Granted, our love story had a bitter end, and I didn't even want to speculate how this would end, but he shouldn't think he had the right to compare the two. "But, it's nice to know I'm not beholden to you for the effort, since it was for our mutual profit."

"Profit?" He matched my aloof tone. "Yes, I suppose. At any rate, that episode will be the nine day wonder of the place. There won't be any doubt that, even if we're not deliriously happy, we're well matched."

"Good thing, too. After all, who else would want us?" I muttered. "Why wouldn't people think we're deliriously happy?"

"Ah, caught that, did you?" He looked into the fire. "A deliriously happy bride does not pull away when her deliriously happy groom kisses her."

"Oh. I…you surprised me, that's all. I didn't expect it."

He turned his head just enough to meet my eyes. "A kiss at a wedding surprised you? Don't tell me he — sorry." He put up a hand. "I forgot our agreement."

"Yes, Cainan did kiss me," I said, answering his unfinished question. "But, it was a completely different set of circumstances."

"Quite so." He stretched lazily. "Well, it's been a long day and it's a cold night. How does a hot bath sound before bed? Did Merdyce show you were everything was? Good. If you need anything, just knock on my door."

I stood, realising that I just been dismissed. "Thank you." At the doorway, I paused and looked back. He was pouring another cup of tea and nibbling distractedly at a sandwich which looked ridiculously small in his hand. *What have I done?* I wondered. *I've married a man who is a complete stranger to me. I don't know anything more about him than he had a tragic nickname and a tragic marriage…and that he claims not to believe in divorce. According to him, I'm married to him for all time. I've done some very foolish things recently, but I believe this is the most foolish thing of all.*

He must have sensed my study, for he turned from the fire, and when he saw me looking at him, he gave me a pained smile. "Do you need something?"

I backed away from the door, guiltily. "No, just trying to collect my thoughts."

"Any luck?" he asked, rising, the cup and saucer balanced in his hand.

"Not yet."

The pained smile looked more pained. "Well, you're a sensible girl. You'll get all worked out, I'm sure."

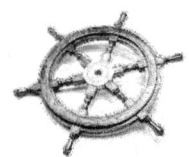

'Sensible girl'. I shut the bathroom door and settled on the slipper chair. *Now there's an endearment every girl dreams of hearing on her wedding night.*

Wedding night!

I looked around the bathroom in search of distraction. It was white, like almost every other room in the house, with few accents. Next to the chair was a towel cupboard with a rack where Merdyce had laid out my white cotton nightgown, freshly laundered and pressed into crisp comfort. My old blue toweling robe hung from a hook on the back of the door. Hardly a bride's trousseau, I reflected, but hearing Jaggar moving around in his bedroom next door, I wished they were flannel and burlap.

I bathed, brushed the tangles of a long drive from my hair, put lotion on my skin – all my nightly rituals, and then wrapped myself tightly in the thick old robe before I left the bathroom. My wedding dress draped carefully over my arm, I went into the kitchen, and filled a glass from the pitcher on the table, just as Jaggar came through, carrying the tea tray. "Where are you going?" he asked with a frown.

"Upstairs." It seemed perfectly obvious to me.

"But, your room is downstairs, now," he reminded me, gesturing toward the hallway behind him.

"Yes, I know." I backed up a stair or two and looked down at him. "But, since all my things haven't arrived yet, I thought it would be easier to sleep up there tonight."

He shook his head firmly. "You will sleep down here tonight."

"But, I have no bed, yet!" Would he have me sleep on the floor on a night like this?

"That's hardly a problem," he said, reaching up for my hand, "since you'll be sleeping in my room tonight."

"In…your room?" My throat seemed to close up and I could barely speak. "But, you said-"

"Yes, my room," he cut off my objections as effectively as my own panic cut off my voice. His fingers curled around my hand and he gave a little tug, forcing me down the steps. "Come along, now." He led me along the hallway and across the foyer. "I believe it is customary on the wedding night." He pushed open a door and gestured for me to step inside.

His room was the antithesis of the rest of the house. Instead of white walls and austere décor, his room was walled in warm cherry wood, with a matching floor, covered with thick rugs of black and blue with hints of red or rose. A massive cherry rice four posted bed dominated the room, the bedclothes drawn back invitingly, to reveal dark blue linens.

I'd never seen bed linens that weren't white or utilitarian grey. I crossed the room impulsively to touch them. They were as soft as silk. "This is *your* room?"

"Yes, of course." He pushed the door closed behind him with a decisive click. "Why?"

"It's not at all what I imagined for your bedroom," I confessed, running my fingers over the smooth wood of the bedpost.

"Really? You imagined my bedroom?" He slid out of his jacket and draped it across the back of a large chair near the window. "I suppose that's a start in the right direction."

"Oh, I didn't really mean imagine," I hedged, admiring a crocheted blanket at the foot of the bed. It looked very old, like one of the heirloom pieces my father had sold. "I just assumed it would look like the rest of the house - white and Spartan."

"Really?" he repeated, tugging at his necktie. He did not seem particularly interested in my opinion. He was just making sounds to fill in the silences between us while he removed clothing. His eyes were dark and veiled as he approached me, working the buttons of his dress shirt with impatient fingers. "If you don't like it, we can discuss it later. Come here, Mrs. Cingesleah," he commanded softly.

I didn't have to move. He kept coming closer and did just what I expected and dreaded, reaching for me and pulling me close to him; so close I could smell cologne and a taste of sherry and something else, a scent so subtle I couldn't place it. It wasn't wholly disagreeable.

"Now," he said, his voice dipping low, "I don't want to startle you again, so I'm warning you, I am going to kiss you." His hands slid over my throat, pushing away the toweling robe and brushing his fingers over my bare shoulder. "And this time we're going to get it right." His lips closed over mine, moving slowly, insinuating himself within my senses, teasing my lips open, exploring my mouth with a tea sweet tongue. His hands, while holding me firmly, also roved over me, finding the knot in my robe's sash, loosening it, letting the robe fall away so that he could touch me and not toweling cloth.

I recognised the scent suddenly. It became stronger, filling my nostrils with the desire emanating off his skin, as his fingers touched and toyed with me, parts of me more willing to receive his attentions. When he slid his hand under my gown, I found my wits again, and pushed away from him, frantically. "No!"

He staggered back, a little stunned. "What do you mean, 'no'?" he demanded, raggedly. "You can't tell me no. You're my wife and I have right to-"

I jerked my robe over my shoulders and tied the sash firmly. "Not those kinds of rights," I denied, backing away from his rage black face. Somewhere, softly, I could hear my mother's advice about men, something about marriage and a woman's duty...but none of it mattered much at that moment. "You said this was a business arrangement."

"Yes, of course," he said, bewilderment and incredulity melting over the rage, "but it is also a marriage. It won't be all business. It can't be." He tried to soften his tone, he even tried to smile. "I did expect to be able to sleep with my partner." He reached for me again, but I darted out of his grasp, and put the chair between us.

He scowled at his empty hand. "Wait one moment. Did you really think I would agree to a sexless marriage?" He followed me around the chair. "Let us get this very clear between us, Mrs. Cingesleah. I am not one of those impotent fools who would agree to a so called marriage of convenience."

"I thought it would be," I said breathlessly as I made a quick dash for the door

"This may come as a surprise to you, but the greatest convenience of a marriage is having someone in the house to keep my bed warm at night." He cut off my escape in a couple of steps.

"Then why did you give me a room of my own," I argued, feeling blindly behind me for the door.

"For your privacy, of course," he countered, still descending on me. "You said it yourself, you're accustomed to your privacy. And so am I, but that doesn't mean I won't want you next to me some nights."

I hugged the collar of the robe to my throat, feeling exposed by his words. His argument had logic, but I refused to lose sight of the fact that he had presented this marriage in a completely different light when he proposed. "But you said-"

He silenced me with a sharp shake of his head. "I never said I wouldn't expect to sleep with you."

"Yes, you did! You said you would never suggest something as crude as the surrender of my virtue." I pointed a finger at him, emphatically. "Those were your very words."

"Of course I said that." He was beyond impatience. "You thought I was expecting to have an affair with you." He shook his head. "I would never ask you to do that, and I also never expected you to resist me within the bonds of holy matrimony."

I was backed up as far as I could get, between the doorframe where he loomed and the armoire in the corner. "There's nothing holy about this."

"All right, if you wish, but it is matrimony." He had me trapped, now, and he hovered over me, apparently expecting my surrender. "Now, get in that bed before I throw you into it."

I stared at him, stubbornly. "No. I never thought you would w-want that." My voice caught and broke, sounding weak and fearful and angry – just the way I felt. "I asked you what you wanted from me and you told me you wanted a business partner." I felt tears on my cheeks and I brushed them away. "That's all you asked for. That's all I agreed to."

Jaggar reached out. "You also agreed to marriage, and sex is a sanctioned part of marriage."

85

I twisted away from his touch. "I would never have agreed to it, if I had known."

"You silly fool," he said in exasperation, "I thought you'd know what I meant."

"Well, I didn't." I was about one breath away from sobbing, or screaming, or both.

"Surely you expected to sleep with-"

"Don't!" I protested, loudly, covering my face with both hands. "It was different. It wasn't like this."

Jaggar swore darkly. It was a deadly sound, but there was something sweetly comforting about it as well, something I couldn't immediately place but it caught me by surprise. I looked at him through my fingers, waiting. "Sorry," he said, curtly. "I shouldn't have said that." He turned away from me with a broad gesture of dismissal. "Ah, I'm in no mood to deal with virginal hysteria tonight." He reached for his own dressing gown. "All right, all right, all right. Not tonight, Mrs. Cingesleah. I can see that you were not properly prepared. But, you had better get yourself prepared," he added, pointing a warning finger at me as he opened the door to the bathroom. "It is going to happen and it will happen soon. Goodnight." He slammed the door behind him.

Chapter Six
The Warning

Of course I had no hope of sleep that night. At the first finger of light in the sky, I was up, dressed and making coffee on the old stove in Merdyce's kitchen. I had spent the night thinking over the situation. It wasn't really as hopeless as I'd first believed. I might as well sleep with the man. I had, as he pointed out, lawfully married him. Despite all the treasured anticipation of those precious moments in the arms of a most beloved husband, I had to recognise that those were the dreams of a girl and I was now a grown woman, forced to embrace reality. The reality was that the circumstances of the night before might have been all that I could hope for, if only he hadn't frightened me, if only he hadn't made me feel so peculiar.

"Running away already?"

I nearly dropped the cup I'd just pulled from a shelf. Jaggar was in the doorway, barefoot, bare-chested, his thumbs hooked in the belt loops of his jeans. I swallowed that peculiar feeling again. "Yes," I answered, willing myself to act as unaffected as possible, "but I thought I'd have coffee first."

Jaggar reached over me to pull down another cup and saucer. "Got enough for two?"

I nodded, backing away from the stove as he crowded me without moving. "Help yourself."

He smiled, a strange and knowing smile, as he filled both cups. "Here."

I accepted my cup, and backed up against the wall, bracing myself for the inevitable barrage of questions and comments.

He matched my pose at the opposite wall, cup in one hand, saucer in the other, watching me. "Ready to go to work?" he asked at length.

I must have given myself away with my startled, "Why — yes, yes, of course." That was not the question I had expected.

He smiled around the rim of his cup. "Do you want me to ask, Sydney?"

I gave great attention to a miniscule blemish in the paint of the wall. "I don't know what you're talking about."

"Yes, you do, so don't insult either of us with that act. Do you want me to ask if you're ready to sleep me?"

"Don't be absurd!" I snapped, putting the cup down before I dropped it. "I don't even want to discuss it."

"Fine," he responded, crisply. "I don't care if we never discuss it."

"Y-you don't?"

"No," he gulped coffee, despite the steam still rising from it, "as long as it happens."

It was the perfect exit line. I waited for him to march out, triumphantly. Instead, he continued to lean against the wall, watching me watch him until his gaze made me so nervous I began to fumble around, looking for something to do. How could his stare unnerve me that way? It seemed ridiculous that the way a man looked, and where he looked, and how long he looked there could have any effect on me at all, and yet, those black eyes fixed on me made my knees a little weak, and my cheeks very hot, and my heart flutter in that most unusual way it had developed since I'd been ill.

"Sex bothers you, doesn't it?" he suggested, after an interminable silence.

"Bother me?" I tried to laugh. "Not at all. What a thing to suggest. I think it's a…normal, natural, beautiful culmination of feelings between married people."

"Ah, now you're going to put feelings into it, are you?" He took a step nearer and although I steeled myself not to move, somehow I backed away from him. "You'll only make me angry if you continue to pull away, Sydney," he warned. He reached out and caught a strand of my hair. "And you don't want me to be angry. Not now." He gave the curl a gentle tug. "Come here."

I inched nearer, even as my back stiffened at the idea being ordered around like a...a pet. Putting my hand up to my hair, I said, "Let go of me. I don't like to be manhandled."

"Really?" he drawled, his fingers twisting into my hair. "Well, you may as well resign yourself, Mrs. Cingesleah, this man is going to handle you any time he pleases." He slid his free hand along the collar of my shirt.

"Don't!" I pushed with both hands, breaking his touch.

His eyes were flashing fire. "Don't you ever tell me no again," he threatened, descending on me as I fumbled my way toward the stairs. "You are mine, and you will answer to me any time I want you. Is that understood?" He caught my shoulders and held me in a painful grip. "Is it?"

"Jaggar, you're hurting me."

"Then stop fighting me, Sydney." His breathing had become ragged and his eyes had that same dark, distant look they had the night before.

I pushed my hands up between us, preparing to defend myself, if he moved another inch.

But he didn't move. There were heavy footsteps in the room next door and Jaggar dropped his hands as if I had burst into flame and marched out of the kitchen, leaving me to wipe away tears of fear and shame before Merdyce came into the kitchen.

"Good morning, Missus," she called cheerfully. "Oh, you've made the coffee. What are you doing up so early? I should think a bride could be allowed to lie in on the morning after her wedding." She turned when she got no response. Seeing me scrambling to compose myself, she took a step toward me. "Are you all right? Your face is as white as the wall."

I nodded, keeping my eyes averted. "Yes, I'm fine, thank you. I've got to get to work." I tried to push past, but pushing past Merdyce was an endeavour.

The housekeeper caught my arm and forced me around to face her. "Did he hurt you?" she asked baldly.

I blinked at her, stupidly. "Only a little. He pulled my hair..." too late I realised Merdyce was asking a completely different question. "No," I mumbled, certain my face had gone from ghost white to dull red. "He didn't."

Merdyce lowered her hand, shaking her head, sadly. "You shouldn't ever try lying to me, Missus. I've got eyes and I've got ears – good ones, too, despite my age. I saw what was happening just now. You better learn another way around him – he's not used to a woman standing up to him. He's gotten used to having things his way."

I straightened my shoulders and said, proudly, "Well, I'm used to having my own way, too. I don't belong to any man – not even the great Jaggar Cingesleah."

Merdyce might have looked less stunned and less pained if I'd dumped the contents of the coffee pot on her head. Her mouth opened, her eyes widened, her body shuddered with a huff. "But, you're married."

"That may be so, but it doesn't give him the right to...to..." my bravado flagged and I pulled away. "No one understands. Never mind." Merdyce reached out to me, but I brushed her off. "I've got work to do."

The day before the wedding, Jaggar had shown me the room at the back of the house where he kept the books for the *Gabriella*, and now I almost ran to it. Shutting the door behind me, I covered my face with my hands, shaking. What was wrong with me? What was wrong with him? Oh, I knew better. After all, I had watched my mother endure loneliness, poverty, infidelity and even violence from my father and never display even a hint of desire to fight back or run away. Once I asked her why she didn't hit back when my father slapped her or pushed her into a wall or a chair. I could never forget the way she smiled through her tears, stroking my hair and saying that ladies didn't hit back. "Well, I do," I whispered fiercely, curling my hands into trembling fists, "if it ever comes to that." All the years on my own had erased the lessons my mother had taught me about a woman's place and duty. The reality was a woman's duty was to survive.

I scrubbed away my tears with my fists, and settled at the desk, flipping open the ledger. Perhaps, if I work hard, I decided, and showed myself to be an asset to the business, he might think I was more valuable as a business partner than a marriage partner and there would be the end of his more intimate expectations.

Numbers and letters swam before me on the pages. I could hear Jaggar moving around his room just beyond the door and as long as he was in the house he would dominate my thoughts. It was only when the front door slammed behind him that I relaxed and allowed myself to get to know the workings of his business and the fortune of the good *Gabriella*.

The boat did a good business. He, like many other fishermen of the coves, inlets and bays of Newfoundland, would commission for long trips, laying his nets several miles out to sea, stopping right on the commercial fishing boundaries. This was a practise I'd always avoided. I only had the one boat, and I could not afford to risk the daily business for the hopes of one big haul that might have to be delivered to St. John's or across the Gulf of St. Lawrence to Quebec. I preferred to send the *Sidonie Stone* to the edge of the Bay and have it back in port by noon or better, to sell her catch to local shops and restaurants. I wondered about suggesting the same strategy to Jaggar until we had the money to purchase a second boat for local fishing, and then send the *Gabriella* back out to sea.

No, the more trips Jaggar made to the outer reaches of the fishing boundaries, the more nights he would be away from home and away from me.

Merdyce brought me some tea and toast around ten o'clock and I closed the books with a sigh. "Mr. Cingesleah is right," I told her, reaching for the cup, "he doesn't know his books."

Merdyce sniffed indignantly. "He's always done well enough."

"He's done better than enough," I corrected, shoving a thumb toward the ledger. "He has more money than he thinks."

Merdyce looked slightly horrified to be privy to the man's financial circumstances and she hurried out of the room without a comment.

Funny woman, I thought, sinking back into the creaking old desk chair. *She has no scruples about listening to gossip or speaking her mind about marriage, but God forbid she hear a word about a man's money. She didn't mind boasting about his position and reputation when he was…*

I sat up and put the cup down carelessly, splashing tea as I reached for the ledger again, turning pages and reviewing numbers quickly. Jaggar had been a banker. How could a banker make these errors? Some were no more than simple addition problems. The only answer was that he didn't miss them because, until he got the idea of marrying me, the errors didn't exist.

What in the world was the man up to? There were so many things about him that confused me, the doctored books, the impulsive proposal, the insistence that there would be no divorce… I closed the ledger again and pushed it away. He had said he did not believe in divorce, and yet Merdyce said he had gone back to Quebec to get one from his first wife. Had he actually gotten his divorce? Was he still married to the first Mrs. Cingesleah? Had I married a bigamist?

"I have to find out, but how?" I pushed away from the desk. "I can't simply ask him and give away the fact that Merdyce told me anything so personal." I began to pace. "But how else do I bring up the subject?" The idea of bigamy repulsed me. My father had a comrade the last few years of his life; Laughing Jack he was called, and if he had a surname no one knew it. Laughing Jack was a tall, powerfully built man with perpetually blue-black stubble of a beard. In contrast, he wore fine clothes, and always carried a gun with intricately carved handles. When he smiled, which was often, he revealed missing front teeth and a mean nature. He always bragged that he had a dozen wives in a dozen ports and he loved the variety. He even told my father once that he was going to make me his thirteenth wife as soon as I 'grew some breasts.'

Just the memory of that statement made me shiver and cover myself. My father had laughed along with him that night, and I always feared that Laughing Jack knew something about my father that would prevent him from protecting me from the man. Fortunately, Laughing Jack died before he could make good on his claim. Unfortunately, he died in the same enterprise that took my father's life. Just thinking the word bigamist made me think of Laughing Jack in his silk shirt and missing front teeth.

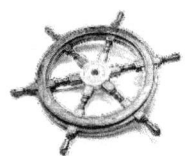

Jaggar returned a little after noon. He had been gone seven hours and he looked as if he had been climbing uphill the entire time. He looked weary and haggard and smelled of rotted fish. Now that I knew this was not his chosen profession, I understood why he always looked so beaten, and I also understood why, despite owning the largest single vessel afloat in the Bay, he had never achieved any notable success. It was up to me to revitalize his business. I was a keen negotiator, everyone knew that. If I wasn't particularly liked, at least I was respected for knowing what my catch was worth, and knowing how to get that price. I was going to have to take over the negotiations.

He met me at the table for tea, noting that, while he had showered and shaved, I had dressed for business. "Going out?" he asked curtly.

"As a matter of fact, I am," I told him, sliding onto the bench at his left. "I've got to see about moving my things, and there are one or two other details I must look into today."

"I've already hired someone to move your things," he reminded me, gruffly, tearing a bread roll apart almost savagely.

"I know, and thank you, but I'd like to supervise." I tucked my napkin into my lap. "After all, they are my things. I'll be back before dark."

He didn't bother to reply since he saw he wasn't going to win the argument, and he didn't want to concede. He took a spoonful of honey and dribbled it over the bread. "How do the books look?"

"Fine, as you well know, since you are the one who doctored them.

I had never imagined a man with such a dark complexion would blush, but he did and it wasn't particularly pleasant. "So you found me out."

"A child in primary school could have done," I told him honestly. "You clearly know your way around a ledger. Why the deception?"

"Laziness," he answered, spreading the honey around. "By the time I finish a day's work, I'm too weary to put any concern into the recordkeeping. I thought it would be nice to have someone else able to do it for me."

I wasn't completely sure that was the truth, either, but I decided to accept it for the moment. "I wanted to discuss the negotiating and commissions with you."

"Don't." He waved the subject away. "I used to love to dicker and haggle, but now it's too much effort for too little result."

"That's because you're so tired." I leaned toward him intently, nearly touching his hand. "Why not let me do it? I have a reputation for being able to drive a hard bargain. I'm the one managing the books. It makes sense for me to do it."

His hard look made it clear I was interfering and it wasn't welcome. "Well, well, well. Where's that little girl I scared squeakless this morning? She's got her sea legs, now, and is going to stand straight and steady."

"I'm serious," I told him.

"I can see that." His hard look turned into a leer. "Are you sure you want to do that? After all," he shot a glance over his shoulder, toward the door to the kitchen, "it will give me more energy and you more fatigue."

"Stop giving everything a sexual meaning," I hissed. "I thought you wanted to make this partnership a success?"

"Stop giving everything a business meaning," he snapped. "I want the marriage to be a success, too."

I was surprised by that confession, and didn't school the surprise from my expression.

He sighed, impatiently. "I mean, if the marriage isn't a success, the business won't be, either. In this situation, one follows the other."

I didn't agree, but I didn't argue, either. That would be sending me out into dangerous waters again. "All right then, let me do the negotiating. Yes, or no?"

"Yes, yes, yes," he said, tiredly, pushing his plate away. "Excuse me, I'm going to lie down a while." His dark eyes met mine, full of meaning. "I didn't get much sleep last night. None for me, Merdyce," he added as the woman came in with an over laden tray. "I'll see you at suppertime." He kicked his chair back with the heel of his boot, and strode out, leaving me very dissatisfied with my victory.

95

Perle Butcher Lyon

The packing and cleaning took longer than I had planned. I didn't realise I had collected so many possessions, so many little worthless trinkets gathered from around the world. A great many of them I threw away, or gave to the men who were hired to take away the furniture and boxes. I didn't even feel a twinge of remorse to rid myself of so many vestiges of my former life. There were a few possessions I had to keep, however: a photograph of my mother and a lace scarf she had made, a map of the place where my father died, a silk fan and a mosaic lamp he had been bringing home to me, a violet woven of horsehair from Cainan and a few love letters he had smuggled to me, all of these things I locked into a small trunk and put the key on a chain around my neck.

As I was leaving the little house for the last time, I started down the muddy, cobbled street and saw a painfully familiar figure striding toward me. It was Mrs. Keel, still draped head to foot in black, her heavy veil and long skirts snapping loudly in the freshening breeze. If it weren't so heartbreaking, she would have made a very laughable figure. She marched toward me with purpose, one black gloved hand outstretched, pointing an accusing finger. "I thought you'd be here," she announced. "I want to have a word with you."

Of course she would come here; she wouldn't dare come looking for me at Jaggar's house. "Not today, Mrs. Keel," I implored. "I'm very late already." The sun had already dipped below the hills behind Jaggar's house and I'd promised to be home before dark.

96

Mrs. Keel took a determined stance on the only part of the road high enough not to be a puddle, effectively blocking my path. "You'll hear me out, young woman," she vowed. "I want you to know that I know why you married Jaggar Cingesleah." By now that accusing finger was barely an inch from my nose. "And I'm going to see to it that you never have a happy moment with him."

It was on the tip of my tongue to assure the woman that she needn't worry on that score, the damage was already done, but my pride wouldn't allow it. "I don't see how you can possibly succeed, Mrs. Keel, nor do I understand why it matters so much to you. You wanted to deny that Cainan and I were married. Since you've cut off any connection I might have with you, my subsequent marriage is of no consequence to you. And," I drew in a deep breath to force out the lie, "I think Mr. Cingesleah and I have a promising future." *Well, that's true; it promises to be a disaster.*

"Don't bother putting on airs, Miss Stone. It can't be that promising if he didn't dare marry you in the Church," Mrs. Keel challenged.

"It's Mrs. Cingesleah." Over her shoulder, I could see curious onlookers gathering for the next chapter of the melodrama. "We didn't marry in the church because we're not Catholic."

"That's how much you know of your husband," Mrs. Keel answered smugly. "It so happens he *is* Catholic. Why, he went to Communion yesterday morning before your so called wedding."

I staggered back, as if she had slapped me. If he were that devout, he would never have sought a divorce from his first wife. Of course, a devout Catholic was not likely to enter into bigamy, either. "Well, I hope you feel better for having told me, Mrs. Keel," I said, trying to sound unaffected. "I just wish I knew why it matters so much to you if Jag-Mr. Cingesleah, that is, and I are happy."

"Why should you be happy?" Mrs. Keel demanded. "You stole my son. You don't deserve to be happy. I'll make sure you never are."

"I didn't-" I pushed away, stepping into the mud to go around the woman. "I've got to be going. I'm late already." Blindly, I forced myself forward, down the narrow streets and up the road to the Mediterranean anomaly that was now home.

Once at Jaggar's door, I reached for the brass handle, only to have it fly back from my fingers. Jaggar filled the door, eyes blazing much like Mrs. Keel's had been. "Where have you been?" he demanded. "You were expected home over an hour ago."

I was too stunned to be angry at his presumptuous and unwarranted reaction. I murmured something about the movers taking such a long time, and slid inside, and out of his reach.

"They were here and gone an hour ago," he informed me, slamming the door. "Where were you?"

I looked up at him, the rest of the story on my tongue but the words would not come out. I couldn't tell him about that humiliating encounter with Mrs. Keel. "I had to clean up after them. I couldn't leave the place a shambles, could I?" *Oh, Jaggar, did you get that divorce, or not?*

"I sent someone to do that," he countered.

"Yes, I know, and thank you." I tugged the wool scarf from my neck and put it on the table in the foyer. "But, you know how it is. I just wanted to leave things a certain way – my way." I glanced toward the dining room, the door closed as if to say 'there'll be no supper for you this night' "Merdyce would understand."

"Oh, I understand well enough." He reached for the collar of my mackintosh and yanked it savagely from my shoulders. Are you sure you weren't trying to melt some other fool's heart in order to get away from me?"

"No!" I jumped out of his reach, rubbing my shoulder. "As if I could melt your heart," I muttered.

"What?" He took a step nearer.

"I said I wasn't trying to melt any hearts," I lied.

"Well, don't even try, my girl," he warned, putting my coat on a hook next to his, "because there's no escaping this marriage. I'll never give you a divorce, no matter how far you run."

Well, that certainly answers that question, I realised, my heart starting to pound. *I'm only one of this man's wives. What if I work myself ragged to turn his business around? Would he leave me and take the proceeds back to his first wife, or worse, move on to a third woman? Suppose, God forbid, he didn't come home one night from the sea. Who would be his legal heir? Who had the legal right to mourn him? How did I get into this situation? And...why did he?*

"Do you understand me?" he repeated, harshly.

"Yes, yes, yes," I said, mimicking his impatient mannerism, "but I wasn't doing anything you'd disapprove. I cleaned up my house, as I told you – "

"This is your house," he corrected sharply.

House, I thought, *not home. How funny that such a distinction should matter to me.* "Yes, the old house. And on the way back..."

"Yes?" he prompted. "What happened on the way back?"

"Nothing," I sighed.

He grabbed my shoulder. "Don't lie to me, Sydney. I will not tolerate being lied to. I'd rather you told me the worst thing in the world rather than lie to me. What happened on the way home? What happened that's filling your eyes with tears?"

I rubbed my eyes, impatiently. "Nothing, I tell you and you'd better learn that I expect to be believed when I state something. My word is good all over this town. It had better be good in this house." I darted around him. "And what is all this questioning about, anyway? I don't owe you explanations for my whereabouts."

"You owe me your very life, Sydney Cingesleah." He was no longer yelling, but his voice had taken on an edge as it dropped. "I saved you from the gutter. I gave you my name, my home. For that you owe me your respect and the assurance that you're not doing anything to bring shame on that name or this house."

Hands behind my back, I counted ten, twisting the two wedding rings around on my finger. "This is my word," I said carefully, "that I have done nothing to bring shame on that name or this house. You'll just have to accept it."

"I do not," he answered indignantly. His eyes narrowed meanly. "How do I know you haven't? What proof have you got?"

I knew what he was implying and the all the wounds inflicted the last two weeks burned hot in my eyes. "You know what proof, Jaggar Cingesleah, and don't you ever insinuate such a thing again."

He was unmoved. "How do I know that this maidenly reticence isn't merely a way of hiding a terrible truth from me? How do I know that you and Keel didn't steal away in the night because you found yourself expecting a-"

Words failed me and I flew at him with unleashed rage and hatred and bitterness and pain – not just for him, but the Keels, and every other cruel, unfeeling person in town, for fate, and for my future.

Jaggar fended off my attack easily, merely keeping me at arm's length until I staggered back, spent, sobbing, and slid down the wall to crouch on the floor, miserably. "Are you through?" he asked, as if amused by the display.

"I hate you," I assured him.

"Of course you do," he agreed, dropping to his haunches beside me. "Are you ready to give me the proof I want?"

"Never." I swung at him again and he caught my hand easily. "I won't tolerate this constant harassment, Jaggar," I vowed. "Leave me alone, or I swear I will walk out of here, even if I'm walking out to a gutter, somewhere."

Something locked into place inside him, his eyes went blacker than night, and his fingers tightened around mine, causing the rings to bite into my flesh until I made a sound of pain. "I'll tell you what I won't tolerate, Mrs. Cingesleah," he said coldly. "I won't tolerate my wife wearing a ring another man gave her." Viciously, he tugged the two rings free and, taking Cainan's ring from me, shoved the other ring back into place. "Here." He dropped Cainan's ring into my lap. "Dispose of it, will you?" He stood and walked away.

I slipped into that little corner room meant to be my haven from the rest of the world, almost as if I feared being heard or seen, before I could close the door and slide the bolt. In the falling light it was every bit as dark and dreary as Merdyce had warned, even with the familiar sight of my own bed. I now understood the significance of my narrow bunk, but I didn't even want to think about that any more. How could supposedly intelligent people make such a stupid, stupid blunder?

I kicked my way through the neatly stacked cartons of my belongings, resenting the boxes which confirmed my displacement. I might have been allotted a room in the corner of Jaggar Cingesleah's home, but I would never wholly belong there. I belonged nowhere and to no one and the only one who had ever belonged to me slept in the sea.

Cainan's ring burned in my clenched fist. Dispose of it, he had decreed. Had he so carelessly disposed of all vestiges of his first marriage? *Well, I am not as indifferent as he*, I decided, pulling open one carton and then another looking for the little cedar box my father had brought me from some mysterious port in his travels. I could put Cainan's ring in that box and lock it in the trunk with my other treasures. As I reached for the key on the chain around my neck, it occurred to me that Cainan's ring would be just as safe there. I unclasped the chain, slid the ring on it, and fastened it again. If I kept my collars pulled up, I could hide any trace of my disobedience, and I could keep Cainan's ring close to my heart. Jaggar would never know the difference.

I went to bed, content with my defiance.

Chapter Seven
The Routine

The days passed, becoming a week and then a month. The weather grew colder and more violent, and more days than not, the boats stayed in harbour, as ice floes were reported in the Bay. Only the most desperate men were willing to pull anchor and face the harshness of a winter sea. This did not stop Jaggar, however, and for this I was daily grateful. With fewer boats going out, the Fishing Commission had plenty of jobs available, and the local merchants were willing to pay a premium for anything fresh.

So our days fell into a pattern: we rose to eat in silence, save the forecasts broadcast from the wireless in the kitchen, and after he left, I would lock myself into the office and work on the books, calculate costs and profits for the previous haul and estimate the current day's sales. Just before noon each day, I would bundle up against the wind and rain, and walk up to the office of the local Commission to look at work for the next day. Then, regardless of the weather, I would go to the dock to meet him, consider his catch and negotiate a sale with the men from the shops.

By the time I returned, in mid-afternoon, he would have had his dinner and gone to bed or shut himself away in his study. I would record the sales and expenses, lock up the ledgers and retreat to my room until tea time. At the table, we rarely spoke, except to discuss the business of the day and the money it brought. On that topic, conversation was very pleasant because, if I say it myself, I am a shrewd saleswoman. After our meal, he would go out for a time, and I would retire and wait in dread for him to return and demand that for which he had been waiting since our wedding day.

And he never let me forget he was waiting. Sometimes I caught him looking at me in angry speculation, and other times he would have a look that got very near to longing.

Occasionally, he would brush against me or touch my hair, and his eyes would glow bright with a light that disturbed me. Sometimes, when he was short with me for no apparent reason, he would catch himself, pat my cheek gently and give me an apologetic smile. Other times, he would not apologise, and turn away from me sharply. He never slept well; I could hear him pacing the long hallway in the night, and sometimes I thought he stopped in front of my door for a long time. I would always pull the covers up over my head and pray he wouldn't knock. Eventually he would move back down the hall and I could breathe again.

The worst part, of course, would be those meetings at the wharf. When I appeared at the gate and carefully picked my way down the slick wooden planks to meet him, I know people stopped to watch us. Under such scrutiny, we were forced to greet each other with warmth and affection; very often he would bound from the deck to catch me up, swing me around and press kisses to my cheek or brow. For that reason I was starting to both long for and dread the noon hour. It was a queer confusion in me; as much as I dreaded it, there was something in the charade for which I longed. To every onlooker, we were the picture of a happy newlywed couple, and no one but we two knew the misery behind the doors of Jaggar's house.

We'd been married five weeks when that façade was tested. When I came in from the markets that afternoon, I shed my dripping foul weather gear in the mudroom and went into the kitchen to warm myself by the stove.

Merdyce brought me a mug of coffee, shaking her head in disapproval. "Look at those hands, they're nearly blue with cold. You shouldn't be out in weather like that, Missus. You just came off a sick bed."

"Oh, nonsense, Merdyce, I'm fine," I insisted, trying to ease the shivering by edging nearer the fire. "But, thank you for being so concerned."

"Someone has to," she sniffed, loudly.

"Dycie," Jaggar called from the hallway, "who are you talking to?" Without waiting for a reply, he came through to the kitchen. "Oh, you're home," he said to me. "Good, I've got something to show you." He turned and went out, just as abruptly.

Merdyce took the cup from me and jerked her head toward the door.

I got up and hurried out, peeking in each door I passed, and found him in his study. He was standing before his desk, a large grey envelope in his hand. "The holiday parties are beginning," he announced, holding out the envelope. "It's an invitation to a dinner party at the Mandells."

The Mandells were second only to the Keels in power and social standing in the area, and upon hearing the name, I realised the gossipy hens I'd encountered in Clarenville were kin to them. "How nice," I said, not taking the envelope.

"Do you think we should go?" He opened the envelope to show me the engraved paper. "It's for Saturday night."

Neither the Mandells nor the Keels had ever shown any interest in socialising with me before, so this could be only a thinly disguised opportunity to put us on display. I scowled at the idea, but perhaps it would also be a good chance to squelch the rumours about us. "It would mean an entire night of being watched for any false moves," I predicted. "Can you bear that?"

He studied me for a long time – at least, he looked at me; his thoughts were clearly elsewhere. "I've borne worse," he said at last. "And it might serve to ease some of the speculation about us, and make living here a little easier. After all, except for a few minutes every afternoon, we're never seen together." He put up a hand. "Now, that's not a rebuke, Sydney, so swallow that bitter retort. It's simply a statement of fact. We have accepted that we are each solitary people, but others might not understand that. I think it would be a good idea for us to go."

"Very well." I reached for the invitation. "Shall I write to them and accept?"

"Good idea." He folded the invitation up and returned it to its envelope. "And why don't you go out and get a new dress for the occasion? I think the books could handle it – even after I doctored them."

It was on the tip of my tongue to protest, but it was undeniable that my wardrobe could not meet the demands of even the most informal gathering, and the Mandells' gatherings were anything but informal. And anyway, arguments with him always ended badly for me. "If you like."

"I like," he said, but he didn't seem especially pleased to have gotten his way.

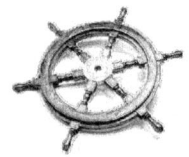

I had seen photographs in newspapers showing what society women in New York and Toronto were wearing to social events: long, body draping silks that exposed arms, bosom and back. Even though I doubted that the denizens of Hickman's Harbour would be seen in such revealing dresses, nothing the shops offered seemed modest or practical enough for my tastes. When I complained to Merdyce about the limited selection, she pulled out her shears and sewing needles and allowed that we could probably put our heads together and make a dress that would allow me to feel suitably stylish but not exposed.

Back in the dry goods store, handling almost every piece of cloth available, Merdyce came home with the makings of a flocked gauze of white over a cotton shift of light brown – in the right light it looked almost gold. She made a cardigan neckline and short cape to cover my shoulders, and gathered the skirt together at my knees to create a ruffle that stopped only inches from my ankles. It was ingenious; with a change of accessories it would make an acceptable ensemble for a dinner party, an afternoon tea, or a Sunday morning at church. The best part was that the modest neckline hid Cainan's ring.

I had no jewellery to my name except my wedding rings, but Merdyce lent me two gold combs to pull my hair up off my neck, and said I should use my complexion and eyes as my ornament.

I did buy a new pair of shoes, flimsy brown things, with tiny heels that made me stumble the first time I walked in them, but they looked right with the dress. In fact, as I passed my reflection in one of the tall, narrow windows of the foyer that Saturday night, I had to admit I was not merely satisfied with my appearance but actually pleased.

Jaggar emerged from his room, busily affixing a topaz cufflink, and when he looked up, his reaction indicated that he agreed with me. "Nice dress. Suits you." He shifted the knot of his dark blue necktie, and smoothed down his shirtfront. "Wotcha think?"

"You look nice," I said. It wasn't the same suit he wore for our wedding, but I liked the colour better. "I'm glad you like the dress. Merdyce made it for me."

"Did she?" He shot a look toward the dining room. "I thought we agreed you could afford to buy ready-made."

"Yes, we did." I picked up the shawl Merdyce had given me for our wedding. "But, I couldn't find anything I liked. It was all either old fashioned and frumpy or too... too..."I scrambled for a word, "new fashioned." I pulled the shawl around me, snugly, before accepting my coat. "I like this."

"Well, as it happens, so do I." He settled the coat over my shoulders and extended his arm. "I had the car brought up. Will you be warm enough?"

It was a funny thing; I slipped my hand into the crook of his arm as if I'd been doing it all my life, and I felt warm all over. "Oh, yes," I squeaked, "I'm fine."

Something amused him, his mouth twisted up and a little sound huffed out, but when I looked at him for an explanation, he turned away, coughed and reached for the door. "This will be good for us," he announced. "It's time the newlyweds emerged on society."

I wondered what he would call those heart wrenching scenes at the harbour each day, but I didn't ask him. Sensing he expected some sort of comment from me, I asked, instead, "I wonder who will be there tonight."

"Does it matter, Mrs. Cingesleah?" he snapped, yanking open the door. "You will be there with me."

"I am aware of that," I protested.

"And for that you are sorry."

Oh, perfect, it will be five minutes to the Mandell home and we're going to spend those five minutes in an argument. Won't that be a fine display of the newlyweds? I waited until he handed me into the car and climbed in on his side. "I am making an effort to be agreeable."

"And it is an effort," he said through gritted teeth.

"Are you determined to think the worst of me? I was merely trying to make conversation."

Instead of arguing the point, he said, "I expect this party is in honour of their oldest boy."

"Leslie?" I tried not to sneer his name.

"Oh? You know him, then." Jaggar didn't seem very surprised – or pleased.

"Not as such. It's more that I knew *of* him. Ca – we had friends in common." I swallowed back my embarrassment. "No, I wouldn't even say friends." I sighed. "But I thought he was making good at some firm in St. John's."

"So I've heard." He started the car with a jab of the ignition and let it lurch forward impatiently. "But, it is the homecoming season, isn't it?" He manoeuvred the car toward the road. "I understand he's here for the holidays, along with a few cronies – those of good family, of course," he added dryly.

"Of course," I echoed. "Given that, I'm surprised mere merchants such as ourselves were even suggested for the invitation list."

"Oh, well, you know how proud Mrs. Mandell is of her illustrious family tree." He rolled his eyes. "No doubt there are a good share of the lower strata invited just to ooh and ahh at the appropriate times."

"I see." I settled back in my seat. "We're to be a sort of Greek Chorus."

He laughed. "That's a good way to put it."

"You surprise me, though. You talk as if you don't care much for her. I'd always understood her to be very involved in charities and other kindnesses."

"Kindness?" he snorted. "Kindness has nothing to do with it. Every time she donates a dollar, she gets her name in the newspapers. Every good deed she does gets her name on a plaque or statue someplace. You're right; I don't much care for her. I have more respect for people who don't need a spotlight to find good deeds to do."

"If you have so much contempt for these people, why are we going?"

He gave me a swift glance as the car rolled up in front of an oversized house on a rise above the high street. "I thought you could benefit from a little hen talk. After all, you are a matron of society now."

I shuddered. What an idea!

As Jaggar had predicted, the house was overrun with friends and family of the Mandells' oldest son, Leslie. Every window was shining with light, casting large squares of gold out onto the cobbled road below, and music and laughter and conversation mingled and spilled out into the street. As we approached the door, I saw something that made me freeze mid-step.

"Something wrong?"

"Yes, very wrong," I whispered. "There, under that tree. That's the Keels' automobile. I can't believe we'd both be invited to the same party. How...how disgusting."

"It is in poor taste," Jaggar agreed, cupping my shoulders reassuringly. "Perhaps Mrs. Mandell enjoys the power she wields in forcing a public confrontation. Do you want to leave?"

"Yes, I do," I confessed, baldly, "but I won't. I wouldn't give them the satisfaction of thinking they frightened me away."

"That's my girl. Let's go in." He rapped on the door, sharply.

As we were admitted, Mrs. Mandell floated through the foyer in shiny yellow that revealed and clung in places a more discreet matron might not wish to have clung to or revealed. My first impression was of a walrus in a satin sack. Upon seeing us, she produced a smile so wide it must have reached both diamond studded ears. "Mr. and Mrs. Cingesleah," she said in a loud, dramatic voice, marching toward us, her hand thrust forward like a bayonet. "It is so good of you to come. I was afraid you two newly-weds wouldn't be able to tear yourselves away from your little love nest."

Only dimly aware of Jaggar's undoubtedly appropriate murmurings, I scanned the larger room beyond. Most of the women wore sensible frocks, like mine, but a few were dressed as Mrs. Mandell, in thin, clingy things more suitable to a movie star's boudoir. In the midst of all the flimsy silks and sturdy muslins - draped in black that wasn't even remotely stylish or even flattering - was Mrs. Keel. It was the first time I had seen her without a heavy veil. And, as she held court, in the centre of the room, she was using her pie dough face and mournful gloom to full effect.

Upon hearing our names pronounced, she had whirled around and the look she gave me as I searched the room and found her was so venomous, I couldn't help wishing the veil had remained a part of her ensemble.

"Let me take your coat, my dear," Mrs. Mandell insisted. "What a...practical thing it is." She held it by two fingertips as she handed it off to someone evidently employed solely to collect unsuitable outerwear. "There. You look quite lovely." She sounded surprised and she knew it and rushed on to cover her gaffe. "Come through, come through. Everyone is in the library. That's right."

I didn't want to go through. Mrs. Keel's stare was burning through the dress Merdyce had created for me, but Jaggar had a hand on my arm and was urging me forward into what Mrs. Mandell had called the library, though there wasn't a book to be seen. We had to pass directly beside Mr. and Mrs. Keel, and though I steeled myself for an assault, there was no acknowledgment other than that poisonous stare.

Jaggar went directly to a bar in a corner opposite the door, and wasted no time picking up two glasses of champagne. "Here's to a short evening," he whispered, tipping his glass toward me.

I nodded and sipped. "Isn't it acceptable even for a model wife to have a headache so severe that the happy couple must go home?"

He nodded, looking concerned. "Do you?"

I was so relieved I almost smiled. "I'll work on it."

"Do. Oh, good, we're about to be introduced to the guest of honor." He indicated the tall man with a mop of white-blond hair being led through the crowd by a determined Mrs. Mandell. "Evidently, even the peasants must be introduced."

"Prepare your oohs and ahhs," I whispered.

"Leslie, look," Mrs. Mandell trilled. "This is Jaggar Cingesleah. You may have heard of him. He owns that boat with the three sails. And this," she paused for a dramatic flourish, "is his brand new bride." She presented us as if we were rare antiques or treasured artwork on display. "Sydney Stone."

"Ah, yes." Leslie had an amused, I-know-something-you-don't-know smile. "I remember Sydney Stone."

"It's Cingesleah now," Jaggar inserted. "How do you do?" He put his hand out in such a way that I could not offer mine, even if I were inclined to.

"Oh, yes, of course, you do. Before Mr. Cingesleah married her," Mrs. Mandell went on, with a delighted smile, "she was married to your good friend, Cainan Keel."

I gasped at her insensitivity. Let people whisper at my lack of discretion but to blurt out the dead man's name in a room where at least three people were still mourning him was more than a social blunder, it was cruel.

And there it was; now, even those who only suspected knew for certain that just two weeks before my surprise marriage to Jaggar, the Dagger, I had eloped with poor, dead Cainan Keel.

Jaggar withdrew his hand sharply, stepping almost protectively in front of me, hiding me from the curious stares and judgemental gawking. "That's true," he said, making sure his voice carried enough that no one could misunderstand him. "While I dislike the idea of benefiting from someone else's misfortunes, I must say that I could not resist the opportunity to help her in her hour of need, and in so doing express my admiration for her as I had never been free to do before."

I was astounded. The man had a gift for speechmaking I had never suspected. Even knowing his true feelings and motives, for a moment, even I was convinced of his admiration.

Mrs. Keel pushed her way through the group. "You must have felt more than admiration if you had to rush her to the altar," she accused. "Cainan had only been gone two weeks." She lifted a black bordered handkerchief and snuffled into it.

Jaggar answered with one of his customary shrugs. "Perhaps I saw no need to wait. She was being displaced at once, she had lost her means of income, and her late husband's family was certainly making no effort to assist her. Why bow to convention under such circumstances?"

Again the room filled with shocked whispers, but this time the discussions and stares turned toward Mr. and Mrs. Keel and the allegations of their treatment of their daughter in law. "It was a shocking disrespect to Cainan's memory," Mrs. Keel protested even as her husband tugged at her sleeve to silence her. "Well, it was," she insisted.

"Wasn't it an even greater disrespect for you to turn your back on the woman your son chose to love?" Jaggar answered with an edge to his voice. "Would your son want his wife to be left on the street to starve? I think your son would approve my solution far more than yours." So saying, he turned a determined eye on his hostess. "I'm afraid we're going to have to leave, Mrs. Mandell. I thought we had been invited to a party, not an inquisition of my wife for the crimes of others."

Mrs. Mandell no longer looked like a walrus in a silk sack; she looked like a burst balloon. Her coup had blown up in her face, and her position as hostess of the elite had been materially damaged by allowing a guest to be publicly humiliated. With a reddened face, tearful eyes and fluttering hands, she began effusive apologies and entreaties for us to stay, while her son Leslie stood by, grinning like an ignorant fool. The Keels, meanwhile, were slinking out of the room.

I had barely managed to sigh in relief when I realised that Jaggar was relenting. The group was being ushered, *en masse*, through another set of doors and into an impressive dining room, where Jaggar and I were separated by protocol and place cards. I found myself wedged between Leslie and his best friend, James. Jaggar was seated near the head of the table, between the daughter of one of the Mandells' neighbors; an achingly beautiful girl who looked about eighteen, and a lovely, brown haired widow in her mid-thirties, wearing almost the same dress as her hostess, but with a figure more suited to the style.

I watched them throughout the oysters, consommé and fish courses. Gleda, the widow, had the air of someone well educated and well-travelled, while Marthe was soft and sweet and blushed a lot. I had the charms of neither woman and it didn't take long for me to stop wondering why Jaggar had never once, since being seated, looked down the table at me.

I suppose I ought to have been content, however, as Leslie and James appeared to be competing with one another to lavish me with attention, tales of their school pranks, fortunate positions and their appreciation of my appearance. They acted and talked so much like Cainan that it was as if he were sitting right next to me, and I suffered for the memory.

Most of the conversation at table was a small, intimate discussion between parties of two or three, although at some point everyone contributed their opinions to the speech King Edward VIII had made earlier in the day, and that kept the table talk lively.

By the time the meat course came to the table, I had decided that if Jaggar could enjoy his neighbours I could enjoy mine. Caring nothing for either man, it was easy to relax and talk freely, laughing at their inanity and en-couraging their pompously parroted opinions. It was clear neither of them had ever had an original thought in their lives, but that wasn't going to stop them from expressing what thoughts they had.

I pasted a sweet smile on my face and turned back and forth between them while my mind turned back and forth between the pleasure Jaggar seemed to take in his dinner companions and the obscene ostentation of the meal. Nearly everyone in town was cutting back and making do. Some were doing without, choosing to go hungry to feed their children, yet this woman was serving at least seven courses to a company of twenty, just to impress and get her name in the newspaper – as if the society pages had any merit in these times! Disgusting.

As nuts, sorbet and a seven layer torte were being served to the requisite sounds of admiration, I was uncomfortably aware of dark scrutiny from Jaggar's end of the table. I turned my head just enough to see him watching me, full lips drawn into a thin line, his black eyes hooded. I gave him the same meaningless smile I'd been sharing with Leslie and James throughout the meal, and returned my attention to my plate.

When staff returned, lining one wall of the dining room with trays with glasses, brandy and cigars for the gentlemen, Mrs. Mandell directed the ladies to the library for coffee. Jaggar rose as well, nodding his excuses to Mrs. Mandell, and Gleda followed. This satisfied one of my questions; it made sense that Jaggar would choose sophistication over maidenly blushes.

Seeing that Jaggar had broken the constraints of custom by going off with a female guest, the group splintered into couples and foursomes, chatting and wandering around the common rooms. Mrs. Mandell tried unsuccessfully to instruct Leslie with meaningful looks to set a proper example, but he ignored her and invited me to tour the gardens with him. As they were reputed to be some of the finest gardens in Newfoundland, and it seemed very unlikely that I'd ever receive another invitation to view them, I accepted.

The fires in every room, and the wines with the meal had left me feeling very warm, but the night air changed that. An icy breeze was coming off the water, and somehow making the sharp turn up the high street to enter the Mandell's garden, as if it, too, had been invited. My dress, no matter how practical for almost any other occasion, simply did not measure up to an early winter stroll at night.

"It is a bit brisk, isn't it?" Leslie laughed when I shivered. "Let's cut into the folly, that will at least block the wind." He had a hand around my forearm and started pulling me toward the tall, well-trimmed shrubs. "Ah, my mother does love a good folly." He let his arm slide back to my shoulder, and around, in a single, casually graceful move.

I stepped out of his reach, one hand in front of me to find my way in the maze.

"Oh, come on," he complained, "it's not as if I'm stepping over my old friend's body. It's not-"

"Leslie," I said sharply.

He ignored me. "It's not even as if I'm stepping over legitimate boundaries."

"I beg your pardon?" I stopped long enough to look over my shoulder. "How legitimate must it be?" I turned to my left, encountered a shrub and fumbled to my right. "I'm married."

"Really? Then who's sharing the moonlight with your husband?" Leslie tried to put his arm around me again. "Cainan always said you were a hot blooded wench." He leaned against me, blatantly. "Come on, warm me up a little."

I had somehow been backed against another barrier. "Will you let me go?" I commanded in a hushed voice. "Whatever gave you ideas like this? If my husband should see you, he would-"

He kissed me, quickly. "I'm not worried about your husband. He's with the glorious Gleda; he won't even remember he has a wife when she gets through with him."

"I wouldn't be too sure about that, Mr. Mandell."

Trust Jaggar to show up at the crucial moment, just like the hero in a novel. I don't know if I was more relieved or annoyed.

Leslie's hands fell away and flopped around helplessly. "I didn't think...er, that is...well, how was I to know, damn it?"

"The wedding ring on her hand should have been a clue, Mr. Mandell." I couldn't see him in the shadows of the folly, but I could see my white lace shawl shining like moonlight as he unfolded it and held it out. "It's late, my dear, and time we left."

I didn't waste any time getting to that outspread haven. "Thank you, Jaggar," I murmured. I didn't love him, I wasn't too sure I liked him, but given his ability to show up whenever I was in need, I was very grateful to him.

He did not reply. In fact, he was silent going to the car, and for the entire drive home. Once inside the house, he glanced over the table in the foyer, looking for messages, and then hung up his hat and coat, wordlessly.

I had the strangest feeling that he was blaming me for the scene in the Mandells' maze, and the even stranger feeling that his attitude mattered a great deal.

Pausing in the hallway, he finally looked back at the door, where I waited. "We'll talk in my room," he said, flatly.

I obeyed. I did not want to. My heart was thudding in my ears as I started to cross the floor. He seemed most dangerous when he was controlling his temper like that. I wished we could talk anywhere but his room.

When he flicked on a lamp and pushed the door shut behind him, I didn't have to look at his expression to know I was in danger. His anger seemed to radiate off his body like heat over an open flame. "Jaggar, I-"

"Shut up," he snapped, shrugging out his jacket. "It was bad enough that we were put through that kangaroo court tonight. It was bad enough that they put every conceivable stumbling block before us." He worked the topaz studs from his cuffs, his eyes never leaving my face. "But do you have to play the part they scripted for you so damned well?"

"Wh-what do you mean?"

He took a step nearer and when I flinched, a little flicker of satisfaction played over his face. "They wanted to see a Jezebel and by Heaven you gave the people what they paid to see. You might not have dressed like a harlot as some of those women did, dripping out of your dress and exposing your nakedness, but you certainly dripped out of your marriage, of your modesty, of your respect for me." He held a fist against his shoulder, pressing hard. "You fell all over yourself to flirt with those two pups and you couldn't wait to get off into the shadows to-"

"Wait a minute! What about you and Glorious Gleda?" I protested. "I noticed you didn't exactly tarry when offered a chance to go off on your own with her, despite the fact that Mrs. Mandell had invited us into the library."

"Oh, you managed to notice?" He tugged his tie from his collar and flung it aside.

"*Everyone* noticed it. It was a great breach of etiquette and everyone was talking about it."

"If anyone had been paying attention, they would have seen that the woman had far too much to drink. I escorted her to the kitchen to see that she got some black coffee and arranged for someone to take her home. When I returned to the dining room, everyone had scattered but there was a lot of whispering about my wife and her spectacular exit with young Mandell." He grabbed the capelet collar of my dress, and I gasped, putting my hands up to ease his hands off the fabric. "I'm surprised at you, in a man's arms that way. Perhaps I shouldn't be so surprised. There were a lot of people who felt that if Cainan hadn't won your heart, he was next in the queue."

"That's a lie!" He was pulling at the collar, choking me, and I couldn't move his hand away.

"Is it? Is it really? Then explain why you're so compliant for a junior executive from St. John's and you're stiff as a board in your husband's arms?"

"Jaggar." I tugged at his hand frantically. "I wasn't being-"

"I'm through waiting, Sydney. It's time we made this marriage everything it is supposed to be." He released the collar and I staggered a little, both hands to my throat. "Take that dress off." He stepped back and pulled his own shirt free, letting shirt studs pop off and clatter to the floor.

I groped for one of the bed posts, trembling and gasping for breath. "Not like this, Jaggar. Not when you're angry."

"How can I be anything but angry around you?" he snarled. "Still dressed? Then that's a shame." With one vicious yank, Merdyce's clever work was ripped away, leaving me in nothing but the basic foundations. He flung the tattered material over his shoulder and reached for me.

I twisted away, thinking I might jump across the bed and out of his reach, but his fingers locked in my hair and he forced me around to face him. His kisses were not tender and his other hand, grasping and groping, was not gentle.

I wanted to fight, every inch of me trembled with the need to resist, to push, to scream, to claw, but I struggled to be still. I could put up the greatest fight in history and he would still win, and he would be that much angrier, and therefore that much more brutal.

He pushed me back onto the bed, pinning me beneath him as he began to do things with his fingers and mouth I'd never dreamed of.

Suddenly he stopped, going as rigid above me as I was beneath him. Backing away from me, his eyes were fixed on the gold chain at my neck. "What's this?" he demanded, snapping the chain and pulling it away.

"Jaggar," I cried, roughly, reaching for it, "please, don't-"

He held it out of my reach. "I thought I told you to get rid of this?" he said, backing away from the bed.

The memory of his command was the last burden my resolve could bear, and I burst into tears. "I couldn't," I sobbed, sitting up, not even trying to cover myself. "I couldn't."

He wasn't looking at me. "Then I will," he promised. He marched to the door and threw my dress out into the hallway. "Get out of here. I can't make love to you with another man so close to your heart. I can't even look at you."

I did as I was told.

Chapter 8
The Revelation

Had anyone been witness to that horrible scene, he could not have been surprised that I got no sleep that night, shaking and crying with a pillow pressed to my face so my despair couldn't be heard. Nor could he have found it strange that Jaggar spent the night pacing his room like a caged tiger, from door to bed and back, growling and muttering. What would have surprised said observer was the way Jaggar and his crew managed to greet the sun from the deck of the *Gabriella*, or perhaps the way I was able to paste on a smile to greet them upon their return. It was surely a testament to our mutual determination to succeed that, without having discussed it, we had both decided that everything must appear normal to the rest of the world, particularly that part of the world that had attended the Mandells' party.

That's not to suggest that I had forgiven him, and it was fairly clear he wasn't pleased with me. After going through the conventions, we parted quickly; he to the house and I to conclude negotiations for the fish they brought in.

The weather was getting cold enough that even the largest boats weren't lifting anchor most mornings, so there was a clamour for Jaggar's haul. I would have felt pretty smug as I bundled cash and receipts for the bank if it weren't for the fact that I knew I would have to go home and face him eventually.

I knew the situation had to be addressed, but I was afraid where it would deliver me. There was no question that I had to go, and the sooner the better. Jaggar was a house of straw and I was a match.

As I struggled against the wind to take the receipts to the bank, I wondered if my new status as a society matron would give me more clout to get a loan against my insurance. If I could manage that, then I could get away. I couldn't go on suffering his resentment, nor could I bear up under his demands. The worst part was that if I knowingly stayed with a bigamist, I might be faced with similar charges.

At the bank, I filled out the deposit slip, trying to work out a plan. If I got an advance on the insurance someone might tell him before I left. I considered the cash in my hands, weighing the possibility of getting the money directly from Jaggar. It wouldn't really be stealing, I told myself; after all, I worked as hard for the money as he, and I would sign over my insurance policy, so he could get the money back within a few months.

Of course I left the money at the bank, but I was still resisting the temptation as I left and started home. The truth was that, whether I got money or not, I had to go, even if it meant walking out with nothing more than the clothes on my back. The next time he took a trip to the open sea, I could... I could walk out on him just as his first wife did, that annoying voice of reason pointed out. "Oh, but that was different," I argued aloud. "He loved her. He'd be delighted to see the back of me." A couple passing me turned to look over their shoulders and nodded to one another, knowingly.

Embarrassed, I darted across the lane, to cut through between two shops and avoid the road up to the house. I hadn't taken more than a step into the alleyway when I saw a car I recognised – probably the only Willys-Knight roadster on the island. I ducked into the vestibule of the shop at the corner and peered out between displays as a woman I knew stepped out of the car and waved gaily as she walked away – who could fail to recognise the figure of 'Glorious Gleda'?

Feeling as if I'd been gutted with Jaggar's long fishing knife, I clutched at the doorframe, dragging in air, and fixed my resolve to escape.

"Good afternoon, Miss," the chemist's clerk began brightly. When he saw that his potential customer was only me, crouching low behind dolls, a toy fire engine and French perfume displayed in anticipation of Christmas gift giving, his enthusiasm dimmed dramatically. "Oh, pardon me, Mis-sus." He emphasised the word. "What do you need?"

"Nothing," I said, peering out between a doll's legs. Gleda should turn the corner and pass by at any moment and then I could leave.

But, she didn't pass by. She reached the corner and turned into the shop.

Thinking as quickly as a muddled head could, I turned to study a display of a new pain relief medicine. The tube of wafers claimed to cure a myriad of complaints; aches and pains, nervousness, stomach ailments and headache. "These," I said, picking up a box. "I've heard they're very good."

He looked as if he was going to demand an explana-tion for my odd behavior, but Gleda interrupted. "Why, it is Mrs. Cingesleah, is it not?" she asked in that soft, sultry voice that must have taken years of practise to acquire.

"Yes," I said, trying to sound glad to see her. "It's Gleda, I believe. I'm sorry, I never learnt your last name."

"I'm not surprised," she laughed. "Last night you seemed to be having trouble with your own last name." Her eyes fell to the blue and white package the clerk was wrapping up. "Alka-Seltzer." She gave me the same I-know-something smile Leslie had given me the night before. "You're going to need those, I think."

"Actually, they're for Jaggar," I lied, digging money from my pocket, "that is, Mr. Cingesleah. Good day."

"You, too," Gleda called after me, still laughing.

With the package clasped against me, head down against the wind, I marched up the hill to the house.

There was no sign of the car, but Jaggar was in the front room, stoking the fire. He glanced up, but didn't really seem to see me. "Oh, there you are," he muttered, distracted, and returned to his task.

I didn't bother to reply. I shrugged off my coat and put the package down on the hall table. I wanted to get the day's transactions recorded and get into my room to begin a discreet packing up of my most precious belongings. Somehow I had to get Cainan's ring back before I left.

"What's this?" I hadn't even realised that Jaggar had left the hearth and come into the hall. He picked up the package and peered in. "What's this?"

I shrugged, avoiding his eyes. "A new kind of medicine for headaches and things."

"Headaches? There is a whole bottle of aspirins in the kitchen cupboard."

"I didn't know that," I answered irritably, taking the package, "and I had a decided need for them at the time."

"Oh?" He was looking down at me, searching my face for symptoms, a mixture of surprise and concern marring his brow. "Are you not feeling well?"

How am I supposed to feel, after last night? I started to ask, but closed my lips together firmly. I had come in expecting another venomous attack, and this unexpected swing in mood made me anxious. "J-just a headache."

"Well," he drew a deep breath, "you've been working very hard. Don't think I haven't noticed." He worked up a smile, "I think I've got the answer. What about another party?"

I shook my head adamantly. "Oh, no, not another-"

"No, you'll enjoy this one. It will be *our* party, just singing and dancing and absolutely no snobs allowed. We'll invite the crew and their families and some friends for a little Christmas gathering. What do you say?"

Christmas! Was it possible that Christmas was coming, even to me?

He seemed to know what I was thinking because he nodded and said, "Time seems to have gone by very quickly. I don't think I'll be able to take the *Gabriella* out more than two or three more times. I'm thinking of taking her down to have her hull scraped over the winter. I guess we'll be out of business for a while. What will you be doing with yourself?"

He knows! I thought, with a frisson of panic. "Well, getting ready for a Christmas party for a start," I answered, too bright to be believable.

He considered my answer, and forced another of his own. "Yes. Mr. and Mrs. Cingesleah will have a party, as well, and set this whole place on its ear."

I couldn't help liking the idea. I'd never been to a Christmas party. Once my mother died, we never really celebrated Christmas. I glanced toward the front room, imagining a towering tree there. "I'd like that."

"We've got some mistletoe growing in back, in the trees behind Dycie's garden, and I'll see about a nice tall spruce for that corner, on my next trek out of the Bay. Somewhere upstairs are some candles and ribbon and tinsel. We'll do this place up like a faerie land."

He looked so happy, when only moments before his face had been black with accusation. I felt almost duty bound to throw myself into the project with enthusiasm. "I've never had a Christmas party," I told him. "I'd love to have one here."

"Never? Oh, my girl, you shall have one, and a proper one this year." He patted my back and left me, whistling something that sounded very festive.

I took the receipts and paperwork into the office and shut the door, feeling a bit like my brain was trying to split in two. On one side there was the desperate need to get away, fueled by the knowledge that he was spending time with 'Glorious Gleda', and on the other was the thrill of having someone care that I'd never had a Christmas celebration, and certainly never a party, with a tree and decorations.

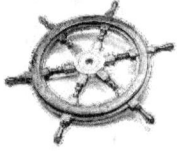

Merdyce threw herself into the preparations much the way she did for every other occasion, scouring cookbooks and reviewing the contents of the larder, going through boxes in the attic in search of holiday décor, sending Jaggar off on mysterious errands, and singing to herself as she worked.

Jaggar wrote himself a large cheque and starting sending off packets of mail, and delaying his return home some days, clearly prowling through shop windows. Some days he came home with treats to go into the kitchen, but one day he came home with a small brass angel to put on display on the table in the hall. It was beautiful. The face looked so serene it reminded me a bit of my mother, and I couldn't help pausing to look at it every time I went by.

I knew I needed to give Jaggar some token for the holiday, but I had no idea what it could be. I knew what he wanted, but even if I were ready for such a step, that was hardly something to be wrapped and put under the tree.

Day by day the house took on a holiday air. Boughs of greenery, with ribbons and silver bells framed the windows and draped across the mantelpiece. The scent of cider was everywhere as Merdyce put up her special recipe in brown jugs with waxed seals. Apples were ordered for pies and dumplings and crumbles, as well, and a bowl full of spiced oranges appeared on the dining room table. Paper rustled late into the evening in the kitchen, and the wireless was switched from the shipping forecasts to holiday music broadcast way down in New York City.

Jaggar prepared the guest list and I wrote out the invitations. It was embarrassing that, though I'd lived in the town eight years, many of the names on his list were un-known to me.

When I had time, I would slip into the office and consider the advertisements in the newspapers and magazines, looking for something suitable for Jaggar. His life was so rough and tumble now, but I had seen evidence that he appreciated finer things in his former life. He had a nice wrist watch, and elegant shirt studs, he had at least two well-tailored suits and linen shirts. He had a pocket knife that certainly hadn't come from the fisherman's co-op.

I suspected that Merdyce was knitting up jumpers for us both, so my meagre talents there would be useless. In fact, anything I could do would be useless. I was useless when it came to holiday gift giving. I might be useless for anything that mattered in a home and family.

I was in a full sulk that Friday morning before the Saturday evening party, elbows on a pile of receipts, chin in hand, scowling at the world in general, when Merdyce brought in a steaming cup of peppermint tea. "It's good for grumblies," she told me, setting down at my side.

"Well, then I could certainly use it." I didn't shift from my pose, and only belatedly added, "Thank you."

Merdyce tipped her head to one side, hands folded before her, looking at me.

I sent her a sidelong look that was full of irritation. "Yes?"

"You're not eating."

"Of course I am."

"Not enough to keep a bird alive."

I shook my head, chin still in hand. "Not hungry."

"Hmm." Her look became more intent. "Stomach troubles you in the mornings, does it?"

"No." I shifted wearily in my chair. "Not at any particular time. Why are..." I lifted my head and gaped at her. "You take that nonsense right out of here."

She held her position. "It's not nonsense. It's been known to happen between married couples." She shrugged a little. "Between unmarried couples, if it comes to that."

"Well, that's because..." I felt my face start to burn, "other things are known to happen first."

"Well then?"

"Merdyce, this embarrasses me. Please stop."

It was her turn to gape. "Do you mean..."

127

"Merdyce," I implored, "please."

"Well." She drew the word out. "That's unexpected." She unfolded her hands and put them on her hips. "Then what's got you so sour and out of sorts? It's not like you."

"Oh, I don't know." I pushed back into my chair with a heavy sigh. "It's this Christmas party. Jaggar's like a little boy about it, with all his secrets and plans." I turned to her, helplessly. "Merdyce, I don't have any idea what to give him."

"Oh, child, is that what has you in knots? He'll be happy with the littlest thing so long as you give it to him."

"I don't want to give him the littlest thing," I complained. "Even though we're not...you know, in love, he's been decent to me. I want to show him I appreciate that. I don't think a necktie from the chemist's shop will convey that, do you?"

"Now, let me think." Merdyce put her fist to her chin for a moment. "He does need a good inkstand. Have you seen the way he splashes ink all around from the bottle? I think I saw some very nice ones at the same shop where he found that dress for you."

It wasn't a romantic gift, but I didn't really want anything that suggested romance. And it did fit with his taste for nice things. "That's a good idea, Merdyce," I decided.

"You ought to go down now, while he's out."

"He's out?" I hadn't heard him leave. "He's always out," I concluded.

"Where would you expect him to be?" Merdyce protested.

"Well, he hasn't had the boat out in a week, but he's always out doing something." I hadn't really put the pieces together until that moment, but if he wasn't working, where was he? Surely he wasn't out shopping for the party for several hours every day. There was really only one answer, and her name was Gleda. "You're right, I should go now." I reached for the cup and gulped down some of the hot tea. "Thank you for the advice, Merdyce."

It was nice to be down in the town, despite the bitter cold, and the high drifts of snow accumulating at each side of the road. It wasn't even officially winter but we'd had three storms with significant snow already. There weren't many people out that morning, and those that were out were dashing from vestibule to vestibule to get out of the wind. It was a shame, really, because no one was taking the time to admire the windows in all the shops which were decorated with tinfoil stars and green paper bunting. The dry goods store had electric candles in the windows. I had seen them advertised in the newspaper earlier in the week. I had to admit they definitely added something to the display.

There was a clockwork Santa in the window of the post office, and a crèche in front of the church. Someone had whimsically tied a scarf around the Holy Virgin's throat. The grocer had candy canes and evergreen wreaths the window, along with a sign that promised condensed milk and oranges – both highly prized at this time of year - inside. At the end of the high street, across from the courthouse, someone had started a bonfire, and a few of the unemployed gathered around it, while someone from the Aid Society handed out paper cups of tea. Someone else was handing out tips from a bottle wrapped in brown paper, to augment the tea. Songs were being sung, loudly, so the bottle had been passed around a few times already

On the other side of the courthouse was the shop Merdyce had mentioned. The door was closed, and there were no goods on display outside, so for a moment I was afraid they were closed, but when I peered in the frosted window, I saw someone at the counter wrapping up a purchase, so I tried the door, and it opened with a jangle of brass bells.

The man at the counter didn't look at me until the other customer had taken his parcel and departed, but then he gave me a pleasant smile. He looked as if he had come from the same far off lands as most of his goods, with dark burnished skin and bright, mysterious eyes. "What could I show you, Mrs. Cingesleah?" he asked.

I was taken aback by his address. "I beg your pardon, have we met?"

"No," he said with a smile, "but everyone knows you. Are you looking for a Christmas present for someone?"

"Yes, as it happens, for Mr. Cingesleah. I was thinking a new inkstand would be good."

"Oh, I have some nice ones. Mediterranean pine with cut glass wells, or quartz in blue or green." He gestured to a shelf across the room. "And glass pens with brass nibs. I'll give you one, free, if you buy." He smiled again.

In the end, I did buy. The polished oak was beautiful and the cut crystal well would look just as nice on a banker's desk as in his private study, so I thought he would like it. The wood reminded me of my little treasure chest, hidden away in my bedroom.

It was more than I wanted to pay, but the shopkeeper did keep his promise and give me a beautiful, swirled glass pen, and some very nice paper to go with it, and put it all into a sturdy box for presentation. I got a bookstand of the same wood for Merdyce to use in the kitchen. I thanked him, took my purchases and hurried out into the relentless wind.

I thought I might take the shortcut up behind the chemist's shop to get home, but it was starting to snow, which would make the path slippery and dangerous. I could slip and fall over the edge and no one would notice, so I stayed in the lee side of the high street and fought my way up to the road.

As I picked my way carefully along the slippery wooden walk, I suddenly noticed that there was a car on the high street ahead of me. It wasn't Jaggar's roadster, but the Keels' Ford, moving slowly along the icy street. I pulled my cap low and tugged the hood of my mac up, ducking my head as I walked. The last thing I wanted was another encounter with one of the Keels.

They managed to get to the corner and turn up the street before I did, and by the time I turned onto the road toward the house, they were gone. I couldn't imagine why they'd have the car out on such a day. It would be useless for shopping, and everyone knew the Keels never shopped in town, any-way. The only reasonable explanation was that they had been on a trip and were only just returning. I made myself cease speculation, because thinking of the Keels just de-pressed me.

When I got back to the house, I could smell coffee brew-ing in the kitchen, and there was a very inviting fire in the hearth, but no sign of Merdyce or Jaggar. I shed my outer-wear quickly and hurried into my room to hide my purchases.

Feeling proud of myself, and immensely relieved, I opened the door of my bedroom and bounced right into Jag-gar's shoulder as he passed, with a loud and undignified "Oh!"

He put his hands up to keep me from falling and his eyes went over me, curiously. "Have you been out?"

I eased away from his hold. "What makes you think that?" I asked nervously.

"Well, the snow in your hair, for a start."

"Oh." I brushed at my hair. "Yes, I was. I wanted to see the decorations in the shops."

"So you went down in the middle of a snow storm."

"It wasn't snowing when I left," I countered. "What's wrong with that? You were out this morning, too."

"Yes, but-" he stopped, and I was sure I saw a little pink in his face. "Yes." He left it at that.

"Well," I said, uneasily, "I should go and finish posting the expenses for-"

"Yes, I left an estimate from the shipyard on the desk," he said, seizing on an excuse to end the conversation and leave.

"Thank you." I turned one way and he turned the way he had come. I had to hold myself in check not to run to the office and slam the door.

I don't know what came over me. I should have been pleased that I had solved (or rather, Merdyce had solved for me) my gift giving dilemma. I had managed to avoid rousing anger in Jaggar for more than two weeks, keeping the house relatively peaceful. I had resolved to leave as soon as he took the ship to dry dock, which he had planned to do Christmas week if the weather permitted. Everything was as good as could be in the circumstances, but there was a sense of trepidation growing inside me. I don't know if it was simply dreading a social situation at which I was not adept, or the uncertainty of my future in the new year, or could it be irritation that he wanted to hold me to such a high moral standard when in public, yet he had no scruples about seeing another woman on a regular basis?

Or maybe I just didn't like the idea of him seeing another woman.

I shouldn't care, I told myself as I dropped heavily into the chair behind the desk. *After all, he's not really my husband, it's just paperwork. He's not in love with me and I...*

The candlelight of primitive emotions flickered into a corner of my thoughts that must have been filled with spiders and snakes and I didn't want to see them. I gave myself a good shake and reached for the ledger. "What he does," I said between clenched teeth, "is his business."

The estimate was under a dark glass paperweight. I'd never paid any attention to it before, but after spending the morning in that shop of exotic wares, I had a feeling the paperweight had once rested on those shelves. It was a deep blue with streaks of white and swirls of grey, which, held at the right angle, gave it the look of birds soaring through clouds. I wondered if he purchased it for himself, or if it had been a gift. It didn't seem like the sort of thing he'd buy for himself, but who would have given it to him here in Hickman's Harbour?

Well, that was another corner of my imagination I did not want illuminated, so I put it down and opened the envelope.

The estimate was quite reasonable, which told me even the shipyard was suffering from the horrible economy which had gripped us all. I wrote out a cheque and tucked it and the estimate back into the envelope.

That's when I noticed the scent. I sniffed the envelope. I knew that perfume. I'd smelled it recently in the chemist's shop, when Gleda was standing next to me. How did her perfume get on the envelope from the shipyard down the Bay?

I didn't have to light a corner in my imagination for that. It was easy to see that Jaggar had collected the post and tucked the estimate in the breast pocket of his coat. I'd seen him do that a dozen times. It was also easy to imagine him embracing Gleda, so that her perfumed cheek rested right above the mail in his pocket.

Angrily, I tossed the envelope aside, and it slipped over the edge of the desk. I slid under the desk to pick it up and put it back in the ledger. I was just being petty and melodramatic. There could be a hundred explanations for the fragrance on the envelope. I couldn't think of any, but there were bound to be.

It was on the far end of the desk, and I had to crouch and stretch my arm under the edge to get my fingertips on it and drag it back. As I did, I caught a glimpse of a small white point, like the corner of a piece of paper wedged under the bottom drawer. I gave it a tentative tug. It slipped free easily enough. When I saw what it was I backed out from under the desk and made certain that the door was shut properly so that no one could burst in unexpectedly.

I eased into the chair and considered my find. It was a photograph of Jaggar, and the woman in his arms with the large sparkling ring on her finger was undoubtedly his wife. I wanted to cry. Even in the faded picture the woman's hair was a glorious pale curtain of silk. Her lips were formed into a warm smile of contentment. Her eyes were dark and wide and turned up at Jaggar adoringly. She was beautiful.

I flipped the photo over, unable to bear the sight any longer. The delicate handwriting on the back simply said Jaggar and Lark, honeymoon, 1930.

Lark. Even her name was incredibly beautiful. How could Jaggar bear to marry someone as plain as me after having possessed someone like Lark?

A few moments later, Jaggar rapped on the door and I shoved the photo into a drawer. "Merdyce called you for tea, did you not hear her?"

I looked up at him, and I know that every feeling was on my face with my tears. *The poor man. He must have loved her so much. How can he bear to be here with me?*

"Sydney?" He stepped further into the office. "Is this what you do in here every day? Sit and weep?"

"Not exactly." I made myself laugh a little, and brushed at my cheeks, ineffectually. "I think it's the season. It gets to me." I stood. "Let's go before Merdyce gets a broom after me."

He stood back and let me come around the desk. "I should have listened to her," he said. "She said you haven't been eating."

"Oh, I have. She's just used to cooking for a man and I don't have quite as robust an appetite." I slid around him and out into the hallway. "I'm fine."

"She cares about you," he said, as he pulled the door shut behind him.

Meaning you don't, I concluded. "I know. She's a very good woman. Let's get our tea."

Chapter Nine
The Revelry

The party came off as planned. Every moment Jaggar and Merdyce had invested in the event was evident in the decorations, the food, the music and the guests' obvious enjoyment of it all. I found that I recognised faces as people came through the door, but I had never attached names to them. There was the man who ran the green grocery, and his two sons, the women who were passing out tea in front of the courthouse the day before, the woman who played the organ at the Church, the magistrate's clerk, the post-master and his wife, and several of Jaggar's crew, with family in tow. Each guest came over the threshold with a smile and warm greeting for me, as if they were welcoming *me* home.

Someone brought a fiddle, and someone else had a concertina, so it wasn't long before Jaggar's collection of gramophone recordings was set aside for some high spirited local music, and some sing-a-longs. Some of the music was traditional Christmas music which I recognised, some were of a seafaring theme, and some seemed to be the kind of rhyming song one made up along the way. The chorus was constantly changing, as people arrived, or wandered from one room to another to talk, enjoy the bountiful buffet laid out in the dining room, or admire the decorations.

With a well stoked fire in the fireplace, and a crowd of people milling about, the unlikely house had never been so warm, so bright or so beautiful to me. And Jaggar…I was seeing him with new eyes, too. He really was like a little boy in his enthusiasm; he seemed to bounce with excitement every time someone knocked at the door, his warmth was genuine, and he couldn't do enough to make his guests comfortable. What a contrast to Mrs. Mandell, who seemed to count each guest as an acquisition.

135

There were very few people who had been on both guest lists, but that was all right with me. The fewer reminders I had of that night, the better.

I drifted from room to room, smiling and receiving smiles, but keeping myself apart from the clusters of conversation. It wasn't that I didn't want to participate, but I wasn't sure I'd be welcome, and I was enjoying the role of observer. On such a night, lit with candles and carols and happy faces, there was much to observe.

"Having fun?" Jaggar appeared at my side as I watched two men break into an impromptu jig in the foyer.

"Oh, yes," I promised, "you've made a wonderful party."

"I didn't make it," he denied, dropping an arm across my shoulder, "they did. Look at them, Sydney, they are Newfoundland. Not the Mandells, not the Keels, not the snooty, high and mighties." He gestured broadly. "These are the true Newfoundlanders. These are the descendants of the men and women who fought the North Sea to start a new life in a new land. They're the people who clung to this rock, refusing to give way to weather, to government, to poverty." He pressed a fist to his chest. "You're watching the heart and soul of Newfoundland dancing in our house."

I was ashamed of myself. I had spent so much of my time here aspiring to the heights of Cainan's world, that I missed the people I passed every day, the people who smiled and laughed and made do and survived. "It's amazing," I conceded on a sigh. How had I never seen this world before?

The two men had been joined by other men and their wives and other men's wives, making a whirling sea of stomping and singing before us. "Come on in, Cingesleah," someone called out, "have a dance."

"I believe I will." Jaggar's hand tightened at my waist and before I knew it I was swinging in a circle of wool skirts and work pants and fiddle music.

I don't know how long we danced. There were polkas and jigs and one rough effort at a waltz. Jaggar got into the middle of a shanty, showing he knew how to lift his knees with the best of them, while the women circled the dancers and clapped to keep time. I was laughing so much my face ached.

There was a banging on the front door as Jaggar pulled me close for another spin around the room. Someone went to open it while he pulled me off my feet and romped around. Behind me there was a general cheer of approval, and Jaggar stopped suddenly, his face split into a delighted grin. "Mummers!" he shouted.

I turned to look over my shoulder. A dozen or more garishly dressed people tumbled into the room; each in ill-matched, ill-fitted clothes, with masks and heavy makeup, homemade wigs of straw and wool sticking out at all angles. They scattered into the crowds, hugging, mugging, poking and pinching, and eliciting shrieks and laughter. It was evident that some men were dressed as women and women were there as men; a very tall, thin person was dressed as a caricature of a glamourous woman, and a small, round-in-the-middle person had on a gingham dress and pinny, but clearly needed a shave. There was a 'man' in an old suit and second hand shoes, with a cigar held in slim, delicate fingers, and another dressed in rain gear, dragging a fishing net, but walking with the unmistakable sway of a woman.

As they snaked through the crowd, one woman with red straw hair and enormous black freckles on a white face paused before us and pushed me away from Jaggar, and with large, red lips open wide, threw 'her' arms around Jaggar's waist and attempted to kiss him. Jaggar took it good-naturedly, but managed to avoid the kiss. Another, dressed as a dog in a suit jacket and necktie knotted around a dog collar, caught me by the shoulders and sniffed my face, hair and neck. Jaggar didn't take that quite as well.

Someone started up the music again, and someone else called out for a song. The 'dog' and the 'lady' abandoned us to take their place in a circle. The group began a slightly ribald version of a holiday song, causing the company to laugh and clap along. Jaggar elbowed his way into the circle and began to dance, arms linked with the 'man' with the cigar.

Merdyce, who had appeared at the first cry of 'Mummers', was in the corner with a tray full of glasses, looking as if she disapproved of the intrusion, the noise, and the naughty lyrics, but there was no denying that beneath her heavy skirts she was tapping her feet to the music.

The tradition of mummers or mummer plays wasn't new to me. I'd read about it in old histories of England and France. It seemed to be an entertainment that knew no class distinction; it was as popular in royal courts as in the house of a commoner. I had not, in eight years in Hickman's Harbour, realised it was a popular practise here during the holidays. Nor had I ever witnessed the custom firsthand. In principle, it should be ludicrous; men and women dressed in outlandish costumes to lampoon aspects of the opposite sex or to mock social superiors and pompous politicians, going from house to house to intrude on parties and dinners with loud and bawdy songs and antics. Yet, as I watched the joy and exuberance of the participants and audience, I wondered why it wasn't a universal tradition and I envied those for whom it was a treasured memory year after year.

I was jerked, literally, out of my reverie by the dog in a necktie. Dragged into the circle performing a parody of a current dance craze, the dog held my waist tightly, bending me back and forth in rhythm to the clapping hands, and making me a little lightheaded. Before I could master the motions and stay in step with my partner, the 'lady' who had attempted to kiss Jaggar earlier, grabbed my arm and slapped the dog, scolding in pantomime. The dog rubbed his nose and pretended to creep off to sulk. This caused a great deal of laughter. When I turned to see if Jaggar appreciated the scene, I realised he was no longer a part of the show. I barely had time to scan the room and see

Jaggar at the door of the dining room, talking to the 'man' with the cigar, when the 'lady' began to parade me around the circle in an old fashioned promenade.

The mummers' antics continued for nearly an hour and when the fiddler finally begged an intermission and a drink, the mummers began clapping and winding their way back to the foyer, and we all followed, clapping with them.

Apparently, part of the tradition meant providing a bowl of Christmas punch to the company, and then guests were challenged to identify their friends and neighbors hidden under the costumes.

Some of the players were identified quickly, and I was surprised to see that they were people I had met at the Mandell's party. The fisherman with the net was none other than Marthe, and the tall thin 'lady' was actually James, Leslie Mandell's friend. I had guessed that the 'man' who showed Jaggar so much attention was Gleda, and I was proved right, and someone else identified the 'woman' in gingham as Leslie Mandell himself. There were a few that no one could guess; one dressed in clerical garb, the dog, and another dressed as posh society dame. When they went unidentified, they bowed and waved and walked out, their identified companions lingering a few moments to chat and have another drink.

I wasn't surprised when Jaggar and Gleda disappeared; Jaggar's expression had been one of grim determination from the moment the revelers were revealed. I'm not sure if he was annoyed that Gleda dared appear and claim his attention or if it was that James and Leslie were there and paid some attention to me. Both men were a little inebriated and seemed in extremely good cheer; every little word or gesture seemed to generate snickers or outright laughter. At first it was fun to try and guess what would make them laugh next, but it wasn't long before they were just tiring and juvenile and I wondered what Mrs. Mandell would have thought of their behavior.

It was nearing midnight and people began to make their goodbyes. Merdyce went off to find Jaggar and make him perform his duties as host. As we stood in the foyer shaking hands and thanking each guest in turn, no one but me would have known he was anything but delighted to have the pleasure of each person's company; his smile seemed warm and happy, his words with full of gratitude and wishes for a safe journey home and the best of holidays. But I could feel the rage roiling in him like a stormy sea; he trembled in his efforts to contain his emotions, and when James and Leslie came to take their leave, he wouldn't offer his hand at all and spoke through clenched teeth.

When the last guest had gone out the door, I went into the parlour to help Merdyce collect glasses, right chairs and wipe up spills on the floor and tables. Jaggar followed us and commanded, "Leave it. It's late and there's nothing here that won't keep until the morning. Let's all go to bed."

Merdyce didn't stop so neither did I. I had collected a tray full of glasses to take into the kitchen, and as I passed Jaggar, I thought he was going to knock them out of my hands. "I said," he said, roughly, jerking the tray from me, "go to bed."

I stared at him and then at Merdyce. She was staring at him, too.

He inhaled deeply through his nose and let the sigh escaped his lips in measured portions before saying, "You both must be exhausted. Please, go to bed. We'll all work on this tomorrow." He gestured with the tray in his hands. "Please."

Not really having a choice, I nodded my goodnights to both of them and returned to my room. I could hear them murmuring as I went from my room to wash my face and brush my hair, and I could hear him come down the hallway to his room, but I did not hear another footstep once the door closed, which was odd. It was almost as if he had stopped just on the other side of his door, waiting.

Once back in my room, bedclothes turned back, window opened just enough to keep the air fresh, I turned off the lamp and climbed up into my bed, exhausted. It had been quite an evening, exciting, fun, surprising, and bewildering all in one colourful dance. I would never have expected Leslie, James, Gleda or Marthe to take part in something as silly and boisterous as a mummer's play, or to come to our house, of all places. Nor would have I expected Jaggar's almost violent reaction to their presence when he realised who they were. I wouldn't have expected Jaggar to insist we leave the cleaning up for the morning, either. For a man, he was as fastidious as a cat.

I got an unexpected explanation for that question, however, as I lay there watching the moon send shadows across my floor. I could hear the soft crunching of footsteps trying to be stealthy in the snow just outside my window and I sat up, almost ready to call out to Jaggar that there was an intruder, when I realised it was Jaggar, walking slowly and carefully toward the road, casting long shadows in the moonlight.

The days before Christmas were quiet, even for that house. There were no more midnight trips, nor morning excursions. Jaggar stayed in his study, or sat in the parlor, staring at the fire. With Jaggar staying ashore, I had no work to do, so I stayed in my little room, reading, planning and thinking far too much. Merdyce was determined to keep the atmosphere jolly, baking gingerbread and apple tarts, and brewing up a tea full of spices, but her efforts were mostly wasted. We kept to ourselves and the festive atmosphere that filled the house before the party was gone.

The day before Christmas Jaggar went down to pick up the post, so I took the gifts I'd purchased into the office and wrapped them in silver paper Merdyce had found in the attic. I was tying ribbon around his gift when I heard his steps in the hall. I scrambled to hide the packages, paper and ribbon under the desk in case he came in without warning, but he didn't even pause as he went by. Slipping out, I crossed the hallway into the parlour and skidded to a stop when I saw him slumped in one of those oversized chairs.

He sat up and indicated the other chair without a saying a word. I shook my head and paused before the Christmas tree. It was really a beautiful thing, nearly ten feet high, with bows and tinsel and hand carved wooden angels and delicate balls of glass. I don't think I had ever seen anything so grand and I said so.

"Oh, little country mouse," he chuckled, "that's not grand at all. I should take you to St. John's. There are some truly grand things there."

"I've been to St. John's," I told him over my shoulder. "It didn't strike me as all that grand."

He leaned forward. "You've been there? I didn't know that. Oh." He settled back in the chair, nodding. "Your first marriage. I'm sorry, I forgot."

I shrugged and returned my gaze to the decorated tree. "When we first came to Newfoundland we settled in St. John's. But," I sighed, "my father made some enemies there."

"Did he?"

I nodded. "It was late 1930, when there was so much talk about giving up our independence and putting New-foundland's government and banks back into the control of England, or perhaps becoming a province of Canada. There were some pretty strong feelings and my father...well, he said a lot of things, but it basically came down to him calling a lot of people cowards."

Jaggar whistled softly. "I'm surprised you felt safe stopping in Hickman's Harbour."

I shrugged. I nearly said that I wished we hadn't stopped in Hickman's Harbour.

"Well," he slapped his thighs and stood. "We'll go back to St. John's and maybe you'll see it in a better light."

"We will?"

"Mm hmm. I have some business there. We'll go up Boxing Day and stay through Twelfth Night."

Business. I'd heard Glorious Gleda was from St. John's. Could his sour mood and stay-at-home behaviour mean that she had gone back? "Oh, if you have business, you won't want me tagging along."

"It won't be all business, and you might have a good time. We can do some shopping and exploring. I haven't been there in many years." He bent and poked at the fire. "Many years," he murmured.

Not since your first wife left you, I thought, looking at his broad back, his shoulders hunched forward in dejection. *Who was she, this wife of yours? What was she like? Why did she leave you? Did you ever care for anyone else? Could you?*

"You look so sad, suddenly. What are you thinking?"

I was surprised to realise he had turned enough to look up at me, his mouth twisted into a strange smile. "No, I was just thinking…" I rubbed my aching brow. "I'm sorry, I'm just tired, I suppose."

He nodded slightly, rising. "I know you are. You work so hard. The trip will be good for you."

It would be good for me to be an obstacle between you and Gleda? I wondered. *No, thank you.* I shook my head and forced myself to smile. "Oh, no. Someone has to be here to look after the business."

"With the *Gabriella* in for repairs and me in St. John's there will be no business." He was facing me, arms folded across his chest. "I had planned for you to come along, anyway. I'm sure there must be one or two things you might enjoy seeing."

"I told you, I've been there before. I've seen everything I'd care to see." If he was going to be gone ten days, I could and would get away from here. "And someone really ought to be around to keep an eye on things."

"Leslie and James are going back this week," he informed me, tightly.

"I…oh!" I spun away and stomped out of the room. *The nerve of that man! Imagine him thinking I'd carry on with another man behind his back. There was only one man I ever wanted to 'carry on' with and that was Cainan, and now…and now…oh, Cainan, why didn't we wait until the storm passed?*

The door of the study burst open. "Don't ever walk out on me when I'm talking to you," he rasped.

"Then don't make stupid and vile insinuations," I retorted, too angry to remember that I was speaking to my lawful husband. "And what about you? Wouldn't my presence interfere with your visit to the 'Glorious Gleda'?"

Jaggar raised a fist, and I think we both wondered if he would strike me, but he did not. Instead, he lowered the fist slowly, working the fingers open and flexing them to make certain they had not frozen in that violent pose. "Rest assured, Sydney," he said quietly, "Gleda is not the purpose for our trip to St. John's. And, I repeat my invitation. It would give me…well," he paused, his eyes fixed on the desktop. "Let's just say it would give me satisfaction to have you with me."

"Why?" I challenged, even when every fiber in my being told me to take my small victory and run. "So you can force me to bed somewhere else?"

"No." He sighed and raised his eyes to mine. "It was brought home to me with painful clarity why you are so unwilling to sleep with me. You are the type of woman who needs more than legalities and conventions. You need more than to fancy yourself loved and in love. You have to have the genuine emotion. We," he gestured between us, "have nothing but a mutual desire to feed this township pomposity au gratin. I guess what I'm trying to say is that I've surrendered. I have no more expectations in the bedroom."

I studied his reserved and withdrawn expression, the rigidity of his person and wondered if Gleda had already provided the salve for his tortured desires. "That," I said coolly, "was a very wise decision. It would reduce complications if you found that you wanted..." I tried, but I couldn't think of a less trite expression, "your freedom."

He scowled. "I suppose you're referring once again to Gleda."

I'm not sure what I did, but something about me confirmed his suspicions and he slammed his fist on the desktop, sending papers flying. "Damn it, I don't want Gleda. I don't need her. I have more than I can handle now."

I suppose you do, I thought wryly. Two wives, kept far apart, might be overlooked, but three? There wasn't enough room on the whole of Newfoundland to get away with that.

"Sydney," there was a vague imploring tone to his voice, "I am trying to be fair. At least give me credit for that. Come to St. John's with me. Please?"

I shrugged. I wasn't going to be moved by that soft imprecation. "We can discuss it later, Jaggar." I gestured toward the mess he had left when he scattered papers here and there. "I have work to do."

"Very well." He backed out of the study with a wounded sigh. "We can discuss it over supper tonight, hmm?"

"Fine." I made impatient shooing gestures with both hands and sank into the chair when I heard the door shut decisively. And I cried.

I cried for Cainan and the dreams we'd had together. I cried for my mother who died before any of her dreams could be realised. I cried for myself, alone in a parody of a marriage. I even cried for my foolish, selfish father. But, mostly, I cried for Jaggar. He had loved, deeply, I now had no doubt of that. If even Gleda could not tempt him and he had relinquished his rights to me, it could only mean his heart still belonged to that elegant, delicate, birdsong of a woman, his wife. His real, lawful wife.

After a while, I heard the front door slam, and I opened the door just a crack to listen. No sound of his voice, no sound of his footsteps, no sound of anything but a faint banging of pots from the kitchen as Merdyce busied herself with plans for supper. Mindful of a creaking board in the hall, I slipped out and went back to the parlour. I looked down at the gifts gathered around the tree; there were far more than I would imagine should be found under a tree for a three person household.

Checking over my shoulder to make sure no one was in the foyer or hall, I knelt and lifted a few packages to examine the labels. There were several for me! I recognised Merdyce's old fashioned style on one soft, squishy package, and knew it was a jumper or scarf. Another was a long, narrow box that didn't make a sound when shook. Another might have been a book. I was reaching under the tree to look at a larger package in bright red paper when something fluttered in front of me.

I caught it and gave it the merest glance, tucking it into my pocket for later disposal. The package in red was not labeled so I backed away from the tree, still on hands and knees, and saw another bit of paper, between the tree and the woodpile on the hearth. I reached for it and gave it a glance. Then I pulled out the other scrap. They were both written on white paper and torn carelessly. Only, they weren't written at all. They were typewritten. I had only seen one other letter typed out and that had been from the insurance company after my father's death.

I looked over my shoulder again, and then poked around the hearth and woodpile, and even the grate of the fire. There were a few more bits of white paper scattered around, suggesting that Jaggar had torn up some correspondence and tossed it toward the fire hastily when I entered the room. I gathered up as many as I could find, pushed them back into my pocket and took them back to the study.

Spreading them out carefully, it took a while to find matching pieces, and enough of the page to determine that it had come from someone calling himself a detective in St. John. Most of the pieces evidently came from the salutation portion of the letter, but I did find two phrases that struck me as both curious and frightening; one was *located here in St. John's* and the other was *legal ramifications*. So, he had hired a detective who had located Lark, and now he had to go to St. John's and work out the messy details of having two wives.

I suppose I should have been happy. All my problems were solved. If he decided to abandon me up in St. John's without a penny I could make things decidedly difficult for him, so I was pretty confident he meant to settle some money on me to buy my silence before he took his first wife, *whom he loved*, home. I should have been happy, that it was all going to work out in my favour.

I should have been, but I was not.

I scooped up the sooty paper bits and sat with them clenched in my fists, and let the tears flow.

The door pushed open unexpectedly, making me jump and try to rub the tears away but it was too late. He had seen the tears. "Sydney, you're crying."

"Oh, Jaggar, go away," I complained, the guilty paper burning in my hands. "Can't you see that I want to be alone?"

"Was it because of what I said?"

It's always about what you say, you fool, I thought, but I shook my head. "Please, just go away."

He hesitated, and backed out with a nod, and I thrust the evidence back into my pocket and rubbed the soot off my trousers, before the door opened again and he came through, talking. "Sydney, I am sorry for what I said." He reached out and pulled my hand from my lap, forcing me out of the chair. "I know you didn't encourage Leslie at the Mandells' party, nor at ours, no matter how much he looks like Cainan Keel."

I was startled by his perception. Until he had uttered the words, I would not have even imagined such a similarity, but there it was; Leslie Mandell did have Cainan's colouring, build and surface charm.

"I want you to know how sorry I am for what I said," he continued resolutely. "I don't want harsh words like that to hover between us."

He spoke with the finality of a dying man seeking absolution for his sins. "You spoke in anger, Jaggar," I said at last. "But the important thing is that you realise I take my vows just as seriously as you." I said the words purposely, watching his eyes anxiously for any revelation of his feelings or plans. I only saw sudden and intense sadness.

He dropped his hand from mine. "Do you?" he asked in a voice I could only call weak. "Which vows, Sydney? The ones you made to Cainan? Or to me?"

I forced myself to meet his eyes. "Cainan is dead, Jaggar."

Merdyce was arranging long stemmed purple flowers in a vase when I came into the dining room that afternoon. "What lovely flowers!" I cried, recognising the rich colour of the blossoms. "I always see these growing through the snow up on the cliffs at the mouth of the harbour. What are they?"

Merdyce kept her eyes fixed on her task. "They've got all kinds of names. Some call them Christmas Lilies and some call them Flag Lilies, but I've always called them Lover's Lilies. There's baked cod for tea."

"That sounds good." I bent to sniff the flowers, but there was no fragrance I could find above the smell of fish coming out of the kitchen. "They're so pretty. I've never seen any up close."

"Yes." Merdyce paused, and frowned at them. "Well, sit down and I'll get the soup."

I pulled my chair away from the table. "Shouldn't we wait for Jaggar?"

"He's gone to make some arrangements for your trip," Merdyce said from the kitchen door. "He said you're to start without him." She brought a steaming bowl to set before me. "So, you are going to St. John's."

It wasn't a question, in fact, it was almost a condemnation. "I said I would discuss it," I countered. "I haven't made up my mind." That was a lie. "Anyway, regardless of what I decide, I hope he goes. It might do him some good."

"Might do more good if you went along."

I twisted in my chair to look at her, expectantly.

She lifted her nose, knowingly. "Might dispel some old ghosts about the place."

"You mean, like Lark?"

"Oh, so he finally got 'round to tell you about her." She went to the sideboard and brought bread.

"N-no." I tried to find a way to explain that wouldn't suggest I'd been snooping into his personal effects. "I was picking up some papers that fell and found a photograph that had fallen down behind the desk." I sighed. "She's very beautiful."

Merdyce gripped my arm, glancing around furtively as if she expected there were spies everywhere. "You found a picture of her?" she hissed. "Don't let *him* know. When he got back from seeing her the last time, he went through the house and burnt every photograph he could find. He hovered just above a catatonic state for months after. I was beginning to think he would never recover. "

I was clenching my spoon and holding my breath. "And you never learnt whether he was able to divorce her?"

Merdyce straightened, realising she had gone too far. "I'm sure he did." She eased her grip on my arm and turned it into a pat. "I wouldn't worry about it."

That's easy for you to say, I thought, wryly, you're not the other wife.

True to his word, Jaggar came in just as Merdyce brought in the fish and brown rice. "Oh, good," he said, coming to the head of the table, "you didn't wait for me."

The rebuke was unmistakable: a good wife would have waited – Lark would have waited. I tried to smile. "Merdyce wouldn't let me. She takes your instructions very seriously."

"Yes, I can always count on her." He dropped heavily into his chair. "I've been making arrangements for the trip. You may as well go," he added, lowering his voice as Merdyce returned to the kitchen, "I arranged for two rooms."

I looked up, slowly. He looked more than tired now, he looked…well…beaten. What pounded relentlessly on his heart to make him look so defeated? Was it me? Did wearing Cainan's ring in secret mean that much to him? Not even Jaggar could be so proud that knowing his wife – his self-determined business partner – preferred the memory of her late husband would torture him this way. Was there something else? Had marrying again reminded him of cherished memories he had banished when Lark left him? Was there still anger or guilt buried in those memories? I looked at the lilies, self consciously. Why should it matter to me? I didn't care a pin for Jaggar Cingesleah or his first wife. The only thing that mattered to me was that I married a bigamist, and that I wanted to get away at the first opportunity.

"Well?" he put down his spoon and drummed his fingers on the table. "You said we would at least discuss it. A discussion requires more than one point of view. So far, all we've heard is mine."

"Yes, I know. I'm thinking it over." I tried to smile again, and gave it up immediately. "How long would we be gone? You said until Twelfth Night?"

He shrugged. "Maybe, maybe less. It depends on how long it takes."

"How long what takes?" I asked, leaping on the statement. "What are you planning to do? I thought this was supposed to be a vacation?"

"No," he rubbed his unshaven chin, "I've found one or two things that must be done and they can only be done up there. But, you can do whatever you like; you can shop or see the sights or... visit friends."

I looked back at him, sharply. Why had he said that so strangely? Was it because he was making the trip to visit a 'friend'... or a wife? "I haven't got any friends in St. John's," I said, stiffly.

"No?" He picked up his spoon and ladled up some soup. "Somehow I thought you did."

I felt my face getting flushed with anger. "Look, if you're talking about Leslie or James, let me tell you-"

"Easy, easy," he cajoled, "I didn't mean either of them." He pointed with his spoon toward the hallway. "Didn't I just tell you that I didn't believe you were interested in either of them? We both agreed I spoke in anger. Do I look angry now? Not at all. I only thought you might know some people there. You lived there once upon a time."

"Well, I don't," I repeated petulantly. He was determined to make me look the worst in every argument.

"Look at us, Sydney," he sighed, "we're fighting again. Can't we just talk like a normal couple?"

"We're not a normal couple," I pointed out.

"Let's pretend," he said, dryly. "Let's go to St. John's and see what's to be seen, and buy the stores out, and just get along for a few days. Can't you do that? I can."

I set my teeth against my tongue to keep from lashing out at his smugly condescending manner. *See what's to be seen? Don't you mean who is to be seen?* "Yes, Jaggar, I can. And I will."

Chapter Ten
The Retreat

I had spent most of the evening in the kitchen with Merdyce for the sake of friendly companionship. Merdyce was not her customary genial self, appearing to be lost in thought with her brow deeply lined with concern. When I probed I was brushed off, and then she would brighten for a while, sharing stories of her girlhood in Quebec and her brief marriage to a Mountie. I would never have guessed she was from Quebec. She had less of an accent than I did. And it was hard to imagine the wife of a Royal Canadian Mounted Police becoming housekeeper to a disgraced banker, but when I attempted to find out where she and Jaggar had originally crossed paths, she shrugged off my questions and announced she was too tired, and excused herself.

Coming across the foyer from the dining room toward my bedroom, I looked into the parlour and saw Jaggar before the great, stone fireplace, slumped in one of the leather chairs, elbows on knees, chin cupped in upturned palm. Something about his forlorn expression touched that lonely little girl deep inside me. Leaning in the archway, I watched him. Somehow, I was overlooking our differences and really seeing the man for the first time.

Once he had been only a name to me, an entity that made my existence that much more difficult. I recognised the face, I heard the stories inevitably linked with his name, I had seen his determined stride down the very streets I walked, yet I had never really seen the man. Now as I looked at him, I had to acknowledge that he was by no means the ugly monster that one mentally associated with the appellation Jaggar, the Dagger. In a wind whipped way, he could be called good-looking, and although his name was synonymous with a ruthless and unbending nature, he really was a soft-spoken man with genuine and deep feelings. My heart went out to him just a little bit.

We had both spent the entire evening brooding over Lark Cingesleah. I had hidden in the kitchen with Merdyce to hide from my thoughts, yet at the same time I had hoped she would reveal something about this woman who had held my title for so long. I couldn't admit to her that I had spent quite a lot of time looking at that contraband photograph; she would have insisted that I destroy it before he found it, and I couldn't do that.

He had clearly spent the evening recalling his own images of those years together. Merdyce had accused her of abusing him in every possible way, but I had a feeling that they had been intensely happy until that terrible something happened to drive them apart. What could it have been? Nothing in my limited imagination could explain such a horrible and complete change. *Poor Lark*, I thought with a sigh, *poor Jaggar*.

He lifted his head at the restless sound, blinking black eyes at me, dragging himself to the present. "Yes?" he called softly. "Did you need something?"

I backed up from the door, guiltily. "No, nothing. I was just going to bed."

"Oh?" He glanced at the anniversary clock on the mantle. "Somehow I had thought you had gone hours ago."

"No, I was in the kitchen with Merdyce." I gestured feebly. "It was warm there." It was nothing more than idle chatter, but it seemed so necessary for us both to reach across that great void of our individual loneliness and make contact with another living, breathing soul.

"You're good company for her." He stretched his hands toward the dying fire. "It's still warm."

I smiled at him. "Well, goodnight."

"Sydney?"

I turned back. "Yes, Jaggar?"

For a moment he just looked at me. Then he said, "Come and sit with me a while." He indicated the other chair, empty and inviting. "I could use the company, too."

I took a step or two, uncertain. "Even mine?"

He ignored that. "I'll make more tea."

"Oh, no." I eased into the chair opposite him. The chair seemed to require a second party to fill the room up. "Tomorrow's Christmas, and we'll have trouble getting up for Church, as it is."

He cocked a brow at me "Church?"

"Well, I assumed you'd go to Mass for Christmas... wouldn't you?"

"You wouldn't."

I didn't even try to deny it. "No, but if you want to go-"

"No." He sighed heavily and settled back in his chair. "How would it look for me to attend Christmas Mass with-out my wife?"

"Like you married a woman who wasn't Catholic," I answered. The chair was more comfortable than I recalled and I had to stifle a yawn as I settled in as far back as I could.

"I can't get to sleep, at any rate," he said. "Maybe I could use a little brandy. How about you?"

I didn't really want any. I didn't like any kind of spirits, but the occasion seemed to warrant it and if I refused, Jaggar might take it personally. I didn't want to ruin this delicate truce between us. "I'll get it." I got up and went to the cupboard where I had seen him take down bottles for the party. There was the cut crystal decanter Merdyce had left out for us on our wedding day, and I put it on a tray with two glasses and carried it back to the hearth. *It's such a simple and intimate scene*, I thought, setting the tray on the table at his side. It was the kind of moment I'd seen described in novels and magazines. If only life could be like novels and magazines.

Jaggar filled the glasses and held one out to me. "Thank you." Of course, it was hard to have a life like novels and magazines with little details like one too many wives.

"Jaggar," I said impulsively, "I don't want to interfere with your...rest or business in St. John's. If you rather I didn't go along, please just say so."

His face darkened. "Still think I'm planning an assignation with Gleda?"

I looked down at the glass in my hands. "No, I know you're not."

"Because if you do, I may as well tell you I could have had my fill of her any time. She's come to this house to tell me she was available-"

"I know that, too."

"-and I let her know in no uncertain terms...what did you say?"

"I know she came the day before the party." I gestured faintly toward the door. "I saw her leaving here."

Jaggar sat forward, stunned. "And you didn't say anything?" He sat back again. "You didn't even ask me why?"

"It was none of my business," I said with effort. I took a quick sip of the fiery brandy, but it didn't burn away the unexpected lump in my throat.

"I would think it was your business," he argued, "if you thought your marriage was in jeopardy because of her. Or, doesn't it matter to you?"

'Because of her', I thought, that's a fine distinction. "Is my marriage in jeopardy?"

He finished his drink abruptly. "No. I've said it a thousand times, Sydney, I don't believe in divorce." He reached for the decanter and refilled his glass. "I once thought I could get a divorce but after thinking about the enormity of such an action, I...I couldn't bring myself to ever consider it again."

The big bowled glass trembled in my fingers. There, in his own words, he had told me he had never divorced Lark. "What if you had no alternative?"

He shook his head slowly, resignedly. "There's always an alternative, Sydney. The only way for us to end our mar-riage would be if..." he sighed, "if we had never married."

There was such a sadness and finality in his voice that I ached to reach out and comfort him. I sipped my drink and stared into reddish grey embers of a dying fire.

"I don't want Gleda, if that's what you're thinking."

"Oh, I told you I know that," I assured him. You just want Lark back. "Whatever we feel for each other personally, Jaggar, I am confident that you are a man of principle."

"Well," he smiled grimly, "that's something."

"What do you want from me, Jaggar?"

I expected a lengthy diatribe, a virulent reaction. Instead, he turned his gaze to the fire, as well. He was silent so long I thought he had either forgotten the question or forgotten I was there. I was tempted to get up, quietly, and leave him, but as my fingers curled around the arm of the chair to rise, he said, "What I want, Sydney, you could never be." He emptied his glass again and stood. "Goodnight."

"Goodnight." He left, and I remained there taking up the vigil of solitary sorrow where he left it. *What am I to do?* I asked the embers. *I must leave – I can't stay, yet I can't seem to bring myself to wound him again, not like she did. He seems so vulnerable with the knowledge of Lark exposed to me. Yet, Lark is the very reason I can't stay, even if I wanted to. Do I want to? If there had never been a Lark in his life, would I want to remain here? Could I?* I looked around the vast, Spartan room. *Would I really want to be his wife?*

I emptied my own glass and stood slowly and carefully. *Well, there will always be a Lark before me, so I will never know.*

Christmas morning was as wintry a morning as I'd ever known in all the years I'd lived in Newfoundland. Overnight, snow had drifted halfway up the tall windows of the foyer, and wind blasted relentlessly against the doors, making the rafters creak in protest. The electricity flickered timidly, so that the lights dimmed and brightened like an old fashioned nickelodeon.

Merdyce, bundled in a thick carpet robe and knitted hat, made a large pot of strong coffee and porridge mixed with raisins and cinnamon for our Christmas morning breakfast. We ate in the kitchen, our chairs turned toward the stove, the only sounds coming from the storm outside, and the scraping of spoons on the bowls as we finished the porridge. While Merdyce boiled water to wash the dishes, Jaggar peeled the last of the oranges and passed them around.

After breakfast, we all went to the parlour, and Jaggar built a fire in the hearth, and Merdyce and I lit the candles on the tree. We all sang Silent Night and Jaggar read the Christmas story in the gospel of Luke. Then we took turns passing out the gifts under the tree.

Merdyce loved the bookstand and Jaggar gave her some nice muslin and broadcloth to make dresses. Merdyce, as I suspected, had knitted thick jumpers for both us, rich in cables and bobbles, in a soft white wool. Jaggar seemed genuinely touched by the inkstand and pen.

He certainly wasn't ungenerous to me; he gave me a fine onionskin journal in a beautiful brocade cover, a very pretty white shirt with full sleeves and a pin tucked bodice – easily the most feminine thing I'd ever owned, my mother's things notwithstanding, a bracelet with purple stones and, in the big package in the corner, was a fine, fawn coloured cape of virgin wool. I was astounded. It was soft and warm and worlds away from my father's old mac.

I could sense Jaggar's anxiety as he watched me open things; he wanted me to be pleased – no, more than pleased. He wanted me to be delighted. Still holding the cape in my arms, I turned to him and sighed. "It's beautiful. It's…it's…I don't have enough words for how beautiful it is. How did you ever think to give me this? Until this moment, I didn't even know how much I wanted something like this."

He didn't smile, as I expected. In fact, his brows knitted together in a frown. "I didn't like the way Mrs. Mandell looked at your coat when we went to that party. You should have been dressed like all the other women there. You *deserved* to be. You didn't deserve the way she looked at you."

I didn't know whether to be hurt or touched. In the spirit of the holiday I decided to believe he meant it kindly. "Thank you, Jaggar. It's the most beautiful thing I've ever seen."

"You'll cut a pretty fine figure on the streets of St. John's," he declared. He held up the inkwell and the jumper Merdyce had made. "Thank you for my gifts. They're exactly what I need."

Merdyce gushed over her 'fineries' as she called them, then announced it was time to get Christmas dinner on the stove. As she shuffled out of the parlour, she was sniffling loudly.

Jaggar and I watched her go, then looked at one another. It was an odd, intense moment full of unexpected and unexplained emotion. Then he stood, and left the room.

I remained on the floor where I had been sitting, my new treasures scattered around me. I had felt uneasy since our conversation the night before. Now I felt unsettled, as well. I knew that our trip to St. John's was going to be the end of our marriage and despite all my plans and fantasies, I really didn't want it to end, but I wasn't sure why.

It wasn't because I loved him, I told myself as I began to gather up the tiny bits of paper and ribbon that Merdyce hadn't rescued and smoothed out to put away in the attic tomorrow. I could never love anyone but Cainan, of course. Perhaps it was just that for the first time in a very long time I felt anchored. I had purpose, I had people who looked after me and expected others to respect me. Those were two good reasons to stay.

It had been arranged that Merdyce would be visiting her people while we were gone to St. John's. This surprised me on many counts; I had assumed she'd be coming along with us, and if she didn't, why shouldn't she stay there in the house over which she ruled? I didn't even know she had people, but apparently she did, and they came to call for her late that afternoon. They were a bright, boisterous family of blonde children and babies, and a youngish couple who either stared adoringly at their children or each other. Jaggar told me later that they were Merdyce's sister's granddaughter and great grand-children. He also pointed out that it made sense for her to go to her family while we were away; with the traditionally bad weather of December and January, she shouldn't be left alone in case the power failed or she fell ill. It turned out that Jaggar had paid for the trip to Hickman's Harbour and back as an extra gift to Merdyce.

Once they were gone, the house seemed extra-ordinarily empty. I ached to think I might never see Merdyce again. By the time she returned from her holiday, I could be gone from the house, and from Jaggar's life. I wandered from room to room, looking at the decorations she had so lovingly displayed, and every touch she added to make this a warm and comfortable home. I tried to memorize every detail so that if I ever got the chance to be a wife again, if I ever had a chance to make a home for someone, I would do it just as she had done.

In the kitchen, I made tea, fingers tracing the painted design on the side of the pot while I waited for the water to boil, remembering each time I had sat in this room, drinking tea and listening to Merdyce tell stories of her childhood, or about Canada and Newfoundland. These were the real treasures I had received while living here.

"There you are. Making tea?"

Jaggar was in the doorway, wearing the jumper Merdyce had given him as if he, too, needed comfort in her absence. "Mmm, yes," I mumbled.

"Is there enough in there for me?"

"Yes," I promised. "I'll bring you some."

"Thanks."

When I looked up again, he was gone.

I made up a tea tray the way Merdyce always did and carried it, awkwardly, to the parlour. Jaggar was standing before the tree, his hands clasped behind his back, staring up at the old china head angel at the top, but he turned when he heard cups and saucers rattle on the tray.

He came to take it from my hands and set it on the sideboard where he kept his liquor. "Thanks."

"You're welcome." I followed him. "I hope I did it right. Merdyce always-"

"Yes." He set the tray down. "Merdyce always keeps things just right. It's quiet without her here."

"Yes." I searched for something to add. "But it was nice of you to send her to her family for the holidays."

He made one of those noncommittal 'hmm's that people make when they don't want to say what's on their mind, and took up his chair by the fire. He held out his hands as I brought a cup to him. "Well, are you ready to go tomorrow?"

"Not quite." I returned to the sideboard to prepare a cup for myself. "I'm not really sure what to take." When I looked over my shoulder at him, he was glaring into his cup. "I suppose it doesn't matter. I don't have that much."

"Take what you can't do without, Sydney. That's what I generally do."

"Hmm." *I suppose you can do without me*, I thought, bringing my tea to the fireside. "Jaggar, do you wish you were taking…Merdyce?"

"No." His face was dark and his mouth was twisted in exasperation. "For the love of-" he put his cup down roughly. "No. I do not wish I was taking Merdyce, or Gleda or the King."

"I'm sorry, Jaggar." I lowered my eyes. "I didn't mean to make you angry."

"I'm not-" he settled back into his chair. "Yes, Sydney, I am angry," he confessed in a ragged voice. "I am angry and I'm frustrated and more, I am worried – no, I am frightened."

"You? Frightened?" What was big enough, what was horrible enough to put fear in the heart of Jaggar Cingesleah? "Of what?"

"Of what might become of us," he answered flatly. "I married you to save your life, not take it from you. I've watched people die, Sydney," he went on in a colourless voice. "I nearly watched you die the night I brought you here. Death is a fearsome thing to hear about, but it is terrifying to watch." He leaned forward, setting his cup down on the table beside his chair. "And since our marriage, I've watched you die a little bit every day. You want to go…and yet, I can't let you."

I don't want to go, my heart cried. *I want to stay with you and make a life for us as if Cainan and Lark never existed. I want to love you, Jaggar and I want you to love me. But I don't know how to make that happen.* "What do we do?"

"I don't know, Sydney." His sigh was heavy with defeat. "I really don't know."

There was another swell of unnamed emotion within me, speckled with flecks of fear, concern, frustration… desire? "Can we be happy, Jaggar?"

He was unmoved by this tide of emotion, sitting as solid as a time worn boulder at the peak of the cape. "I don't know," he repeated. "Can we?" He raised his eyes at last, and lashed over mine like lightning. "Do you want to be happy with me?"

Something pulled me forward until my hand rested against his on the arm of his chair. He put his other hand over mine.

"Do you?" he demanded huskily, his fingers curling around mine.

"I..." I licked my dry lips, crying out in silence, *kiss me, oh, please kiss me*. "I...don't know how."

His half smile was almost triumphant, as he leaned forward, pulling me closer. "Like this." His parted lips brushed mine.

I felt a shiver race down my spine; neither hot nor cold, it was more like electricity, and it made me gasp against his mouth.

His hands freed mine and slid up my arms, cradling my face, tangling into my hair as his kiss became deeper, more demanding. "Like this, Sydney," he whispered into my hair.

I found myself on the floor, in his arms, his hands moving over me, and I don't know how I got there. I struggled against him, not out of fear of his intent, more out of the fear that I was losing control. "Jaggar," I whispered, as his lips moved against my throat, "Jaggar, this is crazy."

He raised his head and looked down at me, his hands still moving, his lips still arranged in that amused half smile. "Do you want me to stop?" he challenged.

I felt, for a moment, as if I was losing my mind. I had held my life in rigid fingers, always in control, always carefully planned and arranged, always my own ever since my father died. The only time I had surrendered control was that ill-fated night of my elopement. Now I felt my life spiraling in the same direction toward desire, longing and madness. "I...yes – no, I don't know, Jaggar," I sobbed. "I don't know."

He rolled away from me and I was flooded with ice and fear. The room was cold and seemed to spin, growing not merely dark, but black. I remained on the floor, biting my lip until I felt blood run onto my tongue, letting tears fall back into my hair, too ashamed to look at him, and too afraid that I was never going to see him again.

I must have made some pitiful sound, for he turned back to me, and gathered me into his arms, whispering soothing words. "*Ne pleur pas* Sydney, *ne pleur pas*."

"*Je regrette*." I buried my face in his shoulder. I had wanted his lovemaking and that frightened me, but how could I explain that to him?

"It's all right. I promise it's all right." He wiped tears from my cheek with a fingertip. "You're just not ready, yet."

His kindness was more frightening than his anger or his passion. Kindness was barely worse than ambivalence. It came with detachment and I did not want him to detach himself from me. "But, I...I wanted to be," I protested. "I do." I eased back to search his eyes. "I want us to be happy, Jaggar, if we can."

"If we can?" he echoed, quizzically. "Why couldn't we be? What would keep us unhappy if we both chose to make this a good marriage?"

I lowered my eyes, searching for a way to tell him that I understood about Lark without admitting that I knew about his first wife. "Sometimes," I began carefully, "sometimes one has an image of what a happy marriage should be, who would make one happy. But, we can't always have that person with us, and that makes it very hard."

"Yes," he said, rising to his knees and then pulling himself to his feet. "That's very true." He reached for his tea cup. "That's true."

I avoided his proffered hand and stood, myself. "But, that doesn't mean we couldn't have a happy marriage," I added hastily, "especially if that other person is no longer around."

Jaggar's frown deepened.

"Jaggar?" I risked touching his sleeve. "Couldn't we keep trying?"

He drew a deep breath and worked to soften his expression. "We'll talk about it in St. John's."

I felt that panic again, as if I were trapped in a hold of a sinking ship and the icy water was rushing in to cover me and sweep me away. "What's in St. John's?" I asked when I could catch my breath again.

He stared at me for a long time. "Who knows?" he said at last. "It could be your happiness. Or it could be mine." He turned and left the room.

Chapter Eleven
The Rejection

I was awake the entire night. I selfishly wished Merdyce had stayed home so that I could have her comfort and counsel, but perhaps Jaggar had displayed greater generosity of spirit than I had thought by sparing Merdyce the pain of a farewell. It had been painful enough for us both when I had broached the possibility of his reconciliation with Lark earlier in the week. When she had complained about my sullen silence one evening as we prepared for the party, I had blurted out, "He's going back to Lark. What can I do?"

Merdyce gathered me against her and held tight. "Now…what makes you think after all this time he'd go back to his wife – to his first wife?"

I tried to pull away, but she held fast. "He is, Merdyce, I just know," I sobbed.

"Oh, you just know." She released me and wiped tears from my cheek with a corner of her pinny. "Well, I know he wouldn't go back to her when he-"

"Merdyce, what's going on? I thought I heard Sydney …." Jaggar, appearing in the kitchen door, paused for a moment and then took a step toward us, jamming his fists into his pockets. "Why are you crying?"

I looked at Merdyce, begging her not to reveal what I knew. "Go along now, Jag," she advised. "The poor girl's been thinking about her lost husband."

Jaggar's face became a mask of granite. "Indeed. Well, thank God we won't be listening to *that* much longer." He stomped out.

No wonder he said his happiness was in St. John's. A chance to be reunited with the love of his life and rid himself of a weepy wife who wouldn't even sleep with him!

Jaggar came into my room early the next morning as I packed. Noting that I had left the beautiful wool cape on a hook in the cupboard, he reached in and handed it to me, wordlessly.

I shook my head. "I don't need that. It will be stormy and wet the entire time we're gone. Better for me to take the old mac on this trip."

"You'd better take it," he said, tonelessly, "just in case."

"Very well." I folded it into the bag carefully. I understood what he was saying and I should have been relieved, but I wasn't: I wasn't coming back with him.

"Are you taking any money?" he asked.

"Some," I admitted, indicating the canvas bag lying open at the foot of my bed. "I don't have much, but I didn't think I'd need much."

"You might." He must have seen the horror in my eyes because he repeated, "You might," as he reached for the bag and snapped open the coin purse inside. "You might want to shop." He counted the bills and then reached into his pocket to produce a roll of money, which he stuffed into the coin purse and put into the bag. "Just in case," he explained flatly.

I nodded, too numb to thank him. At least he wasn't going to leave me stranded in a strange town without money. His gesture stated in ways none of his words could manage that I was not coming back with him. I pulled open the drawers next to the bed and began gathering all of my clothes together. I stopped when I lifted the Indian cotton caftan from the drawer.

"I don't think it would be a good idea to take that," he said, soberly.

He was right, of course. I let it fall into the drawer and eased it shut.

"I want to leave in an hour. Can you be ready?"

I nodded without turning around.

He pulled a long breath, hunting for words. "We can be in St. John's by tomorrow morning," he said. "You can shop if you like," he said once again.

"And you?"

"I...have things I must do."

167

Like visiting Lark? I accused silently. *Your first wife? Your real wife?* "I see."

"I thought that…after…we could go someplace nice for supper." He let out breath, heavily. "We could talk."

"Yes. We can talk." *I'm sure we'll have a lot to say.* I turned around and saw he was still at the end of the bed, watching me. "Was there anything else?"

"Yes." He held out his hand. "It was unfair of me to take this. Cruel. So, I'm returning it to you now." He opened his hand; there on that broad palm was Cainan's tiny wedding ring. "Just in case," he repeated, and backed out of my room.

I held the precious ring in my open hand, waiting for the rush of relief and delight. Only sorrow came. Cainan was dead, and now Jaggaroh, Jaggar!

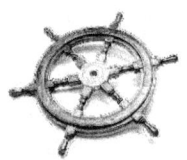

We left the long way through town, driving up toward the ferry landing east of Hickman's Harbour that would take us over to Clarenville and onward to St. John's. It felt as if every person in town came out to watch us drive us away. It felt as if everyone knew I was leaving forever. Jaggar stared straight ahead, his eyes on the road and the future. His face was like rock, jaw rigid, lips tight, not even his hair stirred in the little whips of wind that snapped around the open car.

I knew better than to try and engage him; the man did love his privacy and solitude. He barely spoke to the ferry-men, and if he spoke at all requesting two rooms at the inn where we stopped for the night I didn't hear him. Since it was too late for a meal at the inn, he went out and came back, miraculously, with sandwiches and oranges and paper cups of tea. Delivering my portion of the bounty, he backed out of my room and nodded his goodnights.

I wanted to believe he got a good night's rest, at least, but it seemed he paced all night. I could hear the floorboard near the door creak regularly. Yet, before the sun was fully up, he met me in the lobby, bags in hand. He was a little less stiff that morning, a little more alert to our surroundings, possibly a little more aware of me. Many times as we drove the precariously icy road overland to the Bay, I caught him giving me bemused study.

Then it was my turn to stare straight ahead; but I didn't see a slick narrow strip of black between six foot walls of packed snow. I saw my life in St. John's, alone and empty; I saw my life without Jaggar.

He finally broke the silence as we passed a sign saying that we were nearing the capitol of Newfoundland. "I guess you know, don't you?" he asked above the roar of the engine and the hiss of the wet road.

He's saying goodbye already! I nodded jerkily.

He drove a while longer. "Funny," he said, suddenly, "I thought you'd be happier about it. Isn't it what you want?"

How was I supposed to answer? All along I had maintained, even to myself, that I wanted to be free of him and now he'd chosen this way to set me free. Was it meant to be an act of kindness or an act of desperation? "Yes," I said, trying to hold back tears, "of course."

"Funny," he repeated, "I thought you'd be happier about it."

We were driving through a nice area just outside the main part of town - tall white houses with black shutters and black roofs and tall trees lined the streets on one side, and well-kept shops, still displaying Christmas goods and twinkly coloured lights lined the other - when he tugged his watch from his pocket. "Right on time." He pointed ahead at a brick building with the flags of Newfoundland and England snapping in the wind. "That's the hotel where we'll be staying." He drew up to a curb. "There are some nice shops here. Why don't you enjoy yourself, and we'll meet up later. Get something smashing to wear. What about eight o'clock, in the lobby?"

"Oh, I thought we were having dinner together," I blurted out. Stupid me, he would want the whole day for his 'business', wouldn't he? Or perhaps he didn't plan to meet me at all.

"I'm not very hungry right now." He forced himself up and over the side of the car. "You have some fun and a nice meal. The restaurant at the hotel is supposed to be very good." He came around the car and opened the door for me. "Charge it to me."

"Thank you." I climbed out. "I'll see you later," I finished, with a pathetic note of hope in my voice.

"Have fun." He jumped over the door and settled into the seat in one move, and jerked the car away from the curb.

I watched him manoeuvre himself into the slow moving traffic. *He's very eager to see her,* I thought. *I wonder what she's like? Is she still beautiful? Does she still love him?* Impulsively, I turned back and motioned to the hack waiting up the street. He moved up the curb as if he had been expecting me to hail him. "Follow that roadster," I commanded, sliding into the back seat.

The driver laughed loudly. "Just like in the fill-ums," he said, indicating his origins with a broad Irish accent.

"Yes," I said patiently, sliding down on the hard leather seat.

Jaggar drove through town at a slow, even pace, passing through the best and worst of St. John's. "Where's 'e headed, Miss?" the driver asked as Jaggar seemed to double back on himself, cruising through neighborhoods as if he was looking for something and had no idea where to find it.

"To see his wife," I answered miserably.

"Ohhh, I see." He must have done because he didn't say any more.

We followed at a discreet distance, as Jaggar turned onto another fashionable street. He seemed to be meandering, with no apparent purpose, until he slowed before one particularly elegant address, gated and hidden behind tall trees. "Stop here," I hissed. "Otherwise he'll know he's being followed."

"There's one of them 'lectronical gates, Miss," the driver pointed out. "If he goes in, there's no way we'll be able to follow."

"No, I suppose not, so we'll just – oh, look, he's driving on." I pointed over the seat. "I wonder why he even stopped." I considered the ornate iron fence as we passed. *Could that have been his home once? Or was it hers? Poor Jaggar, no wonder he despises Hickman's Harbour. He had lost so much.* "Drive on, quickly."

Jaggar had turned back toward the bay, this time with purpose, stopping only once, at a flower cart on a nearly deserted corner. He held out money and took possession of a dozen red roses.

"Odd," I mumbled, over a pang of jealousy. With the exception of my wedding bouquet, Jaggar had never brought so much as a lover's lily for me.

"Why?" the driver crept around the corner as Jaggar pulled in at another black, iron gate. "Shall I follow him in?"

I sat forward and looked at the gate. "No. I'll get out here." Words were an effort around the lump of anxiety in my throat. I fumbled into my bag and pulled out some of the money Jaggar had given me. I thrust it at him, not caring about the exact amount of the fare. Climbing out of the taxi, I hurried across the wide, empty street and darted inside, past the slowly swinging gates.

Jaggar had parked the roadster at the bottom of a sloping lawn and climbed the hill, flowers tucked under his arm, hands thrust into pockets, head down, a portrait of utter misery.

I ached for him, uncertain what drew him up this dismal hill, to stop beneath a tree. He put a hand on the trunk of the tree for a moment, and even from behind I could tell he was reining in emotion before he knelt to put the flowers down.

I crept up behind him, quietly, staying behind trees until I was close enough to read the name on the marble headstone. It said Lark Cingesleah. "Oh!"

Jaggar whirled on me. "What are you doing here?" he demanded.

"I...I followed you," I confessed brokenly. "I wanted to see what she was like."

"What who was like?"

"Y-your wife." I gestured faintly toward the red roses on the edge of the granite marker. "Lark. I wanted to see what she was like, only – only I didn't know she was d-dead."

"Lark..." Jaggar looked over his shoulder at the roses, and then looked at me again. "You knew I had been married before?"

"Yes." I frowned, too. "I thought you knew that I knew."

Confusion wrinkled his brow. "No...how could you think she was still alive? I married *you*."

"I know." I twisted my hands together, miserably. "I thought you were going back to her."

The confusion vanished, replaced by pain. "But I'm married to *you*," he repeated.

"I know. But, I thought you were going to leave me, to...to free me."

"I don't believe in divorce."

"I know you've said it many times."

"Then how could I be married to you if Lark was..." his black eyes widened. "You thought I had committed bigamy? You thought I had two wives?" He threw his head back and laughed, but it was a grim, hollow laughter and it sounded eerie as it echoed back to us on the wind.

I watched him, bewildered and amazed. I had expected rage, indignation, accusation, but certainly not laughter. "I'm sorry, Jaggar."

He held out a hand for me. "Let's go get something to eat."

That was as unexpected as the laughter. "I thought you..." I didn't pursue it and accepted his hand and let him assist me as we went down the slick hillside.

"How did you get here?"

"I got a taxi." Lark was dead. I hadn't married a bigamist after all. So, he was leaving me here just because he was tired of me?

He was still smiling, a twisted, bemused smile. "I suppose you leapt in and yelled 'follow that car' just like in the movies."

"That's what the driver said."

"Is he waiting for you?" He caught my hand as I stumbled on the incline.

"No, I sent him on." I liked the touch of his hands, warm and strong on mine. Why didn't I notice that before? "I'm really sorry, Jaggar. I had no idea."

"You had ideas enough, if you thought I'd marry you while I was still married to her," he scolded, the smile disappearing entirely. "I assume Merdyce told you."

"Everything she knew. Don't be angry at her, Jaggar. She was trying to protect me."

"You should have known better. And if you thought me capable of being a bigamist, you oughtn't have married me."

"How could I know what to believe, Jaggar? You told me you didn't believe in divorce and even Merdyce didn't know she was...was dead."

He stopped, rubbing his chin. "I suppose I never did tell her when I found out." He turned and sent a glance up the hill. "I should have done."

We walked the rest of the way down the hill and to the car in silence. I had finally achieved parity with my enigmatic husband, but, oh! at such a cost. I would have given nearly anything to spare Jaggar the pain I had suffered at Cainan's death. As Jaggar started the engine, I reached out impulsively to touch his hand. "I am so sorry, Jaggar."

He didn't look my way. His teeth settled on his lower lip for just a moment and he glanced over his shoulder, as if preparing to merge into nonexistent traffic. "She left me, Sydney. Did Merdyce tell you that?"

"Yes." What was I to do? Lie?

That hurt him. I saw a momentary droop in his shoulders. "She left me," he repeated, his voice getting a little stronger. "She destroyed my business and tore my family apart and yet I couldn't bring myself to divorce her. When I learnt-" he broke off and frowned at me. "Are you sure you really want to hear this?"

"Only if you really want to tell me."

He weighed his feelings for a moment. Then he began again, in a toneless voice. "She left me to go to my brother, Gale. I left home to be away from them. Oh, some would say I left to avoid the gossip, humiliation and financial ruin, but I think I could have withstood that. It was seeing them together, shameless and in love, that drove me as far from them as I could get. Of course, I was never really free of them. Each one of my sisters wrote to me in turns, telling me what was happening." His voice tasted of bitterness. "Eventually, one of them wrote to me that Lark was going to have a child – Gale's child." He paused for a moment, swallowing hard. "That's when I went up from Hickman's Harbour – I'm sure Merdyce told you about that?"

I nodded, guiltily.

He made a face; it only lasted a moment, but it was telling. "I decided to give her the divorce she was begging me to give her. Only," again he paused, "I waited too long. By the time I got to Quebec, I was told she and Gale had moved away…here, to St. John's, to avoid scandal. Evidently it was all right to defame your husband and sleep in his bed with his brother, but it was too much to produce an illegitimate child. So, I came here, too. But, I was too late."

I couldn't even muster another 'I'm sorry.' I settled back in the seat, recalling his words: *I'm afraid of what will happen to us*. Did he fear the same fate for us?

He must have taken my silence as disgust or rebuke for his voice changed, grew crisp, almost impatient. "Well, now you know."

"Yes." I sat quietly as he drove back toward the hotel. "Jaggar," I said, as we turned onto the street where the hotel was situated. "The house where you stopped..." I couldn't finish the question. "Never mind."

"You missed nothing, did you?" He pulled up before the hotel. "That is the house they bought with my money. They intended to live there as man and wife and raise the child. Ironically, I recently learnt that I inherited the house in my brother's estate, but I could never live there so I was arranging with an estate agent to sell the property." He stopped the engine. "Let's go inside and get our rooms."

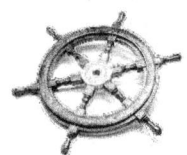

It was a nice room. Crisp white linens and dark green curtains and chair rail. There was a sturdy, single bed and a rocking chair near the window, and if I stood on tiptoe, I could see the water of the bay. There was fresh lavender soap next to the basin, and the pitcher and bowl were replicas of a Dutch patterned china I'd seen in a magazine, only instead of blue windmills and flowers, they were dark green. It was the sort of room my mother would have appreciated. I wanted to appreciate it, but that single bed disturbed me.

175

True, he had told me he had reserved two rooms, and true, the trip had not begun on the best of terms, but hadn't the air been cleared somewhat? Why hadn't he changed our reservation when we got to the hotel? It was disheartening to realise that nothing material had changed in our marriage – except now he had more proof that I was a fool.

Jaggar had hinted there were still some things to discuss over supper, but he also encouraged me to dress up and look my best, so maybe he intended to suggest that we change the circumstances in a more meaningful way. Perhaps getting two rooms was merely a precaution in case I rejected his advances again. That was very like Jaggar. He was practical, he was pragmatic, but most of all, he was proud.

He came to the door as I was watching the lamplighters on the street below. I knew that most larger cities had electrical street lamps now, but, to me, there was something romantic about the gaslight glow on the snow below my window, something refined about someone going down the street making each lamp come alive.

At the sound of his knock, I caught myself getting fluttery of breath and heart. Lark wasn't able to interfere in our marriage, but it was still presumptuous of me to assume that he'd find his happiness in St. John's with me.

He was wearing the suit he'd worn at our marriage, and he looked unusually tall in that narrow hallway, at the threshold of such a shallow door. I stepped back to let him enter while I went for my wrap and the old fashioned reticule Merdyce had lent me for the trip.

"You look nice," he said, but without much enthusiasm.

I glanced over my shoulder and realised he was frowning at the seam of the dress, which was slightly crooked. I was wearing the dress I'd worn to the Mandells' party. It was my best. "Merdyce mended it for me," I said huskily, recalling how he had ripped it off me that night. "Do you mind?"

He glanced away. "No, it's just right for tonight."

How sad he looks, I thought. *He doesn't look like a man who is trying to rekindle a marriage.* My dying hope gave birth to a new fear. "Jaggar," I blurted impulsively, "are you going to leave me behind in St. John's?"

For a moment, he looked as if he was going to deny it vehemently, and I felt the surging waters of relief, but his face hardened into an impassive mask. "That's really up to you, Sydney. Come on, now." He reached for my arm. "Let's go eat."

I avoided his grasp. "But, Jaggar-"

He held up a hand for silence. "We'll discuss it over supper, Sydney." He turned the hand over and held it out to me again. "Shall we go?"

Our conversation at the table, what there was of it, was very bland and innocuous. Jaggar seemed fascinated by his wristwatch, looking at it at very short intervals. Once, he ventured, "This is a nice hotel, isn't it?"

I didn't want to discuss the hotel. I didn't want to talk about anything but his intentions. "Yes, it's very nice," I said, irritably.

"It's elegant...refined...the sort of place elegant, refined people would stay if they were financially...embarrassed," he continued, looking at his watch again.

That comment alarmed me. I did the books and I knew we were not 'financially embarrassed'. Did he mean it would be a good place for me to stay without worrying about appearances? Or was he trying to tell me there was some unknown obligation that would wipe out our financial stability? "I'm sure it is," I mumbled, glancing around. *Just the right sort of place for the Keels to stay while in St. John,* I thought wryly. *That is, if the rumours were true.*

No sooner did I think that than I thought, for a moment, that Mr. Keel himself was striding across the lobby just

177

outside the dining room. I shook my head and looked back at Jaggar. He was looking at his watch again.

He looked up. "Are you wearing his ring?" he asked quietly.

I felt my face burn, guiltily. It was back on the chain around my neck. "Yes."

He held out his hand. "May I see it, please?"

There was something about his tone, neither angry nor threatening, but certainly compelling, which made me reach up to unhook the chain with trembling fingers. I slid the ring off and held it out to him.

"Hmm..." He gave the band great study. "And may I see the other?"

I had to blink back tears as I twisted the ring from my finger. 'The other' he had said, not his ring. He had identified the other ring by a pronoun, but not the one he gave to me. "Jaggar, what's going on?" When would I be able to express *my* feelings? When would I be allowed to tell him that I didn't want to be left behind? When would I be able to tell him that I-

"Hmm," he muttered again. "Interesting." He laid Cainan's ring in my palm while casually dropping his into his breast pocket. "Ah," he said, looking up. "I believe you'd like to be alone now." He stood.

"Jaggar!" I protested, not caring that nearby diners turned to look at us. "I thought it was going to be my choice."

"It is," he said quietly. "Look behind you."

I turned slowly. "Oh, my God."

He stood rooted to the floor, half way into an embrace with his father, his flashing blue eyes shooting arrows of disbelief toward me, a boyish grin frozen on his pale face.

I'm not exactly sure how it happened. Somehow he reached the table. Somehow his father evaporated. Somehow he embraced me. Somehow my heart stayed in my breast. "Sydney," he groaned.

"Cainan," I whispered, numbly.

"How are you? I didn't know you-" he broke off and looked over his shoulder. "They told me that you were... lost."

That explained a great deal. I dropped into my chair. His parents had played a very cruel trick on both of us. "And I was told the same about you."

He sat, uninvited, reaching across the table for my hand. "It's so good to see you. Are you alone?"

"No, I-" the chair where Jaggar had been sitting was empty, the napkin dropped next to a plate, money to pay the bill tucked discreetly beneath that. "I'm with you. Unless..." another horrible thought on a day full of them – had Cainan, in his own confused misapprehension, made a mistake similar to mine? "Unless you're with someone else."

He looked around, confused, then smiled at me. "No, I'm with you."

"Your mother does know, doesn't she?" I demanded. *So this was Jaggar's way of giving me a choice? Could the man be more cruel or stupid?*

"Yes, of course," Cainan scoffed.

"That's interesting," I said, thoughtfully. "The way she acted, no one would have ever guessed. She treated me...well, she certainly didn't tell me you were still alive." I stared at him, coolly. This entire situation was starting to stink like a hot day at the fish stalls.

He squirmed under my gaze. I'd never seen him squirm before and it was very unattractive. "Damn it, Sydney," he blurted at last. "You know why she didn't."

"Oh, yes, I know. What surprises me is that you never came back to Hickman's Harbour. Everyone there thinks you drowned."

He shrugged. "They thought it was best. No bad memories, no unpleasant explanations."

The way his face twitched around the lie reminded me of his mother and I'd never realised just how much he favoured her. "You don't seem very happy to see me."

"Oh, well..." he looked flustered, "I'm in shock, I suppose. I never expected to see you again. I thought I was seeing a ghost."

You mean you were shocked to see me here in St. John's, I thought meanly, *not merely that I was alive and breathing.* I was starting to suspect that the horrible trick had been played on me, and Cainan had a part in it. I looked around the dining room again, wondering where Jaggar was, and if he was watching this horrible melodrama.

"You don't seem terribly pleased to see me, either," he added.

"Hmm?" I focused on him again. "Oh, it's as you said. I'm in shock." *How could I have ever fancied myself in love with this...this child? How was I swayed to risk everything for the sake of having his name? And where is Jaggar when I really need him?*

"I'm sorry no one ever told me you had survived," he said, his thumb tracing a path along the underside of my wrist, a gesture he once used to thrill me. "You don't know how much I've been suffering."

"You should have asked your friends Leslie and James," I told him, easing my hand away. "I saw them both over the holidays. I should have wondered why they both seemed so amused."

Cainan spluttered. "I didn't know," he insisted. "I haven't seen either of them since...well, since everything happened."

"Really?" I looked at him. "Well, someone had seen you." Could Cainan's amazing survival have been the reason for all those clandestine meetings between Jaggar and Gleda? "How did you manage?"

"Manage?" he echoed, stupidly. "Manage what?"

"Getting off the Sidonie Stone. They looked everywhere for you. Men risked their *lives* looking for you, Cainan."

"I swam to shore."

"On a stormy night, in icy water two miles from shore? Obviously you had an angel looking after you." *Or a friend with a boat nearby.* "And when you got to shore, why didn't you contact anyone?"

"I...I was sick, and then..." his face darkened again, looking more and more like his mother's. I could almost imagine a thick veil dropping down over it. "Now, see here, are you happy to see me or not?"

"I'm happy to know you're alive," I conceded. But I wasn't, really. In the time it took for me to speak those words, I understood, with horror, Jaggar's bitter laughter when he found out I thought he was a bigamist. I was the bigamist, and I didn't even know it!

He was quiet for a moment, even though his lips wobbled with words that didn't quite make it out of his mouth. Finally, he straightened in his chair. "The *Sidonie Stone.* It sank, didn't it?"

"You were there," I reminded him. "It was lost." I put my hands, palms down, on the table and covered his ring.

"I'm sorry." He reached out again, covering one of my hands with both of his. He was no longer wearing his ring, either. "But, surely you got quite a lot of insurance money for it." His voice regained its familiar warmth and affection. "Didn't you, my dear? You appear to be doing all right for yourself."

So many little bells began to ring in my brain like a carillon of truth: the gossip about the Keel's true financial state, the things Jaggar had said about this hotel and then finding Cainan meeting his father here. "You've been staying here?" I asked abruptly.

He seemed surprised by the change in tack. "I have been, but now I think I'll go home. After all, if you're all right, and – and everything."

"I'm not all right," I lied impulsively. "Father didn't have the boat insured. I lost everything." I cocked a brow at him. "I'm surprised you didn't find that out when you attempted to claim my estate, as my husband."

I could see him working frantically for a counter to that accusation and I waved it off. "It seems I have nothing at all." *And if I don't get up this moment and go, I might not have Jaggar, either.*

"No?" His hands slipped from mine. "Oh, my dear, that's too bad. Now, Sydney, please don't misunderstand what I'm about to say, but you can't expect anything from me. My family had the marriage annulled. We're not married."

I sagged in my chair. *Thank God.* For those few moments I had been all the worst of what I had accused Jaggar of being. "You're sure?" Now I knew Cainan had been in on the whole trick. Why would his parents have a marriage annulled when it was presumed to have ended in death? Could it be that they had all used my infatuation with Cainan to get their hands on the *Sidonie Stone*, or its insurance? The circumstances seemed so obvious now it should have blinded me.

"Oh, I'm sure," he said firmly. "I have documents to prove it."

I stood, gathering my things. "I can't tell you how that fact floods me with relief," I said coolly. "Now, if you'll excuse me..." I left, leaving Cainan's ring abandoned on the table.

I ran up the stairs, not caring that I was making a spectacle of myself. I was determined to tell Jaggar the truth, I was going to tell him that I loved him and I didn't care if he ever loved me as long as he didn't leave me. I was going to tell him how grateful I was that he had shown me the truth of Cainan Keel. I was going to tell him...

"Jaggar!" I knocked on his door. "Jaggar, please, I've got to talk to..."

The door opened slowly as I knocked. "Jaggar? The bed was made, the bureau top was bare, the room looked unused, undisturbed. "Oh, Jaggar, no!" I pulled the armoire open. A solitary hanger swung lazily on the rod. "Oh, Jaggar, no!"

He had gone.

Chapter Twelve
The Resolution

The desk clerk protested loudly when I brought my bag down and asked for a taxi. "But, you can't be leaving. Your room is paid through the week."

"Then send the reimbursement to Mr. Cingesleah," I snapped, "because I'm leaving tonight. Do you have a train schedule?" I shifted my bag from one hand to the other and slammed the key on the desk.

"But, Mrs. Keel, I-"

I cringed. He didn't even leave me his name. "My name is Cingesleah," I said distinctly, "Mrs. Jaggar Cingesleah."

The poor desk clerk lost his composure. "Well, this is just the damnedest thing," he complained, flustered. "Just the damnedest."

I ignored his profanity. "Yes, yes, it must be. May I have my receipt?"

The man was beyond hope. "First Mr. Cingesleah checks out, muttered about messing with another man's wife..." he stopped and eyed me suspiciously.

"I am not another man's wife! I am *his* wife." I felt people in the lobby turn to stare at my outburst. "Did he leave a message for me?"

"Started to," the clerk admitted. "But then he said 'what the hell' and he crumpled it up and threw it away." It must have finally occurred to him that his language was not acceptable in such a public place for his face turned a very bright red. "Begging your pardon."

"Where?" Even half a note was better than complete silence. "Did you see where he threw it away?"

The clerk looked at me as if I had just crossed off the last thing on his list so that he could truly say he'd seen everything. "Over there," he mumbled, dumbfounded. "In the brass basket."

"Thank you." I abandoned my bag and raced to the basket, dropping to my knees in front of it. "He's only just left," I told myself. "It must be right on top." I began to pick through the discards of patrons with more care than I'd use picking through offal at the fish-seller's stall.

"Oh, Sydney."

I lifted my head. Cainan was coming out of the bar. "I can't bear to see you this way." He reached for my hand just as my fingers closed around a crumpled note with familiar handwriting visible between the creases. "If things are that bad, I'll give you some cash. My father's here in town. We can see him tomorrow. Come on, come on." He urged me upward. "Come away from there."

"Oh, don't be ridiculous," I snapped, shrugging free of his grasp. "I don't need anything from you. I don't need anything from anyone."

"But, you said-"

"I lied, Cainan," I answered carelessly, smoothing the note open between my fingers. "I've got plenty of money. I've got more than you do, if rumours are to be believed." I skimmed the note quickly. *Sydney*, it read, *I hope you have more success in your first marriage than I had in mine. If it doesn't work out ...*

"But, why?" Cainan cried, aghast. "Why would you lie like that?"

I folded the note carefully and tucked it into the reticule. "For the same reason you lied about believing I was dead," I answered levelly.

For a moment he looked as if he would deny my accusation, but he surrendered the plan quick enough when he saw I wasn't going to accept any further explanation from him. "What do I say, Sydney?" he asked softly. "My family didn't approve of our marriage. They said it was better this way, with you believing I was dead."

I returned to the desk to collect my things. "Did they tell you how I took the news?"

"They said you were quite ill," he answered slowly. "But you did recover," he asserted as if that excused all before it. "In fact, I was told you didn't appear to be heartbroken at all. Mother said some very mean things, in fact." He reached for my bag. "But, I knew that was just your way. You'd never mourn me overtly. Funny." He stopped suddenly.

I accepted my bill, not bothering to look at him. I wanted to find a train schedule, or hire a car, or catch a ferry, or...who knows, fly in an aeroplane to get back to Hickman's Harbour. "What's funny?" I asked, as I reached to take my luggage back.

He fell in step beside me as I strode toward the exit. "Someone mentioned another man."

"Another man?" I chuckled grimly. *Jaggar was more than another man, Cainan Keel, you child. He's my husband. He's my life.*

"Is there another man?" he asked, sounding pained. "Sydney, there can't be another man," he rushed on. "You're *my* wife. You belong to me."

I almost laughed in his face. "But, Cainan," I said, managing to school the bitter amusement from my voice, "you said our marriage had been annulled."

"But that was just a terrible mistake," he cried.

I'm sure you see it as a mistake now, I thought, stepping out into the night air. It was strange to see people milling about on the street after dark, strange to see cars go up and down the avenue, and strange to see shops and cafes still doing business. But, even that strangeness was welcome when I saw there were also taxis on the street.

"It was a mistake," he insisted. "My parents didn't understand how I feel about you." He dropped an arm around me, trying to urge me back inside. "I'm sure if we went back together and explained the situation-"

"I haven't got time." I waved my hand for a taxi. "I'm going home."

"Tonight?"

"Yes."

"How?" He followed me to the curb.

"I don't know. Train, ferry, this cab if need be." I reached for my bag.

He hoisted my bag up and out of my reach, as if holding candy out of a baby's grasp. "There's no train that will take you back to Hickman's Harbour, and the ferries only run during the day. I'm pretty sure this driver won't take you there, either."

"Give the lady her bag, Mister," the driver said gruffly.

"Is there a train station?" I asked the driver. "Or a... a...oh, what are they called...an air field?"

"Train station's six blocks from here," the driver said, giving Cainan the eye. "Ain't no air fields in these parts."

"Can I get a train out tonight?"

"Mebbe. Depends where you're going."

"Hickman's Harbour. It's on Random Island." I sighed when he didn't respond. Didn't these people know their own country? "In Trinity Bay."

"I knew where it was," he told me, archly. "I was just remembering where the trains go. Mebbe Clarenville."

"Yes, I know where that is. Could you take me to the station, please?" I jerked my bag out of Cainan's hand. "Let's go."

Cainan caught the doorframe and wouldn't let me shut it. "You can't go out there tonight, I won't let you. At least stay the night and leave in the morning. I've got an apartment here." He smiled at me in what I suppose was meant to be invitation.

I recoiled at the idea. "I haven't got time. Now let go of this door."

"I won't let you go," he repeated. "You're my wife and, well, damn it, I said you were staying here."

"Look, lady, I don't like being in the middle of marital situations."

Perle Butcher Lyon

"This isn't a marital situation. I am not his wife." I turned to look at Cainan. "I am not your wife. Now let go of the door, or this driver will be forced to summon a constable."

Cainan let go of the door, but only to force his way into the back seat. "I'm going back with you. We'll get this all settled."

"Want me to throw him out?" the driver offered.

"No," I said, sliding as far across the seat as I could. "Just drive, please."

"But, Sydney, what's the rush," Cainan protested. "Wouldn't tomorrow do just as well? We could go back with my father. He has his automobile."

I suppose if Jaggar had never come into my life, I might have given his persistent offer more thought. I might have even accepted. But Jaggar had held up a magnifying glass to the foibles and childishness of the man I once loved and I could never love him – or trust him – again. "I'm going back tonight. With or without you."

"All right, all right." He nodded at the driver. "Let's go."

The train station was probably the most imposing edifice I'd ever seen, larger even than the capitol building I had seen when my father made his incendiary speeches six years prior. It was made of a grey stone, and with a severe roofline, and dark windows. There was very little to indicate that it was even open, but I was prepared to believe that in a big city like St. John's, the railway would be running. After all, hadn't Sir John Hope-Simpson recently arrived to make everything all right in St. John's?

I left Cainan to settle with the driver, and darted up the stone steps. The enormous doors were unlocked, and inside, there were ticket booths and doors of light marled wood, and shiny marble floors. A few men clustered in a smoking room, with newspapers and opinions, and a woman with two active children sat on a bench near the doors. A tall, thin man in an impeccable uniform pushed a broom across the floors in a steady rhythm, whistling brightly, and a Morse key clack-clacked from the Western Union booth. Despite the noise of children and politics and communication and brooms, there was a sort of hush over the whole place.

Cainan caught up to me as I stood before the bank of ticket booths, trying to determine how near to Random Island and Jaggar I could get by train. The taxi driver had guessed correctly when he suggested Clarenville.

"You left me behind," he said peevishly.

"It was your choice to come along," I answered, equally peeved. How was I to get from Clarenville to Hickman's Harbour? I'd just have to work that out when I arrived. I stepped up to a booth and a man poked his nose almost to the grill in the glass. "Where ya want to go?" he demanded.

"Clarenville, please."

He quoted prices for a drawing room, berth and lounge car. Even though it was a night and day of travel, I decided on sitting up in the lounge car. "One, please."

"One?" he repeated, and I realised he was looking at Cainan.

"Yes. One."

"Sydney!" Cainan protested.

He stamped tickets with enthusiasm and set them on the counter, just out of my reach while he repeated the fare. "Train leaves at ten o'clock."

I opened my bag and counted out money. "Thank you." I turned to Cainan, who was red-faced and open mouthed as he stared at me. "Your turn. If you're coming."

189

I picked up my bag and went to find a bench.

He followed me, indignantly, huffing like a steam engine. "You're serious about this?"

"Whatever gave you the idea I wasn't?"

"But why?" He stood before me, hands on hips. "We can settle everything right here in St. John's."

"No." I folded my ticket carefully into the reticule. I'd never ridden on a train before and I was both excited and a little anxious. "We really can't, Cainan."

"Oh, all right. If it matters that much to you." He spun on one heel and marched back to the ticket booths.

I turned my head enough to watch him go. *How could I ever have thought I loved him?* I asked myself for about the fiftieth time that evening. *He was nothing more than a handsome and spoilt child. His parents should be ashamed to produce such an heir.*

He got his ticket, and came back to wedge his way onto the bench between the rail and my bag. He tried to start a conversation, but when I didn't respond, he got up and wandered around the vast room, eventually stopping at the smoking room door, to listen in on conversations.

I picked up a booklet about the history of the railway in Newfoundland, and studied the map and the grainy photographs of famous people who had travelled thus. There was a long piece about Thomas Lodge and a famous speech he had made. There was a menu for the First Class Dining Car and a brief mention of coffee and sandwiches available for other passengers. *Class distinction is everywhere*, I thought with a sigh.

Finally, a man in a dark blue uniform with gold epaulets and a round hat came in and announced our train. I gathered up my things, smiling sympathetically at the woman trying to herd her two exhausted and unhappy children toward the door. The smoking room expelled a few men who walked with newspapers tucked under their arms, and cigars clamped between their teeth, only to be told that smoking was not allowed on board.

I boarded the train and followed directions to the lounge car, half hoping Cainan would have changed his mind, or missed the boarding call, but just as the train jolted into motion, Cainan bounded in, breathless, and dropped into the seat opposite me. "You didn't wait for me," he complained.

The sudden and sharp motion had startled me, and I sat, gripping the arms of my seat, watching steam billowing back from the engine like smoke. I confess the initial experience was alarming. "I didn't want to miss the train," I told him through clenched teeth. "Oh!" We chugged a few feet further on the track and slowed again.

Cainan laughed at my reaction. "Sydney, have you never been on a train?"

I answered with a shake of my head, watching a man in a similar uniform, step up quickly, and catch a handrail, leaning out over the track and waving toward the engine. "Never."

"Well, relax. It's a very comfortable way of traveling. Vastly superior to boats, I assure you."

The train began to pick up speed, rocking and rattling and bumping forward. The lights in windows of buildings along the track began to skip past and soon were just blurs in the darkness. The man who had jumped onto the train at the last moment came into the car calling "Tickets please. Let's have your tickets."

Cainan pulled his from the breast pocket of his coat, and I fumbled around in the reticule, not certain which parts he needed. I finally just handed everything to him.

The man – called Conductor, I later learnt – smiled at me, clipped a few holes in my ticket and returned things to me. "Enjoy your trip," he said kindly.

We bumped and banged around a turn and then picked up speed. The noise and movement made me very uncomfortable.

After a while a lady with a trolley came by, with a cistern of coffee, and some biscuits, cakes and sandwiches. I looked at Cainan, who looked at the trolley and then back at the window. I had a feeling he was hungry, but had no more cash. I actually felt sorry for him at that point. "Yes," I said. "Two coffees and two sandwiches, please."

Cainan turned around and took an interest in the proceedings once I'd opened my coin purse. The lady prepared coffees and I chose two meat paste sandwiches and she gave us each a cookie, as well. Cainan showed me how to set up the folding table between us, and I arranged our impromptu meal. "People are very nice on trains," I observed.

Cainan stirred his coffee idly. "I said it was better than going by sea."

I invited him to talk about what he'd been doing in St. John's all these months, but I didn't really listen to him. It took all my concentration to stay upright as we rattled along and, in truth, I didn't really care.

It started to rain around midnight, and that did not do anything for the bone rattling ride. And as we moved further north, the rain turned to sleet, and the windows began to frost. I dug into my bag and pulled out the wool cape Jaggar had given me for Christmas, wrapping it around me like a blanket.

Cainan paused in his dissertation and gave the garment some consideration. "That's pretty," he said in a speculative tone. "Very nice." I could almost see his mind trying to assess the price and wonder how I had the cash for holidays to St. John's and wool capes and train rides.

I did not feeling like explaining, so I snuggled deeper into the warmth of the cape and said, "Thank you."

"You didn't buy that in Hickman's Harbour," he allowed.

"No," I answered truthfully, "I did not." I barely stifled a yawn. "You were saying about James?"

"Oh, yes, I didn't know you'd met him." Cainan's face darkened. "There's quite a lot about you I didn't know, it seems."

"Because you never bothered to find out." The warm cape was a mistake. Now I was drowsy and I couldn't afford to fall asleep. I pushed it off, and sat up straight.

"You make me sound selfish," he complained.

"You are what you are, Cainan."

"What does that mean?"

"It means, you were raised a certain way, and for good or bad, it's who you are. Now, go on with what you were saying."

But, Cainan was no longer in the mood to talk. He turned toward the window, and sat, sullen and silent for a long time.

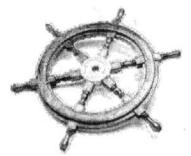

As it was growing light outside my window, the train slowed, and we pulled into a station. The sky was still a steely grey and rain spattered the frosty windows, but people stood on the wooden platform ready to board. The conductor came through the car announcing a fifteen minute water stop.

Cainan roused himself and announced to the car in general, because he would not look directly at me, that he was going to stretch his legs. I decided not to follow, and merely stood up, rubbing my shoulder, and adjusted my bags in the seat. Other passengers came in and found seats in the car, smiling or tipping hats as they passed.

I was settling down in my seat again as I heard raised voices on the platform. I couldn't see clearly, so I pressed my hand against the glass in an attempt to create a window in the frost. I cleared just enough to see that a woman was talking to the conductor and pointing across the platform. Shifting in my seat for another view, I saw Cainan, looking indignant.

"Another rude young man," a man said as he passed my seat.

I'm sure Mrs. Keel would love to hear that, I thought, looking out the window again. Cainan was standing near the car, and bowing low in a mocking gesture to allow the woman to board ahead of him. She was dressed in a coat which was clearly threadbare, and I could see a patch on the elbow even from my limited point of view. I didn't have to see what had transpired to know that Cainan had assumed that he could board ahead of the woman, since he was of a superior station in life. Once again I was flooded with relief that I was not connected to him or his family.

Cainan came into the car, face red, eyes bright, mouth twisted into a furious pout. It was clear he meant to complain to me and I cut him off quickly. "That was quite a display out there, Cainan Keel." I deliberate raised my voice so that witnesses might note his name.

"Wasn't it?" He dropped heavily into his seat. "Some people!"

"Yes," I said dryly.

"I mean, people like that oughtn't even be allowed aboard. Did you see her hat?"

"I did. She looked like a woman who was trying to look her best, despite her situation."

"Well," he rolled his eyes at me, but didn't argue the point anymore.

I was thoroughly disgusted. I didn't even want to sit near him anymore. I gathered my things and stood.

He caught my arm. "Where are you going?"

"The air's fresher on the other side of the car," I told him distinctly.

His lip curled up. "I'll bet it smells just like fish."

He might as well have slapped me. I stepped into the aisle and chose a seat at the back of the car, tumbling into it just as the train lurched forward again.

I could see him from my new position, though I tried not to look. For about fifteen minutes he shifted and sighed, crossing his legs this way and that, rolling his eyes, drumming his fingers on his thighs. Finally, as the train got to full speed, he got up and came down the aisle, smiling pleasantly at each passenger, as if all was wonderful in the world. "I'm sorry," he said, taking the seat opposite me without invitation. "That was mean of me. Let's write it off to lack of sleep and that wretched woman."

I turned to look out the window.

"What? You're going to ignore me now? How petty, Sydney."

"I? Petty? I'm not the one who nearly knocked a woman down because her coat was a little shabby. I'm not the one hurling insults at people and acting like a spoilt child." I pointed up the aisle toward the seat he had vacated. "Go up there and sit until you realise you can't go around treating people like that – no matter who they are."

"That's a fine way to talk to your husband."

I sighed, aggrieved. "For the last time, Cainan Keel, we are not married. You told me so yourself."

"But, we're as good as," he insisted. "That's what this whole trip is about, isn't it? To set things straight with my folks?"

"Cainan, please. I'm tired, too. Be quiet."

He didn't move, but he didn't try to talk, either. Once again we bumped along in silence. At the next stop a family with five boisterous children boarded and the next few hours were filled with laughter and singing as the parents tried to keep their children entertained. They left the train just on the other side of Buenavista and another woman with an infant took their place. Cainan got off at one stop, and was so long in coming back I was certain he had missed the train, but he showed up some time later with newspapers and paper cups of tea. "A peace offering?" he said, settling into his seat.

In truth the tea was very welcomed, and I found the newspapers a distraction. They were full of dismal news, as always; quite a lot of reporting of war in Spain, and what King Edward's speech would mean to Newfoundland. There were editorials about the Fishing Council and that Nazi airship invading North American airspace. There were predictions of higher unemployment and another terrible winter and lots of speculation about what the gold market was doing to the Canadian economy. All of it made me sad, and anxious to get home to Jaggar. I peered out the window, looking for familiar landscape.

"You know, it's a shame about the weather," Cainan said, dropping his newspaper onto the seat next to him. "If it were a clear night, we'd have a fine view of the Northern Lights. It's hard to see them from our side of the island."

I answered with a shrug, and shifted a bit so I could see around him.

"You must be in a big hurry to get all this straightened out," he said, smiling. "I was beginning to think you really didn't care about me."

"Cainan, you've no idea." I chewed a fingernail nervously. I had to get home before Jaggar started taking actions to remove me from his life. How could he have thought I'd choose an infant over a man?

"It will be all right, Sydney," he assured me, gleefully. "We'll take the insurance money from the *Sidonie Stone* and move back to St. John's. It will be wonderful. You'll love living there. I do."

196

I shook my head as if a gnat were annoying me. "I'm going to stay in Hickman's Harbour," I told him, staring out at the darkening scenery.

"Why?" Cainan wailed. "There's nothing for us there. It's so dull. No theatre, no nightlife. Nothing ever happens."

"Not to me," I told him. "Everything I have is there."

"I want to live in St. John's," he insisted.

"Then live in St. John's," I retorted, "I assure you, I don't care."

"But, what about us?"

I looked at him, finally. "Cainan, there is no us. I am not going to marry you. Now stop all this."

"But, you love me!" He stood up, hovering over me. "Why wouldn't you marry me?"

"Cainan, sit down, you're making a scene."

He pronounced a word I didn't suppose he'd ever heard in the Keel residence. "Why won't you marry me?"

"Because I'm married to someone else," I answered impatiently. "Now, do sit down, everyone's staring at us."

"You *what*?" He pounded on the arm of my seat. "Sydney, that's bigamy."

"Why?" I shrank away from his fist. "I *thought* I was a widow. And you told me yourself that the marriage was annulled. That made me free to marry someone else." Behind him everyone in the car had turned to look at us. "Cainan, sit down."

"Who is it? That foul fishmonger from Clarenville who is always giving you the eye?"

"Cainan, you have no right to ask me-"

"The chemist's clerk? He always stared at you when you walked down the street. I wanted to smash his face in."

"Cainan, please," I implored. "Sit down."

Something flickered over his face like foul weather. "Not that Quebecker with a nose like a fish knife. He's got a woman in every port. Didn't you notice how he hung all over that blonde at the Christmas par..."

197

I knew it before he gave himself away, I just didn't realise what I knew. "It *was* you! The mummer dressed like a dog. How dare you come into my husband's house? How dare you put your hands on me in his house?"

"You're not married to Jaggar, the Dagger. I won't have it. I won't have you going from me to him."

"Cainan, listen to me. You have no say in the matter. You told me yourself, we are not married. I can go to anyone I please."

"But, I lied!"

"What? Cainan Keel, tell me the truth: Are we married or not?"

There was confusion in his boyish blue eyes. "I don't know," he confessed. "Father said not to worry, that he would take care of everything if I would just go to St. John's and wait."

I felt tears of my own spill over. We couldn't be married. We just couldn't be. Then Jaggar would be right about all the things he had said about Cainan – and about me. I dug into the reticule and pulled out a handkerchief. "We'd better not be married, Cainan," I warned, dabbing at my eyes, "because if you've lied to me, I'll divorce you and it will be the biggest scandal in all of Newfoundland. I'll make sure it is."

"You wouldn't." For a moment he looked frightened, but then he grinned. "You're bluffing. You want me, you know it. You've always done. It was so easy to convince you to go away with me. As simple as..." he snapped his fingers. "And if we're still married, you'll stay married to me. You'll see."

"No, I won't," I sniffed. "I don't love you. You don't love me. I won't be trapped into a marriage that is based solely on your avarice. Now, get away from me before I call someone to take you away."

Cainan slapped me. I saw it, the way his hand flew up and swept down in an arc, but I didn't move. I watched, horrified, as his hand came smashing against my cheek, and for a moment I couldn't see anything at all.

"That was really stupid, Sydney," he rasped, raising his hand again. "But then, you never were too bright. No one with half a brain would have risked sailing half way round Newfoundland in one of the worst storms of the season. I'm only sorry you woke up before the stupid ship sank. You were the one who was supposed to be lost at sea, not me." His hand came down in the other direction, slapping the other cheek.

I put my arm up to block any further assault. "Don't you touch me again," I warned.

"Who's going to stop me?" he mocked, pulling his fingers in to form a fist.

"I am."

"And so am I."

Two men, other passengers in the car, were standing behind him, one with a grip on his forearm, the other with a grip on his shoulder. One of the men turned to his woman companion and instructed her to call for the conductor. The other, putting a little muscle into his grip on Cainan's arm, asked me if I was all right.

I was in pain, I was humiliated, but I was relieved beyond words. I nodded, dumbly, fumbling for my handkerchief.

The conductor came, and Cainan, despite his howls of protests and threats to call his father, Thomas Lodge and the King of England, was taken away. Someone else brought me ice and another cup of tea. Passengers in the car gave their accounts of the argument to railway staff, and I was questioned, as well. I don't remember what I said. My brain was just one dull thrum at that point, but my statement must have satisfied people because Cainan was taken off at the next stop and handed off to two members of the newly established Newfoundland Rangers, who had been alerted to expect him.

The only anxious moment I had after that was the worry that one of the Rangers would contact Jaggar. When they asked me my name and address, I gave them as Mrs. Jaggar Cingesleah of Hickman's Harbour. Correct inform-ation, of course, but suppose they decided to contact him? He might be very concerned to be contacted by authorities in regard to me, or he might brush off the enquiry by denying we were married. I could only hope they wouldn't try.

Chapter Thirteen
The Reckoning

Of course, there was something else I should have been worried about, but it really hadn't occurred to me once since boarding the train; how was I going to get from Clarenville, across the Sound, and up the shore of Random Island to Hickman's Harbour and home? This concern reasserted itself when I found myself on an empty platform at Clarenville Station, outside the town, late in the evening, woozy and hungry and cold.

I paced around the station as the train pulled out, my cape pulled high over my head against the rain. I felt too faint to cry, and too miserable to faint, so I paced, and fretted and wondered what to do.

The porter came to his window and called out, "Miss? Where's your party?"

I turned around to see a rather dour face peering at me. "I have no party. I thought I might…" I looked around the station, "hire a car?"

"No cars here. Not at this hour." He tsked at me, and then gestured toward a door at the end of the platform. "Come in out of that weather, at least. Can't have you freeze there overnight."

He met me at the door, and let me in. The station was nothing like the one in St. John's. It was small and smelled musty and had no smoking room or benches. "Might as well come through," he said, holding the door just long enough for me to cross the threshold. "There's a kettle going."

"Thank you." I followed him into the office, which was lit with one of those big, bright lamps used in offices and factories.

As I sat down on the battered chair near an oil fire, he gasped loudly. "Gads, what happened to you?"

My hands flew to my face. "I…I'm not…is it bad?"

201

"Is it? Woman, you look as if you walked into that train, face first." He fumbled around on his desk and came up with a small tin mirror.

He was right. My face was swollen and starting to shadow with bruises. I knew this look. I'd seen it on my own mother's face. "I was struck by a passenger aboard the train," I said. I would not lie for Cainan the way my mother had lied for my father.

He didn't seem particularly shocked. He nodded and dropped a tea bag into a cup. "Seen it before," he allowed. "Is that why you're here in the dead of night, with no party waiting?"

"Not really." I touched my cheek gingerly and handed the mirror back to him. I couldn't go to Jaggar looking like this. "I am trying to get to Hickman's Harbour. This was the nearest stop."

"It is." He poured hot water into the cup. "But there's no ferry at this hour. I might be able to find you a cot at the firehouse. It's the next nearest place before town."

"Thank you." I took the cup he offered. "That would be very kind." Seeing myself filled me with shame. I had become all that I despaired of in my mother, something I had vowed never to do. Was I wrong about everything else? Maybe Jaggar didn't want me back. Maybe I should have stayed on the train all the way to the Strait. Maybe I should have stayed with Cainan, after all.

"No answer at the firehouse. Not surprising."

I looked up from my tea. I hadn't even noticed he had left the office. "Well, may I wait in the station until the ferry comes?"

He rubbed the back of his neck, clearly uncomfortable with the idea. "I suppose," he said with a hint of a question lifting the end of his statement. "I'll hafta call my wife." He shuffled away again.

It was a humorous notion – that I might be tempted to trifle with the porter, or that he might be tempted to trifle with me. I didn't laugh, though. I had discovered there was far too much about marriage that I didn't comprehend or appreciate.

Within the hour I was proved wrong again. The wife bustled In, dripping wet, red-faced, and breathless, but her hands were full of blankets and a hamper of food. She was considerably younger than her husband, round and good natured and reminding me of the old childhood rhyme about Jack Sprat. She giggled and chattered as we set up a cot, and she put out tea and sandwiches for me and her 'old man.' She tsked and fussed over my bruised face, and applied witch hazel and cold rags and gave me some aspirins for pain. She asked a lot of questions, but left no room in her remarks for me to answer. I was quite content to sit there and let her ramble on.

I suspected the success of their marriage was due in large part to their odd shift work. He probably worked all night and slept all day, so they got along famously. I was convinced he was all meekness and tolerance and she the boisterous, domineering type but when they were both in the office while I changed out of my wet things, I could see in their silhouettes the way he patted her cheek affectionately, and kissed her brow.

By the time I had changed and eaten, and she had packed up the hamper, I was exhausted. I barely remember thanking either of them before I fell asleep on the cot.

I woke a few hours later with a terrible headache, but my face didn't feel so tender and swollen. It was still dark, but it was the time of year when our days got very little sunlight. The clock on the wall over the platform door told me I'd managed six hours sleep. There were already people out on the platform waiting to come in.

I sat up and dug my comb out of my bag and ran it through my hair. By the time I'd put everything away and folded the cot and clothing, the porter had boiled water for tea and brought me a cup. "Thank you for all your kindness, and your wife's," I said as I gathered up my belong-ings. "How can I repay you?"

He dismissed it with a shrug and fumbled in his pocket for the key. "First ferry's on its way, if you're planning to go across the bar on the morning tide," he told me.

"Yes, thank you." I shrugged the cape over my shoulders, and picked up my bags.

He opened the door and I stepped outside, to the arched brows of surprised passengers awaiting the morning train.

I had to take a bus from the turnout to the ferry's dock, and by the time I reached it, the rain was falling again, and the wind was whipping up dangerously. The few people who had come across were coming down the planks slowly, turning their collars up, and ducking their heads.

I recognised one head, one blonde and elegant head I'd seen too many times for comfort. What was *she* doing on Random Island? As if I didn't know! He didn't waste time, did he? I turned away sharply.

"Mrs. Cingesleah! Sydney!"

I wanted to keep walking, but the mere fact that she called out to me – and used what I considered my proper name – forced me to turn around. She was walking swiftly toward me, waving a sodden scarf, not caring that the rain was ruining her coif and causing that thick kohl around her eyes to run. I didn't walk toward her, but I stood still, under an overhang next to the ticket taker's booth, and let her approach me. "Gleda," I said.

"Well, I'm glad to see one of you has-my God! What happened?"

I touched my cheek, self-consciously. "A bit of an accident. What are you doing here? I thought you were in St. John's."

"A bit of a bust up, you mean. The same could be said of you." She reached me, and slid an arm around my shoulder, drawing me away from the queue of people waiting to purchase tickets. "Tell me Jaggar didn't do that?"

"No," I said quietly. I knew what the next question would be.

Once again, I was surprised. She turned me with both hands to face her, and then she looked back toward the island, hardly visible in the rain. "Then he'll kill the person that did," she said. "Come on." She pushed me back toward the queue.

"What are you doing?"

"Taking you back. I was on my way to St. John's to get you, anyway."

"Get me? Why?"

"Stop asking so many questions." She gave me a rough shove. "One of you needs to have some sense. He's gone raving mad, so you must."

"I don't understand. I can't go back now. Not when…"

"Not when what?" She stepped up to the booth and asked for two tickets. "That? Forget it. There are more important things to deal with. Stop asking questions. I'll explain everything when we get back across." She pushed the tickets into the pocket of her coat and grabbed my arm.

I stopped arguing, and stopped assuming things. I'd been wrong straight across the board. I let her get us on the ferry and secure a place away from the rail, where the rain wouldn't slash at us. True to her word, she said nothing as we wobbled and lurched our way back to the island side dock. She said nothing as we disembarked, dragging my bags between us. She said not a word until we were tucked inside her old Ford.

Once we'd managed to tug the doors closed, she fished her scarf from a pocket and wiped it over her face, making the kohl streaks more symmetrical, and giving her face the suggestion of a tiger, which was, in my opinion, apt. "Well?" I demanded as she pumped the lever to start the car.

"Just answer one question for me, first. Did that little fop hit you?"

I touched my cheek again. "Yes."

"Hmm...and is that why you're running back to Jaggar?"

"Who said I was..." the indignation left as quickly as it came. "No. I was on my way back to Jaggar when it happened, actually. What is this all about?"

"Well, I'm glad to know one of you is capable of sense." she stated once again, and swerved away from a clot of people rushing toward the ferry. "I saw Jaggar yesterday evening. He was in a state; swearing to leave off women entirely, sell his stakes in that little backwash he called home and head off to parts unknown."

"Leaving? Why?"

"You don't know? I'm sure I don't. Of course, it might have something to do with him thinking you've left him for that Keel boy, now that's he's been raised from the dead."

"You knew Cainan was alive, didn't you?"

"I did. What I didn't know, until I came visiting Hickman's Harbour, was that he was supposed to be dead. When I attended that party – what a disaster *that* was – and heard the gossip, and saw how he felt about you, I had to warn him."

"It wouldn't do to warn me?" We hit a bump and the top of my head hit something in the car, making me gasp.

"Don't come over all indignant. I didn't know you. I've known Jaggar for years. The word I'd gotten was that you were a little gold-digger, and I was trying to protect him from another horrible mistake."

"H-horrible mistake. You mean Lark?"

"Yes. Of course, after I'd been around a few days, and asked some questions, I came to understand that you weren't out for his money. You weren't liked in town, but it was because you knew how to make your own way. You and Lark are like night and day. Well, were."

I turned to her, still rubbing my head. "So he hired someone to investigate."

"Yes."

"And found out Cainan was living in St. John's."

"Yes."

"And his family knew all along."

"Oh, yes. From bits and pieces I picked up around town, it seems the Keels are...well, as we used to say, financially embarrassed. Very," she added, sending a look my way, "embarrassed."

"So, why did he marry me?"

"Because you had that biiiiig boat and even today a thing like that would be worth something."

I remembered Cainan's words, flung so cruelly at me on the train. "Yes, evidently, I was supposed to sink, not the *Sidonie Stone*."

"Yes, well, I didn't know that part until after I got back here. And Jaggar doesn't know that part at all, or that bay would be chockablock with the bodies of Keels."

"But, why didn't he leave it to me to make a choice? Why did he just abandon me there?"

"Pride, I expect." She shrugged. "And guilt."

"He had nothing to feel guilty for."

"He thinks he does." She looked at me again. "He told you about Lark, so you know how she died."

I shook my head. "I just know she's dead."

"She was pregnant with his brother's baby, and because he wouldn't divorce her, they ran away from the family. They took Gale's boat and crossed the strait on a stormy night."

"And they..."

"Sank? Yes." Gleda's amusement sank, as well. Her face grew dark, and sad. "Gale died in the wreck. They found her clinging to a half-submerged dinghy, one arm wrapped around his body. She died a few hours later."

"I'm so sorry." So *that's* why he helped me! Guilt!

"Jaggar never got over it. He felt it was his fault for not giving in to the divorce. He didn't want to see you end that way."

"But, I didn't ask for a divorce."

"No?"

"No. He just…just left me there in St. John's."

She looked at me again, her brows drawn together, making her look shrewd and cold. "What about while you were in Hickman's Harbour?"

"I…I never…not really…" In my mind a dozen images, two dozen moments, a hundred words all ran together to paint a picture of a pathetic woman who was hopelessly unhappy. That was what Jaggar saw every day. "So, he's done with me?"

"More to the point, are you done with him?"

"I came back, didn't I?" I protested. "The moment I saw he'd left me I did everything I could to come back."

"Was it then, or was it when you knew the Keels had no money?"

"Stop the car."

"What?"

"Stop it right now. I won't have you saying that to me. What right have you got to make such a horrible suggestion?"

She let the car roll to the side of the road, banging and hissing and rattling. She twisted in the seat and looked at me. "What right? I was Gale's wife. I saw what Lark did to our family."

"Gale's…ohhh."

"Yes." She twisted forward again, her face very dark. "Well, he was a bastard, but I wasn't prepared to see it happen all over again." She buried her face in her hands, and her shoulders shook, but she didn't make a sound.

Of course, I had to explain after she had shown me all her scars. "I knew about the Keels and their money. I knew about it for months. I didn't know Cainan was still alive, or that it was a horrible plot to get the *Sidonie Stone*, but I knew they weren't rich anymore." I sat there for a moment, not knowing what to do. "I...thought I loved Cainan. He was the only boy who ever showed me any attention. He was flash and funny and he made me feel flash and funny, too. And the horrible way I thought he died made me hold on to that feeling too long. But, it wasn't love. Love is...well, it's deep and solid and real and respectful. Cainan was none of those things. Jaggar was."

Gleda lifted her head after a while, released the brake and worked the car back onto the road. "I was right. You've got some sense."

"Where are we going?"

"Where you belong. Why do you think I was on that ferry this morning? After talking to Jaggar last night, I was coming to get you to see if I could talk sense into you. You deserve one another. You're both stubborn and overly romantic, the pair of you."

"Romantic," I laughed, grimly. "Not even close."

"Oh, don't be such a child. That's your problem, you know. You define romance out of the things you see in movies and read in novels. Romance isn't like that. Romance is a sense of...oh, purity, I suppose. It's a desire to see things right and fair and without ulterior motives. Jaggar is hopelessly romantic. He still believes in true love and happily ever after with the one that's meant for you."

"Does that even exist?" I sighed, wistfully. "My parents never had that, though I suppose they were both romantic in their way. My father was more like Cainan, though. Flash and funny and full of big plans and adventures. My mother believed in that forever and ever kind of love. Jaggar believed it with Lark, and you-"

"Don't delude yourself. Jaggar was an infatuated pup when he met Lark. She broke his heart within minutes of their vows. He was just resigned to it. And as for me...well, let's say I'm more pragmatic than he is. When I saw how things were going between Gale and Lark, I let him have his divorce. I loved him, but I accepted that he no longer loved me. Don't feel too bad. I got a fair piece of the Cingesleah pie for my generosity."

"Sounds more like the Keels than the Cingesleahs," I observed. "Oh, people are awful."

"Yes," she agreed.

We drove in silence after that, and I didn't ask her the most important question of all.

The house was as dark as the morning sky when we arrived. I didn't have a key to the latch, but Gleda did and she let us in. There was no fire in the hearth, and the stove in the kitchen was cold as the ice on the windows. "Where's Merdyce?" Gleda asked.

"She went to stay with some of her family for the week," I explained, getting matches from the shelf. "It was Jaggar's idea."

"Sounds like him. He's adored her since he was a child."

"Was she his nanny?" I shoved crumpled newspaper and some kindling into the stove and struck a match.

"Oh, no. She was nanny to one of his sister's children, and when they got too old for one, she was going to pension her out. Jaggar came along and brought her here." She opened cupboards and eventually found a tin of tea.

I blew out the match. "I wonder where Jaggar is?"

"He'll be along soon, I'm sure. He was going someplace to bring his boat back here."

"He's out in the bay in this weather?" I cried.

Gleda seemed unconcerned. "I suppose."

"I have to go." I let the cast iron lid of the stove drop with a heavy bang. "This is no weather to be out on the bay."

"Where are you going?"

I didn't answer. I grabbed my mac from the bag I had dumped in the hall, and ran out the door, slipping and sliding on muddy snow as I hurried toward the road. From there I had a panoramic view of the straits, and with hands cupped over my eyes to shield them from the rain, I could just make out the masts of the *Gabriella* swaying as it zigged and zagged against the wind.

I started down the road, barely able to keep my footing, but I paused now and then to find the *Gabriella* and make sure it was still there, wrestling the wrath of Mother Nature.

By the time I reached the *Gabriella*'s berth, the emptiness of the harbour was eerie in its silence. Most of the boats had been dragged up and tied down on shore, and those still the water bobbed and sloshed and rattled their sheets in vain against the wind. The usually busy docks were empty, and the lack of human sound or activity made it feel as if I'd stumbled into a nightmare.

The dock was slick, and water rushed through the planks with each gust of wind, but I still walked all the way to the end, hands outstretched in a ridiculous attempt to maintain my balance, before I reached one of the thick, wooden supports, wound with fraying rope and thickly smeared with tar. Wrapping my arms around it, I stared out to the mouth of harbour, waiting for some sign of the *Gabriella* limping home.

As I waited there, terrifying memories whistled past me with the wind. Not so very long ago, I had stood just a little way up the beach, wet and numb, watching nearly a dozen men search in vain for my husband. Was I about to lose another man to that heartless mistress? "No," I implored, but the wind carried my words away before it reached my ears, "not this time."

The urgency of my pleas surprised me, even in the confusion of the day's events and my own fears. What would I lose in Jaggar's passing? Was there some great passion to be explored between us or, now that I understood his motives in marrying me, was his passion borne more of anger than longing? To this point there were few cherished memories to savour, there were no silly, private jokes, no mannerisms sprung forth from affection. All that remained between us was a grudging respect and our individual miseries from the past; that was a painful sort of intimacy.

There was something else, something not quite defined, a sorrowful acceptance, yet rebellious resistance to the end of our marriage, something that said losing Jaggar would be a greater loss than Cainan's alleged death.

Could it be love? It certainly wasn't the heart tugging, head spinning feeling that sent me out in a storm much like this to marry someone in secret. It was what I had said to Gleda earlier; it was a bond, a deep, constant tie to another person's soul. Maybe my heart wasn't even involved. Loving Jaggar was a matter of the mind. It was practical, it was right and natural and logical and completely impossible.

I scanned the horizon again. There. Something dark and tall just over the breakers. No, it couldn't be the *Gabriella*. The sheets were full. This ship was sailing. *Gabriella* would be coming in under power. Only a fool would let loose their sails in this weather. I rose up on tiptoe as if I thought it would give me a better view of the boat.

The wind shifted again, and as the boat came full across the breakers I could see the yards swing hard, bringing it starboard. I could see the jet and red of the hull. It was the *Gabriella,* but why wasn't she under power? I almost wept with relief and then with frustration.

It seemed like hours for the great boat to come alongside the dock, but it was probably little more than twenty minutes once it was inside the safety of the harbour. I heard the chains of the anchor rattle down, and the gangplank bumped and thumped down to the dock. I scrambled to catch the line as it came over the rail, but it didn't come. Jaggar didn't realise I was there to catch it.

"Jaggar!" I shouted against the wind.

"Sydney?" He slid down the gangway, and caught my arm, pulling me against him. "What the hell are you doing here?" He brushed my wind whipped, rain dripped hair back from my face in what I wanted to believe was a loving gesture. "My God, woman, what are you doing here?"

I dug my fingers into his rain gear. "Why were the sheets up? Why weren't you under power?"

He gave me a smile that showed straight white teeth and more than a little regard for my unspoken fears. "It was the only way to get back home. There wasn't enough fuel aboard so the engine conked out half way down the strait. Now, what are you doing here? I thought I left you safe in St. John's. Woman, you weren't long ago on a bed with pneumonia. This is insanity."

I didn't answer, I couldn't answer. I was choked with relief and a new fear: What if he didn't want me now? "Why did you go, Jaggar?"

He eased me away, and looped the line over a post. "We'll talk about it at the house. How did you get here?"

"Oh, whatever way I could. Train, ferry, Gleda's car. I would have flown, if I could."

"Gleda?"

"She said you were leaving here. I had to get back before you left."

"That woman..." he let the words go. "If she's here, I assume she's at the house?"

I nodded, shivering.

"I hope she has the sense to make some tea." He dropped an arm around me, using his body to shelter me from the increasing wind.

"She was trying when I left. She told me you were bringing the *Gabriella* back, and I thought...I thought..." I felt tears and I swallowed hard.

"Hey, now...you weren't worried about me, were you?"

I looked at him. "Don't I have every reason to? Wouldn't you have worried if it were me?"

He didn't answer. He stared at me. "Sydney, what happened?"

Once again, I was reminded of how I must look. I shook my head. "We'll talk about that at the house, too."

"The hell we will." He swept me up and carried me down the dock toward the stalls. Setting me down roughly, out of the wind, he took my shoulders and gave me a shake. "Did he do this?"

"Jaggar, please, I don't want to talk about it."

"Well, I do. Did that whelp hurt you?" He dragged me into a tight embrace. "Because if he did, I swear I'll-"

"Oh, Jaggar, I was so scared." I clung to him. "I should never have told him about you. Not until we were back home. He...he just went wild."

"You told him?" His dark eyes sought mine. "Why did you do that? I would have let you go quietly. He need never have known."

"But, I didn't want you to let me go," I blurted out. "Oh, Jaggar, I thought you said the choice was mine? How could you just walk out on me like that?"

"I thought that's what you wanted." He pressed his cheek against my hair. "I couldn't bear to say goodbye."

"I came to your room to tell you what happened, but you had already gone." I pulled away from him. "You know the whole thing was a set-up, don't you? That he wanted the *Sidonie Stone*."

"Whatever for? The only good that boy would serve on a boat is ballast."

"He didn't want the boat, he wanted the money. He used me. He lied to me. His family lied to everyone here in town. When I realised that, it made it very easy to accept the fact that I..." I couldn't say it.

"That you what?" he probed, catching my face between his hands. "That you what?"

"That I was in love with you," I confessed, in a broken whisper.

He gathered me up and held me close, wordlessly.

"How could you, Jaggar?" I wept into his chest. "How could you leave without giving me the chance to say it?"

"Because I wanted you to be happy," he said, finally. "I thought you would be happier with him, the man you chose, the man who was taken from you."

"He wasn't taken away from me. He ran away...but you knew that, didn't you?"

He nodded sadly. "I saw Gleda before I left St. John's. She filled my ears with some pretty grim facts. Unfortunately, I was in no state to think of the mess I'd left you in. I convinced myself you were going to be happy at last, and I came back here determined to settle up and get out of here, turn my back on everything and everyone." He drew up a keg of rock salt and dropped onto it, heavily. "It really wasn't until I was coming back here this morning that the part about the insurance scheme started to fit and I realised that I could have left you in grave danger."

"Yes, the insurance scheme." I shivered.

He shrugged out of his mac and settled it over my shoulders. "Then Gleda told you."

"No, actually, Cainan bragged about it. He insisted on coming back here on the train with me last night. Up to that point he really believed he could convince me to reconcile, but when I made it clear I was done with him, it all came out. Every horrible detail."

Jaggar called him a name. "I ought to pound him to paste for striking you."

"Don't worry. He was taken off the train by two rangers. I'm pretty certain his family won't be bringing him back here. Too embarrassing, I should think."

"That family. There's not a scruple among them. How could you have loved him?"

"I don't think I ever did. I was in love with being in love, I suppose. But I knew when you started talking about going to St. John's that I really didn't want to be left there without you."

"You didn't give me any indication you wanted to stay with me," he complained. "I thought I was doing what would make you happy."

"And that's why I didn't say anything. I thought Lark was still alive and I wasn't going to do anything to prevent you from going back to her."

He touched my hand, his face pulled long with remorse. "I should have told you the truth about her from the start," he admitted. "But our own relationship was so tenuous at the time, I didn't think you'd hear me, or care if you did. And I never thought for a moment that you'd suspect me of..."

"Collecting wives?"

"Exactly." He chuckled, ruefully. "We're a pair of fools."

"That's what Gleda said. Oh, Jaggar, thank you for being there when I needed you – both times."

He wound his arms around me. "I'll always be there for you. I love you, Sydney. I have for years."

I pulled away from him. How could he mock me now? "Of course you did. Even when I refused to sleep with you."

"Even then. Maybe especially then. I think I've loved you since I first arrived here.

"Oh, nonsense," I said, brushing tears from my cheeks, gingerly. "You didn't even know my name until we got married."

"No," he admitted, "but I've always admired you. You've always been a practical, level headed young woman, a young woman who had been dealt hardship and made it work for you." He thumbed away a stray tear. "That's why I thought the marriage proposal might work. You would see it as a practical solution to a couple of impossible problems – and you did. Of course," he surprised me with a swift kiss, "the fact that you're a remarkably beautiful woman certainly didn't make the decision any harder."

"I'm not beautiful. Gleda's beautiful. Lark was beautiful. I saw a photograph," I confessed on a rush.

"You saw…" there was a momentary flicker of pain in his eyes, but it was almost as if it was merely a habitual response. "Yes, she was a beautiful woman, in her own way. You, my dear Mrs. Cingesleah, possess a great inner beauty and it gives you a sort of…" he gestured as if trying to grasp a word from the air, "glow that is almost intoxicating. I've always admired that about you, too. Do you think I'd risk my neck for just anyone?"

"Yes," I answered honestly. "If you thought you could help, you would have marched into the bay and righted the *Sidonie Stone*."

Jaggar stiffened and looked away, almost guiltily.

"It wasn't your fault, Jaggar. It was mine for listening to such wild schemes. It's a miracle I even survived. Cainan made it clear he didn't expect me to." I shivered again, this time from the memory of icy water dragging me down. "I'm not even sure how I survived. I felt so weak."

"You were probably drugged so you would sleep through it all," Jaggar suggested darkly.

"But, that would be murder!"

"Do you think your precious Cainan wasn't capable of such a cold blooded act? And if not him, then what about his family? They were desperate, Sydney. They owe everyone."

"He certainly wasn't above attacking me on a train full of people. I don't think he's evil…just very, very stupid." I touched my face again. "Anyway, I don't remember much about it after that, except standing there on shore watching the men searching for him. You..." I looked up at him in surprise. "You were there, too."

He shifted a little, so I couldn't see his face, but I could see the colour rush up from his collar. "I had gone down to the docks to make sure the *Gabrielle* was moored properly and I saw that the *Sidonie Stone* was gone, but it had been there earlier when I came in. I went to the lighthouse to see if there had been any distress calls, but there hadn't been any. I was coming back when I looked up and realised you were coming in, very close to the breakers, so I climbed out on the wall to watch. The boat went down pretty quick, but I saw you out there, flailing around, struggling against the tides, so I waded out there and dragged you back.

"So you've saved my life twice."

"To tell the truth," he continued, still avoiding my eye, "I had hoped that saving your life would make me a hero in your eyes, let me insinuate myself into your life. I was actually angry to find out someone else had gotten in first. That's probably why I was so cold to you at first. Wounded masculine pride: no one else touches the woman I love."

I was suddenly more storm tossed and bewildered than I had been that night at sea. "Why are you telling me all this now?"

"You should know. I don't want you believing that I married you out of pity, or just to take advantage of your good business sense." He drew in a deep breath. "Thanks to your good business sense, however, we could probably leave here and go back to St. John's, or Montreal, or anywhere you'd like to be."

I had found a buoy in the storm and I clung to it. "Anywhere," I promised, "as long as it's with you."

"Are you certain? I know I'm the reason Lark and Gale are dead. If I hadn't been so pious and stubborn about a divorce, they'd be alive and happy now."

"No, I don't think they could be happy for long. They both had good, loving spouses, and they left them for the flash and fun. They weren't very romantic, were they?"

"Romantic?" He arched a brow at me. "Ah, yes, Gleda's theories about us. She says we're both romantic fools. Ridiculous," he scoffed.

"No, I think she's right. Now that I truly understand what it means to be romantic, I think you're every bit the real romantic hero. You would have stayed by Lark, in the end, when she needed you. For that I would have set you free, even if it broke my heart."

"All the way home yesterday I was praying you'd see him for what he was: a spoilt, selfish brat. But, even then I never wanted you to see him as a murderer. I would give anything if you never had to know about that."

"It's just as well." I reached out to touch his cheek. "I think we've had enough secrets between us. Oh, there is one more thing: just how legitimate is our marriage? Cainan changed his story so many times, I'm not sure if our marriage is valid or not."

"According to the local priest, the Church annulled it. He mentioned it to me the day of our wedding. I thought it was odd that the Keels would seek to have the marriage annulled when he was supposedly dead, but the father thought it might be to keep you from trying to claim any estate from them. So, have no fear, *ma femme*," he smiled at me in such a way as I'd never thought possible, making me shiver again, but in a deliciously warm way. "We are legally wed, and are the only spouses either of us have. My plans for you are both legal and moral."

"Oh," I sighed.

He stood and pulled me close to him again. "I've wanted you for so long." He kissed my brow, my temple, my lips. "*J'taime, j'taime.*"

"That's it!" I pulled away. "In spite of all of our arguments and hard feelings and dark suspicions, when it came down to it, I've always felt safe with you. It must be when you speak French, like my mother. It was like being in a safe place."

He chuckled, and bowed his head slightly. "*Merci.* And now I want to hear you say it."

"*J'taime,* Jaggar. *J'taime.*"

The End

About the Author

Perle Butcher-Lyon is from a long line of historical observers. Her favorite occupation as a child was listening to the stories of her parents, grandparents and great grandparents, when they were growing up. Her goal was to create romantic ephemera of a period that represented the best and the worst of humanity.

If you enjoyed *The Wreck of the Sidonie Stone*, if you have questions or constructive comments, you may contact her at PerleB@inknbeans.com

Other books by Perle Butcher-Lyon:

Dutch Doctor
Rebel Wife (coming Christmas 2014)

More From Inknbeans Press

Emjae Edwards, *You'll Wake Up One Morning*
Annarita Guarnieri, *The Importance of Being Shine*
Jim Burkett, *Shadows of Bataan*
Candy Ann Little, *Murder of an Oil Heiress*
Rusty Coats, *Out of Touch*
Kitty Sutton, *Mysteries From the Trail of Tears*
Dawn Hood, *Pray and Bring Chocolate*
David Rowinski, *The Book of Complements*
Dorothy Legge, *Poems of Faith and Love*
Kristann Monaghan, *The Running Experiment*
Michael Gryboski, *The Man With Ruby Eyes*
Eric Pullin, *The Magical Tree*
Hugh Ashton, *Without My Boswell*
Andy Boerger, *I Like You More Each Day*
Denise Kenney, *I Wish I were*
Jt Sather, *Reasonable Malice*
Virginia Czaja, *Get Real*
Liam McCaughey, *Collected Werks*
Pico Triano, *Let Sleeping Dogs Lie*
Ey Wade, *Tripping Prince Charming*
R.H. Ramsey, *Just Beneath the Surface II: Landon's Story*
Rose Salsman and Claire Turtlemoon, *The Travis Tales*
Robin Bee Owens, *Dabby and Maxie*

Fresh Books Brewed Daily

www.ingramcontent.com/pod-product-compliance
Lightning Source LLC
Chambersburg PA
CBHW060139130626
46556CB00006B/2418